The Secret of Clonacool

Tuatha de'danaan Series

Book Two

Carole Mondragon

ISBN: 979-8-6570-4350-1

CONTENTS

ACKNOWLEDGEMENTS

My deepest thanks to Peter Kirlew for restoring our 200 year-old cottage, and bringing me to live on the edge of an Irish bog in the wonderful world of western Ireland.

A big thank you to Sariah Thompson-Wood for patient book editing and cover design; Paul Cookson for his creative direction; Bill Moylan for his willing advice on correct formatting; Esme-Rose, Mira, and Kieran for their other-worldly qualities; Ariel and Jared for believing in me, to Catherine, mother of all things and to Old Jake the bike nut.

A curtsy to my muse, for each day that I walk across the meadow and into the Faerie circle within the hawthorn grove, where I call on Eiru of the Tuatha de Danaan and write what I am gifted there.

DEDICATION

For Emma, the Light in our Lives

PROLOGUE

Kay McKierney has returned to the west of Ireland with Liam and their daughter Aoife. Their cottage sits on the edge of a meadow leading to a Faerie circle, where strange things occur as the mist gathers beneath the moon.

Kay hopes they will live quietly in the village of Clonacool, where she can protect Aoife from the unusual abilities that have begun to set her apart. But Aoife's budding powers cannot be hidden, and she is soon drawn to those who would guide her.

Unknown to Kay, Liam has discovered Ogham runes matching those found on an ancient stone menhir within the Faerie circle. He believes this to be a portal leading to the place beyond, the home of the Sidhe of the mythical Tuatha de Danaan.

Liam's attempts to enter the portal captures the full attention of the Tuatha de Danaan. They recognize Kay as one who still owes them for services rendered and her child as one of their own.

The Secret of Clonacool

CHAPTER 1 – MICE IN RESIDENCE

The child Aoife, chestnut curls bouncing about her ears, ran in from the bedroom with a closed fist held out before her, "Look what I found Mommy."

"Not now darling." Her mother, Kay McKierney, was engaged in a quiet but urgent conversation with Sean, their neighbor from the farmhouse up the lane.

"But Mommy."

"Not right now dear."

Aoife shifted her weight from one foot to the other.

"Hello now and who are you?" asked Sean, smiling.

"I'm Aoife. That's like ee-fer." She flopped one hand back and forth to indicate the two syllables.

"Is it now and what does that name mean, do ye know?"

"Of course. It's an Irish name. Mommy said it means beauty." The little girl pirouetted with a smile, still holding her fist closed.

"Well done you, with an Irish name. And clever your mother is for giving it ye," Sean nodded to Kay. "It's lovely eyes she has. Unusual I'd say, long and green like that." He wrinkled his forehead and turned from contemplating Aoife, to peer at Kay's round blue eyes.

Kay's face, usually pale, pinked right up. She dipped her blonde head slightly so that her shoulder length hair fell across her face in an effort to hide her embarrassment. Her quick intake of breath was masked by her daughter's insistence.

"D'you want to see what I've found?" asked Aoife. She held out her hand again and danced between them.

Her movement caused Sean to take a step back, "Well it's full of energy ye are, to be sure."

Kay blinked, her wide mouth still working to form words, a reason why Aoife could possibly have such green eyes. There wasn't one person in Kay and Liam's combined families to explain it. The moment passed as Sean responded to the little girl.

"Just a minute now Aoife," Sean laughed and raised his hands against her verbal onslaught, "I've to help your mother here and then I'll come back to ye."

"It's so cute. You should look," Aoife insisted, puffing out her cheeks, pink with impatience.

"Aoife, please!" Kay gave her daughter a gentle tap on the shoulder. She turned back to Sean, "I'm grateful to you Sean, for coming over so quickly."

"Ah! Tink nothing of it. Anything I can do to help."

"It tickles too," the little girl giggled. She looked from Sean to her mother, but getting no response, she wandered off.

"I've no idea where to get another," said Kay.

Kay and Sean turned together to investigate the wood burning stove. The glass door that usually kept the heat in and the coals from falling out, had cracked in two places from the top to the bottom. Kay had placed a metal fire guard in front of it, just in case the glass fell out and with it, a piece of wood or turf that might roll onto the rug, "I'm sorry to call you to help with this Sean but I didn't know what else to do with Liam being away."

"Sure, don't fuss yourself. We'll get it fixed for ye in no time.Now why don't ye find me an oven glove or something thick so I don't cut myself while I'll take out the glass so."

Kay bustled off to the kitchen while Sean studied the small fire door to see where he could get a good hold on the glass. It looked to him that he could probably take the pieces out quite easily just so long as they didn't break while he did it.

He pushed one of the pieces tentatively. It gave in the corner and he began to maneuver the edge of it, careful not to cut himself or to get too close to the fire as he did so.

Kay returned with the oven gloves, glancing briefly at her young daughter who seemed preoccupied by something under the dining table. She noted that one of her cooking pots was under there too. Handing the gloves to Sean, Kay gingerly retrieved the dirty fire guard from behind the wood stove and placed it to one side. She wanted it ready to cover the fire if Sean succeeded in removing the glass.

Sean donned the oven gloves and opened the door of the stove. The glass piece now hung from its housing, threatening to fall out completely.

He carefully pulled out the offending piece of glass, only to find that the one next to it immediately fell into the space left by the first.

Kay looked anxiously at Sean. He was concentrating hard. She chewed her lip, holding back the motherly instinct to admonish him to be careful.

Sean placed one oven-gloved hand on the second piece of glass. He carefully tugged and wiggled away at the ends until it too, came away from its housing. Pulling it out, he laid the glass carefully on the stone hearth beside the first.

They watched apprehensively to see if a third piece would fall. It stayed in place. Sean gave it a little tug just to be sure. It held fast.

"There now." He stood, folding the oven gloves. "I'll take of this tomorrow, don't you worry."

Kay sighed with relief and placed the wire guard in front of the fire to keep the carpet safe from hot falling turf.

Sean watched her action and nodded with approval. Unable to hold back his inquisitiveness he said, “Now! Where did you say Liam is?”

“He’s on a hiking holiday.”

“A hiking holiday is it? Well now,” said Sean scratching his head, “I’m thinking walking is what you mean. And I have to ask, what’s the matter wit here? Sure, a walk through the country lanes of Ireland would keep himself as active as he’d want so.”

“I know. I know,” Kay nodded her head and sighed. “He’s hiking, I mean walking, in Greenland.”

Sean sucked his breath in surprise, “Greenland is it? Well I never! What put that idea into his head now?”

“It’s something he’s always been interested in, hiking that is. Greenland came into it when he joined a group of hikers. They had already made plans for Greenland. He just tagged along really.”

“Sure, I never heard him say a word about it in all these years.”

“Well,” Kay reflected a moment, “to be honest neither did I. The urge for adventure began while he was sitting in an office all day. He’d gotten a bit of a belly.”

“Ah! Is it the belly fat is it?”

Kay put a hand over her mouth to stifle a giggle. Liam might not be too happy about her mentioning his belly to Sean. It was a small village after all. Word got around quickly and Liam had been determined to lose a little weight before coming home to Ireland. He didn’t want people thinking he’d gotten soft, as they said here. “He’s fit now though, Liam is. He started working out and then he connected with this group. They told him about Greenland and Liam was hooked. He said he’d always wanted to do something like it. And now, there he is …”

“There he is,” echoed Sean. “In Greenland. And here we are, surrounded by green. Forty shades of it no less.” He looked mystified. “Well now.”

Sean turned his gaze back to the fireplace. Kay thought he was probably still wondering what had possessed Liam into taking such a vacation and to Greenland of all places.

Sean broke the silence, "Well now, I'll put this glass in the coal bucket here and take it with me. Can't be too careful with the little one around so."

Sean was always a kind neighbor. He'd been a good friend to Liam too and had known him since he was a boy. She was glad he was here and a bit miffed that Liam was not.

Kay had not wanted to return to Ireland at first. It was Liam's idea that they leave the States to come live in this cottage. He said he'd a hankering for the simplicity of village life. His work was in finance. He'd said he could do his job online.

"There, there now," Sean said, misinterpreting her expression, "the place will warm up eventually."

Kay looked away, peering through the window into the gathering dusk. She listened to Sean with half an ear as she thought about her husband. Liam could be charming and fun to be around, but he was obsessive. This brought its own set of challenges.

Six years ago, Kay had seriously considered ending the marriage, to the point where they had almost divorced. Liam had convinced her to keep trying and she'd countered by insisting on counseling. This had brought good results, mostly because they had kept going with it.

Liam's obsessiveness often meant he became so focused that Kay would feel excluded, even neglected. Prior to counseling she reached the point where she had begun to devalue who she was. Now she looked for ways to nurture her inner self, which resulted in her looking for an outlet. She found this in learning to ride a motorcycle. It had become a passion, part of her life now.

It was satisfying to Kay that Liam was not able to join her when she went on motorcycle jaunts through country lanes back home. Her motorcycle gave her an immediate outlet on occasions when her frustrations with Liam became too much.

Then Aoife was born, and they had both loved her. Kay believed it would be all right and it was for the most part.

Sean brought her back to the moment. "Sure, it's the old stone cottages are cold you see. Over two hundred years old this old place is. So it will take several days to heat the walls, for they're quite thick. You have to expect it Kay, despite a good fire roaring in the grate there."

Kay nodded her head in agreement but continued to look through the window where a storm appeared to be gearing up. The wind swished loud through the thick forest of firs and blew the branches of the holly trees to-and-fro. She shivered and not just because the house was cold.

Sean continued to prattle on, "How long has it been now Kay? Almost six years this place has stood empty. In old cottages like this, the walls and even the furniture quickly become foisty. You can smell it can't ye now?"

Kay nodded and looked about the room. She had taken all the dust sheets off the furniture as soon as she had arrived. But there was a stale smell. What did Sean call it, "foisty?"

"Nothing a good fire won't fix," said Sean. "Lucky for ye that Liam fitted the dry wall and insulated the old place. Give it two or three days of a roaring fire to get hot water through the radiators and the whole place will be warm as toast, so it will."

Kay noticed the pause in Sean's prattling. She looked up to find him watching her carefully. "I'm sorry Sean, what did you say?"

Sean looked closely at Kay and placed a steadying hand on her arm, "I said don't fret now Kay. The weather will clear up for tomorrow. Sure, isn't the warm weather forecast for the whole week?" He smiled encouragingly.

"It's not that really, I ..." Kay's voice trailed off.

Sean tried again to interpret her sighs. “Ye’ve done the right thing Kay, you and Liam bringing your child back to Ireland to bring her up in the place of her ancestors. She will thrive here. It will be a fine life you and Liam and the child, if you put your mind to it so.”

“She belongs here,” said Kay without thinking. She felt a slight discomfort as she remembered Sean’s comment earlier about Aoife’s eyes. Glancing up at Sean, she saw nothing but concern on his aging features. She pasted a smile on her face. “You’re right Sean. This is a good place to bring up a child. And thank you,” she added. “I’m grateful to you for airing the place over the years and keeping the garden in check.”

“Ah! ‘tink nothing of it.” Sean got back to business, “Now! You told me there was something else gone wrong wit’ the place. Was it the clothes dryer?”

“That’s right. The dryer.” She led the way and Sean followed through the kitchen into the utility room at the back. “It’s not that it won’t work. It just isn’t heating up. It means I can air the sheets, but I can’t dry them.”

“Ah! That’s a disappointment for ye now. Well I certainly can’t do anything about that at the moment. But maybe ye can leave it ‘til Liam gets back or we can get the man out from Clonacool or Sligo to help ye. When will Liam get back here?”

“A little over a week. Yes, I suppose I could leave it ‘til then. But the sheets, they’ll never dry.”

“Sure, now and they will. Ye’ll have to hang them in front of the fire so. They’ll soon air, don’t you worry. With fresh sheets on the bed and the cottage warm and cozy, it will seem like home soon enough.”

Kay pulled the sheets and pillowcases from the dryer and carried them into the living room. Sean helped her set up the drying rack and positioned it as close to the fire as they dare, with no glass door to prevent a fire hazard at that moment.

Aoife came out from under the table. She held out her hand again, “Aren’t you going to look Mommy. It’s so cute.”

"What is, darling?"

Aoife opened her hand to display a fat little mouse.

Things happened very quickly from there.

Kay jumped onto the coffee table with surprising agility, accompanied by a loud scream. Aoife let out her own scream in response to her mother's. The mouse saw its opportunity to escape and jumped from Aoife's cupped hands, whereupon she screamed again at the loss. Sean looked up at Kay in surprise.

"Mommy, the mouse!" Tears sprang to Aoife's eyes.

Kay, realizing her error and not wanting to make her child afraid, stepped off the coffee table but could not suppress her shaking fight-or-flight response.

"It's all right darling. Mommy was just being silly." She turned to Sean and whispered urgently, "Where'd it go?"

Sean was amused, "Ah! Don't worry yerself now. The little creature probably came in to keep warm during a cold snap and stayed on for the comfort in the place."

Aoife dived under the couch after her new pet. "You've scared her Mommy."

Kay gripped the sleeve of Sean's sweater. "Sean I can't have mice in the house. Do something please," she implored.

"Well now, I'm not sure I can do anything tonight."

"Sean please!"

Sean sighed, "I might have a mouse trap or two. Will I go and fetch them for ye?"

"What?" Kay was shocked. "No! Sean I can't do that! Poor little creatures."

"Ah well, I may have one o' them traps that closes behind them when they go in after the food. Then you can let them go outside in the lane."

"Thank you, Sean." Kay was relieved, certain she would never forgive herself if she had actually hurt the mice.

"You have to get used to living in the country though." Sean pulled on his jacket. "There will be mice," he said darkly. He pulled the hood of the jacket over his head and walked out into the rain. His farmhouse was only up the road but given it had threatened to rain cats and dogs, he had opted for the convenience of bringing a vehicle. He drove off, his headlights soon rounding the bend in the lane that led to his cottage.

Kay retrieved the cooking pot from under the table. Holding it with one hand, she spent ten minutes pulling the living room apart looking for the mouse. First, she looked in and around the two couches, then the chair, under the cushions, in the corners, over to the table, under the bench, along the curtains and back to the cushions which were now strewn all over the floor. All the while, she held the pot ready to catch the mouse.

Aoife stood in the center of the room watching Kay's progressive search with mounting alarm. "Mommy, what are you doing with that pot?"

"I'm going to catch the mouse darling, that's all." Kay spied the mouse cowering in the corner behind the couch. She advanced with great caution, not knowing how the creature might respond to a perceived attack. 'Let's face it,' she thought to herself, 'if she were a mouse, that is most definitely how she would perceive it.' Kay spoke reassuringly to Aoife, "I'm going to let the mouse go, outside where it belongs."

"But Mommy, she's my friend. I've given her a name."

"Darling, please don't give her a name. I have to set her free."

"It's too late Mommy. Her name's Cara."

"Cara?" Kay advanced on the creature.

"Cara's my friend. Mommy!" Aoife pulled on Kay's arm, jerking it up and down to get her attention.

"Well Aoife," Kay struggled to maintain her composure, "Cara can be your friend, but she doesn't have to live in the house with us." Kay advanced on Cara with the pot held carefully in position.

Noticing the determined expression on her mother's face, Aoife cried urgently, "Okay! But don't do anything to hurt it Mommy. All right!?"

"Of course, darling," said Kay advancing on the mouse. She thought she might possibly be more frightened of the mouse than the mouse was of her. Gingerly, she tried to capture the mouse by slowly bringing the pot down over its hiding place. The little creature thwarted her plan by running towards her, right between her legs. In her fright, Kay let the pot fall. It clanged against the stone floor.

Aoife, thinking Kay had attacked the mouse, roared her disapproval. She stamped her foot and glared at Kay, her green eyes blazing. "Mommy! You scared her!"

But Kay was dedicated to her task. She retrieved the pot and hopped about the room, throwing cushions from the floor to the couches and back again in an effort to find the poor mouse.

There was a knock at the door. Aoife flung it wide. Rain dripping from his cap, Sean stepped high to avoid the mouse as it escaped. Aoife screamed and tried to pass Sean in pursuit of the mouse. Kay reached out to grab Aoife's arm to haul her back into the cottage but missed. Aoife ran off into the yard. With surprising strength, Kay pulled Sean inside and slammed the door. She positioned herself with her back to the door to prevent the mouse returning.

"Well now," Sean gasped. "You've left Aoife outside in the dark."

"Believe me, she's more at home here than I will ever be." Kay glanced up quickly at Sean's surprised face and smiled reassuringly, "She's a child, afraid of nothing. You know how they are."

Out in the garden, ignoring the storm crashing about above her, Aoife knelt down in the wet grass and held out her hand. "Come!" she said enticingly, looking into the darkness as if she could see clearly. "Come on. What are you waiting for?"

She smiled then as lightning revealed the mouse creeping forward, one tiny paw after the other, until it nestled in the palm of Aoife's hand. She peered down at the mouse and whispered reassuringly, "Mommy didn't mean to upset you. She just didn't realize that you're my friend. But she doesn't want mice in the house, so now you have to find another home. I'll come visit you okay." Aoife stooped down and released the mouse, which scuttled off into the shadows.

Suddenly, she stiffened and listened carefully. She looked out into the darkness beyond the driveway, where the forest began. There was a lull in the wind and the rain seemed to sweep sideways for a moment or two. The child gazed steadily forward, sensing a presence. Finally, she turned and walked slowly toward the cottage as the wind resumed its wailing and the rain continued to fall.

The mouse scurried between Aoife's legs and paused, looking up at her. Aoife leaned down, scooped up the mouse and slipped it into the pocket of her pants. "You don't want to be outside in the rain, do you?" She patted her pocket. "And why should you? I'll look after you, don't worry," she added quietly as she opened the door to the cottage.

Kay apologized as soon as she saw Aoife. "I'm sorry darling. But did you see how quickly the mouse ran away. And now you're all wet. And what's this on your knees, mud?" Kay grabbed a towel from the airing cupboard beside the fireplace. Quickly, she rubbed Aoife's hair and face with the towel.

"Ew!" Aoife protested. "That towel smells bad."
Kay held the towel to her nose. "You're right. I'm sorry Aoife. I'll wash the towels as soon as I can, but I had to dry you."
Aoife scowled at her mother. "You scared the mouse into running away Mommy! She's my friend."

"No darling. She wanted to leave. Didn't she Sean?" Kay looked to the old man for support.

"Aye! Aye! She did that. She thought she had the place to herself do you see? And when she found she hadn't, well she decided to avail herself of the outdoors." He tried to soothe the child. "Don't worry now. She'll come back when she's ready."

The little girl looked from Sean to her mother, who was clutching the edge of the couch and mouthing at Sean "No!" She smiled at her daughter.

"Let's have chocolate milk," Kay changed the subject with an encouraging smile. "I bought the ingredients earlier today. You get started and I'll come help you mix."

Aoife studied Sean. The expression on his face must have been convincing, for Aoife went off to the kitchen to do her mother's bidding.

Kay immediately demanded, "Did you find a trap Sean? Do you have it with you?"

"I do," he confirmed. "I have two little cages."

"Two! You think there's more than one mouse?"

"Better safe than sorry. I'll put them in the bedroom so." Sean went through into the bedroom, set the traps with tiny pieces of chocolate and walked back into the living room. Before he had even closed the door behind him, there were two clicks as the trapdoors snapped shut behind their surprised occupants. "That was quick!" He turned and went back into the bedroom.

"Oh my goodness." Kay felt faint. "How many could there be?" She sat down on the couch and raised her legs off the floor, afraid to move.

In a few moments, Sean came through from the bedroom holding a cloth over the cages, which protected them from being seen. "I've caught two already. Maybe don't sleep in there tonight if you don't want Aoife upset." Sean didn't stop walking but went right out through the front door to release the mice into the night.

*****

Eventually, Kay and Aoife bedded down on the two couches. Funny that Liam had bought a big purple couch and a smaller gray one, as if they were purchased with his wife and future daughter in mind.

Usually Kay loved sleeping to the sound of wind and storms. She often took comfort in the cozy glow of a fire when the wind howled through the trees. Unfortunately, her anxiety had been raised by the presence of mice in the house. She pessimistically wondered if slates might fly off the roof, for strong winds and the occasional crack of a branch breaking could be heard from the lane outside.

Kay had one eye on the fire to ensure it didn't go completely out. She had quite irrationally fixed her blanket so that it didn't touch the floor, thinking to avoid providing a pathway for a mouse to climb onto the couch.

It was a long time before Kay was able to sleep and just before she did, the thought crossed her mind that the Faerie Folk were at work here, initiating her back into life in rural Ireland.

CHAPTER 2 – PAM AND DERMOT

"I know you're in there, Kay. Wake up! Wake up now!"

The storm had passed. The sun streamed in through the skylights, in the high ceilings Liam had built when he'd taken off the old tin roof. Kay sat up on the couch, hair pressed flat to her head from sleeping on one side. She looked around in alarm. The pounding continued. Aoife rushed to the door, pulled on the handle and opened it wide.

"Hello," said Aoife.

"And hello to you Aoife," said a female voice. Kay turned in the blankets to see her good friend Pam swing Aoife up in her arms, so that she laughed in delight.

"You know my name?"

"I do. I was over there to the States to see you once, but I don't think you remember. Don't you know you're an important person?" Pam winked at Kay. "Ah sure, we all know you here."

Aoife puffed out her little chest with pride, not having realized this before.

Kay got up to greet her friend, impeded by the blankets which dragged along in her wake. "Pam. Thank heaven you're here. Come on in."

Pam staggered into the cottage with Aoife hanging onto her legs. Tall and wiry, Pam's brown curls hung over auburn eyes. She pushed her hair back with one hand. A bird sang in the garden. Aoife let go of Pam's leg and ran out to investigate. "Now," said Pam, by way of greeting. She held her arms wide.

Kay walked into the proffered hug. "I'm so glad you're here Pam. You've no idea the trouble I've had since I arrived in Ireland."

Pam laughed. "Sure, you haven't been here 24 hours yet. What trouble can you have had?"

"Oh! You won't believe it!" Kay rolled her eyes and told her friend about the mice, the broken glass on the door of the wood stove, the dryer not working and the worry of being assailed by mice all night.

"Well," said Pam. "you do realize you're in rural Ireland so."

"Why do people keep saying that? Hang on. I have to pee." Kay ran to the bathroom.

Pam sauntered into the kitchen to find the kettle, laughing at Kay's naivety about country living. "Sure, don't you have mice back home?" she called through the open bathroom door.

"Well yes, but not like this. They've taken over the place!"

"Ah! Well that'll happen when you leave a cottage to its own devices for so long." Pam's tone became reflective, "The land takes back its own."

A sudden yelp from the bathroom caused Pam to pause in her search for cups. "What's wrong?"

"Toilet seat!" yelled Kay.

"What about it?"

"Cold. Why are toilet seats so cold in Ireland?"

"Are they?" Pam considered this, "It might improve as the cottage get aired out and the rooms warm up."

"Nope!" Kay said with certainty, "This toilet seat is always cold, no matter how warm the cottage gets. And it's not the only one I've come across in Ireland." She shivered at the memory of her bum touching a public toilet.

Pam pulled cups from a cupboard and inspected them for dust. "That can't be true. I'm pretty sure the toilet seats at the pub are warm." She blew into the cups one by one. "Hm. Not bad," she pronounced.

"What's that?" Kay asked.

"Not much dust in the cups," said Pam. "Well, considering they've been in a cupboard all this time."

"Oh! You should wash them Pam."

"Maybe." Pam inspected the cups again and muttered to herself, "Nah! They're fine." She answered Kay's earlier question, "I keep it level day and night."

"What?"

"The temperature in the pub."

"Oh! Right! Day and night? What, are you expecting a bus-load of people at 3 a.m. someday?"

"Ha! Funny, aren't you! No, it's better for the alcohol, wine especially. Can't have the temperature going up and down." Pam began to fill the electric kettle from the tap, thought better of it and let it run awhile. Better to be safe than sorry, as deposits can build up in the pipes when houses remain empty this long. She missed Kay's next remark. "What?"

The toilet flushed and the tap ran as Kay washed her hands and came out, flicking drops of water. "I said, I've come across this quite a bit. In Ireland I mean. Cold toilet seats. It must be the style of buildings."

Pam was unmoved. "So, buy a wooden one." She plugged the kettle into the socket and flipped the switch.

"A wooden what?"

"A wooden toilet seat."

"But… isn't that a bit unsanitary?"

"Why would you think that?" Pam found the teapot, checked it for spiders and rinsed it under the tap.

"Well isn't it like using a wooden spoon? You can never be sure to get the bits of food off. They can get caught in the wood."

Pam turned from the sink and eyed Kay, "Are you worried you'll get splinters in yer bum, is that it?" She searched in the cupboards until she found a box of tea bags and leaned against the sink, waiting for the kettle to boil. "I don't know how you exist in this world. You're too finicky by far Kay."

"I just don't want a cold bum. Is that too much to ask from a toilet seat?"

Pam waved the tea bag at her, "Install central heating. That'll do the trick, keep the place warm day and night like I do the pub."

"We have radiators, but they rely on having the fire lit to keep the cottage warm."

"What I mean is, convert to oil heating. Have an oil tank installed, preferably out back of the cottage."

"That's a thought. I don't think Liam would go for it though. He loves chopping wood when he's here. He stacks it by the fire every morning. Like the sun rises every day, so you'll find Liam working at the fire."

Pam laughed. "I love a turf fire. The smell of it; sweet and earthy at the same time."

"No, I'm serious," Kay nodded earnestly. "You know he gets obsessed with things, like the fire for example when we were here last time. He'd clean out the grate, wash the little window on the fire door, and sweep all around the fireplace. Then he'd bring in the turf and stack it on one side and then the wood, to be stacked on the other side."

"He likes things to look tidy," Pam observed.

"You could say that," there was a tone to Kay's voice. "Then he'd roll bits of paper to make a base for the fire and carefully place the tiniest piece of fire-lighter on the paper. The smaller the better just to see if he could beat his own record."

"He's hilarious that man." There was a touch of admiration in Pam's voice as she said this.

"It's a ritual. No don't laugh, it really is."

Pam poured boiling water into the teapot, then the tea bag, and set the pot on the counter to steep. “A bit like me with the keeping of the pub I suppose.” She looked at her friend, “You sound a bit critical Kay.”

Kay reflected on this, “I suppose I do, although I think it’s more of an observation. He can be obsessive my Liam.”

Pam picked up the tea pot, nodded at the cups for Kay to bring and led the way into the living room. “We all have faults Kay. If I asked him to list yours, would he be as quick?”

“Maybe not so much now.” Kay poured the tea.

“When I came to visit you in the States, you and Liam were working with a counselor. I noticed things seemed a bit strained between the two of you occasionally. Can I ask how things are now?”

“Good, for the most part anyway. I’m glad we went to a counselor. I guess what I’ve learned is, it’s a relationship so there will be ups and downs. I’m not sure if he can change, not really. It’s too ingrained in him, this obsessive perfectionist crap. But at least he’s become more aware of it. We still have our moments though …” Kay stopped as she lost herself in a thought.

“Come on, spill the beans girl.” She put her face close to Kay’s, “Earth to Kay. Where are you?”

Kay shook herself. “Liam and me. Well, I try to be more fun now and not take life so seriously, more spontaneous, you know?”

“Right.” Pam thought about this for a moment. “I should try that. Be spontaneous and take off away from the pub when the mood takes me, which can happen at least once a week so.”

Kay laughed. “I can imagine your regulars, wondering where the publican’s disappeared to.”

“They’d soon be round the bar serving themselves, all in the name of helping out of course.”

“Maybe!” nodded Kay. “I can see how that would be a problem. How about something less drastic then? Maybe just dance on the bar counter when you feel the need to be spontaneous.”

"They'd love that!" Pam sipped her tea.

"Good for business I'd think," Kay said with a straight face.

"Sure," agreed Pam.

"You could advertise it. Not just a singing pub, a dancing pub too." Kay giggled.

Pam looked at her friend under half closed lashes. "And here was I thinking it's my job to see you have a good time in Ireland. I see you've a thing or two to teach me.

Kay laughed, "Well I can tell you this, I'm certainly happier than I was before. Before, you know, that thing happened." She blushed as her voice trailed off.

"Ah sure, it's been a long time Kay." The two friends exchanged a look of understanding. "Speaking of which," said Pam darkly, "I'll not want there to be any full moon shenanigans like last time."

Kay sighed. "I try not to think of it, Pam."

"Six years is a long time eh?"

"Exactly. It doesn't seem real now."

"Well that's good then," said Pam, relief evident in her voice. "And no going out into the mist. In fact, if you see a mist over the Faerie circle down there in the meadow, come inside and shut the door."

Kay nodded and took a sip of her tea.

Pam wagged an admonishing finger at Kay. "We don't know what you'll find in that mist. Well, we do know what you'll find but I'm telling you now like I told you before, no good can come from calling up the Sidhe. And call them up you will if you're foolish enough to go into that circle."

Kay nodded again. In doing so, she had the memory of it. The mist and the moonlight and the feel of Mac as he pressed her against the soft moss under his hard body.

Involuntary tingles ran through Kay. Her nipples hardened. She folded her arms across her breasts to hide evidence of the exquisite sensations. Kay swallowed a sigh and glanced at Pam, not sure her friend was convinced.

Pam hadn't noticed. She was preoccupied, watching Aoife through the open door. "Well," she said, turning back and suddenly all business, "what do you have planned for today?"

Kay rolled her eyes. "Well for starters, I'm afraid to unpack for fear of finding mouse droppings in the closets and drawers."

"Ah get away with you, scaredy-cat. We'll tackle it together. Get dressed and I'll start the fire going so. Then I'll fill a bucket with hot water and we'll clean the place. You get milady in off the wall there and give her breakfast."

"In a minute. I'll get dressed first." Kay smiled at Pam as she bustled off. "Since when have you been so into cleaning?"

"I'm just happy you're here Kay. If doing a bit of cleaning helps you settle in faster, then I'm your girl!" Pam laughed and riddled the knob on the side of the woodstove to make the excess ash fall through the grate into the pan below.

While Pam banged about with buckets of wood and turf, Kay folded blankets from the night of camping on the couches. She then turned her attention to finding something to wear.

Kay had lifted the suitcases onto the dining table the previous night while she'd searched for pyjamas. Now, she pulled out blue jeans and black t-shirt. It was pointless wearing light colors today, when so much cleaning was called for, along with the sweeping of cobwebs and similar delights.

It was good to have a friend who cared. Not that she didn't have friends back home, but Pam was different. Pam had come through for her in a way no other friend could have.

Kay changed quickly and brushed her teeth. Childish laughter drew her to the doorway. Aoife sat on the garden wall swinging her legs and talking to the birds in her sweet little voice. She called to her daughter, "Let's get you dressed and some breakfast inside you, Aoife."

Aoife ran her small hand lightly over the moss atop the garden wall. "Did Daddy build this wall?"

"Yes." Kay took her daughter's hand to pull her down from the wall, but Aoife was not to be dissuaded from her reverie. 'Much like Liam in that way,' thought Kay. Since it wasn't genetic, it must be a learned thing.

"But how did he get all the stones different colors? That's very clever isn't it, Mommy? He made the wall special. They're even different sizes." Aoife took Kay's hand and jumped down from the wall. "Daddy knew I wouldn't be able to get up by myself, so he made these for me to walk up to the top. See!" She demonstrated by hopping onto the two steps Liam had built into the wall like the steps of a stile.

Aoife walked along the top of the wall, holding out her arms for balance like a high wire trapeze artist. Kay told her daughter that the stones had come from the cottage next door, which had belonged to Aoife's grandmother, and her great grandmother and before that, her great-great grandmother.

"I have a great," Aoife's head dipped here as she mentally negotiated having to say the word 'great' twice, "great … she was very great, my grandmother."

"Yes, she was," said Kay, smiling at the seriousness of the child.

"Where did she live, my great-great?" asked Aoife, effectively shortening forever the reference to her ancestor.

"She lived right here in the village."

Aoife's eyes widened. "Is she still here?"

"No, she's long gone."

"Where did she go?"

"Hmm," Kay paused here. Not wanting to get into a deep discussion of death. "She went the way of all things."

"The way of all things," echoed Aoife. "And did she paint these stones all different colors or was that Daddy?"

"Ah!" said Kay thinking, now it was getting complicated. "Well no. Daddy didn't paint the stones. Your grandmother painted the stones. They were part of the wall of her cottage you see. Every summer she would give her cottage a fresh coat of paint and always a different color each time."

"Why did she do that, different colors?"

"Well," began Kay, "because, er, that's what grandmothers do."

"Because they like different colors?"

"That's right darling, because they like different colors."

Aoife looked into the distance and changed the subject. "So, I have a great and a great-great?"

"Yes," agreed Kay, relieved. "You have a great and a great-great."

"I'm very lucky, aren't I? I don't know if any of my friends have a great and a great-great."

Kay smiled and held her daughter's face in her hands. "Yes, you are so lucky Aoife."

The little girl threw her arms around her mother's neck and hung off her body, planting a wet kiss on her cheek. She slid down to the ground and announced, "I think I'll take a walk to see great-great's cottage."

"No. We have to get you dressed first, out of those pyjamas."

But it was too late. Aoife was already running.

"Wait!" Kay sighed. Aoife was headstrong and yet Kay didn't want to curb her independent spirit. She wanted Aoife to be stronger than she was herself, so she often let the child have her head unless there was an obvious danger in it. She wondered if there was much traffic on this road. There didn't used to be, but times change. She watched Aoife's lithe little body as she headed along the lane toward the old tumbledown cottage of her grandmothers, just twenty yards along the lane.

"Don't worry Mommy, I'll come back."

Pam came out of the cottage with a bucket full of ash. Seeing Kay's look of concern, she waved her free arm dismissively. "Ah let her go. So, she's in her pyjamas. Who will know?" Pam walked across the driveway and dumped the ash over the wall of the rockery just as Liam used to do. He'd say it had to go somewhere out of sight and that it added potassium, especially if it was dug into the soil. She supposed Pam must have a similar view.

"I'm more concerned about traffic," said Kay.

Pam laughed. "Traffic?" The dumped ashes rose in a little cloud behind Pam as she trudged back to the cottage swinging the empty bucket. "There can't be too many turf cutters coming along the lane these days."

Kay was about to voice her opinion that she was sure there were, since it was mid-April and the start of the turf cutting season, but Pam went on. "If there were any vehicles, they'd come at a crawl because there's so many potholes. Sure, I was obliged to do that myself just now, or wreck the car. I tell you, the local council should be after fixing it. Hasn't it been like that since donkeys pulled wagons full of turf from the bog?"

"Maybe so," agreed Kay. "But Sean brings his cows along here from one field to the other. I've seen them passing by when I was here before. They run all over the lane if they get spooked by a car, or a kid."

Pam plonked the empty bucket by the cottage door and placed her hands on her hips. "And can you hear the mooing of cows right now Kay?"

They both listened a moment.

"No," Kay said.

"No," Pam confirmed. "So, they're not being moved today. Don't waste your thoughts on it now. Why don't you ask Sean which days he moves the cows and then you'll know, won't you?"

"Oh." Kay laughed. "I didn't think of that."

"Ah you'll soon get the way of it, when you've lived here long enough."

"I suppose." Kay gave up.

The two women worked on through the morning until most of the little cottage looked spic and span. It was close to lunch time when Pam suddenly called out, "What the feck!" as she peered through the diamond paned windows.

Kay rushed to the window, her blonde head popping up beside Pam's brown curls. Two pair of eyes, agog side by side. Kay gave a whoop and ran to the door. Flinging it open, she danced on the step in her excitement.

A van backed into the yard, pulling a trailer behind, its bulky contents covered with a tarpaulin.

Pam joined her at the door. "It looks like a motorcycle!" she said unnecessarily, its identity plain to see.

"It's not just a motorcycle. It's a Kawasaki Ninja!" Kay ran over to the trailer. Impatiently pulling off the tarp, she stroked the motorcycle lovingly.

"Hello," she said to the motorcycle.

"Hello," said the van driver.

Kay looked up. "Oh hello. I'm just happy to see this here so fast. Although to be fair, I had it shipped almost two months ago." Kay signed the proffered delivery slip and pocketed her copy. She guided the bike as the van driver wrestled it off the trailer. "Careful now," admonished Kay.

Pam stepped forward to help with the proceedings, until the bike was safely off-loaded and the van had disappeared down the lane.

"Liam has a motorcycle?" Pam was surprised. "I didn't know he was even interested in them."

"It's not Liam's. It's mine." Kay swung her leg over the bike and settled into its leather seat. "Ah!" she said with satisfaction, stroking the dusty green tank. "I've missed you my friend."

"You have a motorcycle? Why do you have a motorcycle? You never mentioned it to me." Suddenly a light blinked on in her mind. "Hey wait a minute." Pam took a step back putting her hands on her hips, "Is this because of…" she frowned at Kay. "Of you know who? Is it?"

"Shhh!" cautioned Kay. "No. Well yes." She held up thumb and index finger close together. "I mean, maybe a little bit." Her tone became briefly wheedling. "Look Pam, it's all I've got from that time."

"You never even rode on his motorcycle."

"I know. But I never forgot… him, you know? How could I forget?" Kay's eyes drifted off to the lane where Aoife had danced away minutes earlier.

Pam broke the silence, her jaw dropping. "Aoife's his. Mac's child. She is, isn't she?" She snapped her fingers at Kay. "Why didn't I know that?"

"I'm sorry Pam. I thought the fewer people that knew, the better. Even talking about it now makes me anxious. I don't ever want Liam to know. It would hurt him deeply."

"You didn't tell Liam?"

"Tell him what exactly? That I had an affair on the edge of an enchanted mist with someone who may or may not have been one of the Sidhe." Kay shook her head. "He'd have thought me mad if I tried to explain that. I've felt guilty about it all these years."

Pam relented. "You shouldn't feel bad. You were separated Kay, almost divorced. The decree nisi had gone through already hadn't it?"

"Yes, but we stopped process before it was finalized."

"Sure, but that was after. You stopped the divorce after the fling with Mac." Pam considered for a moment. "Did you know you were pregnant Kay?"

Kay sighed. "I knew the moment it happened. I knew immediately."

"Wow!" said Pam.

There was silence between them, both thinking of the implications of such a decision.

"And you kept it to yourself."

"Well," said Kay. "Now you know, so that makes two of us."

"Will you ever tell Liam?"

Kay looked her friend in the eye and slowly shook her head. "No!" She wet a finger on her tongue and rubbed anew at the dust on the motorcycle until the green shone through in that one small spot. A chaffinch called to its mate across the trees and they both looked up, shielding their eyes in the bright, April sun.

Kay rocked the bike gently between her thighs. Her long legs reached the ground as she steadied the bike. Leaning forward, she slid herself against the tank, reaching forward until her hands grasped the handlebars. "Making love with Mac was … it was …" She sighed, lost for words. "I'll never find that again Pam. I'll never see him again and that's okay because I have Liam. We're happy and I thought that would never happen."

Pam wasn't convinced. She grabbed a fold-up camping chair from where it rested against the cottage wall, flipped it open and plonked herself down in it. "I still don't understand Kay. If you're happy, why buy the bike?"

Kay sat up on the bike seat. She shrugged her shoulders. "I guess…" her voice trailed off. She began again. "Look, I could say it's the sense of freedom it gives me, riding a motorcycle. And that's true. When I saw it, I had to have it, but it also helps me cherish the memory of that time."

Pam frowned at her friend, but Kay persisted. "Aoife is a fact of life. I can't ignore who she is or where she came from. I made the decision not to go with Mac. If I'd gone with him into the mist that night, I wouldn't exist here today, would I?" Kay swung her leg over the bike and pulled it back on its stand. "The bike brings me comfort. Please don't judge me Pam. I'm here aren't I?" she repeated. "Not there with Mac." She looked away. "Wherever there is. I'm here with Liam. With Aoife."

"Hmph!" Pam snorted. "If it wasn't for me, you'd have been through that mist with Mac and then what? We'd never have seen you again that's what!"

Birds called to each other across the silence between them. Kay shivered slightly.

Pam spoke up at last. "So, you bought a motorcycle. You weren't joking about being spontaneous. Looka you girl!"

They laughed delightedly at each other. "Try it for yourself Pam," she urged.

"Me? You're not getting me on one o' them things."

"Okay, don't say I didn't offer."

They turned back into the cottage just as a vehicle arrived from the direction of Sean's farmhouse. "So much for there being no vehicles on this lane," muttered Kay. With a sidelong glance at Pam's retreating back, she went to greet her visitors.

The truck rolled across the pebbled driveway until its engine was level with Kay's motorcycle. Sean and another man emerged from the truck. Their attention was immediately drawn to the motorcycle, which they spent some minutes admiring. Kay realized she knew the younger man.

"We've met, haven't we?" asked Kay, shaking his hand.

"Connor it is. I was here last time you were in Ireland. It was a flooded bathroom then if I recall."

"It was. You're a man of many talents Connor. One day you're a plumber, the next day you're a mechanic," Kay smiled. Connor turned his attention to the car. Liam had asked Sean to procure it prior to their arrival in Ireland.

Producing cables to jump-start the car, Connor got to work. He seemed pleased that Kay remembered him. "You're looking well now Mrs. McKiernan," he said.

"Kay please," replied Kay. "You were not much more than a boy when I saw you last but look at you now, a grown man."

"Sure, he's a wife and two babbies already." Sean was not to be left out of the conversation.

"Two babies already?" Kay conjured astonishment. "So, you must have been almost married when I saw you last?"

"I was, engaged anyway to a lovely girl from over to Ballina. We were married that very summer after you left."

"Well. Congratulations and thanks for helping me out again."

"Ah don't mention it, tis no bother so."

"Well now Connor," put in Sean, "this is a good little car, but it may need a bit of attention for oil and such like."

"You leave it with me," Connor grinned, "I'll soon have it right as rain so."

Connor walked around the car kicking the tires while Sean popped the hood. They soon had their heads together, chatting companionably over the merits of the car.

Surplus to requirement, Kay left them to it and returned to the cottage. Pam came out of the bedroom carrying a mouse cage. Kay's eyes opened wide in dread but Pam, always down to earth, said dismissively, "What's that face about? I'm releasing it aren't I? You do realize you live in the country? Ye have to expect such things."

"That's what Sean said."

At Kay's expression of distaste, Pam relented. "Don't fuss yerself Kay, we'll soon be rid of them I promise ye."

"I don't want to actually hurt them," said Kay. "I'm glad we're using the catch and release method."

"Oh, you are eh? From your face, I can see you'd be running a mile from the idea of catching mice and releasing them down the lane. You're afraid of this one and sure, the poor creature can't do you any harm at all, being in a cage and so." Pam walked on passed Kay and out of the door. "Good morning Sean. Connor, how are your babbies doing? It's been a while since I've seen ye in the pub to ask after them."

"Ah they're grand so," came Connor's voice from under the hood. The two men went back to mumbling together about valves and starter motors. Pam walked across the lane and into the small forest, where she opened the cage and watched as the mouse ran off into a thicket of ferns. She came back swinging the cage and whistling tunelessly.

"Now," she said, walking through the cottage into the bathroom, "I'll just wash me hands and then we'll get back to it. Come on now Kay. Do the unpacking while I finish cleaning the kitchen. And then we can think about another cup of tea so."

Tea, strong and sweet was a feature in Pam's life. She could easily drink ten or twelve cups of tea in a day. It was the custom in Ireland, more so than coffee, although coffee shops had sprung up here and there, even in the small towns. Nevertheless, tea drinking reigned supreme, the habit of generations.

Just then, the sound of another engine could be heard coming down the lane from the direction Aoife had taken. "Pam!" yelled Kay in a mixture of alarm and recrimination. "I thought vehicles hardly came down here!"

"You've only yourself to blame. It's you that's causing all these people to come here isn't it?"

Kay could not say otherwise, so she went out to greet the newcomer. "Hi," she said before the driver could step out of his vehicle. "Did you see a little girl down the lane?"

"I did not." he said, his gaze on the motorcycle. At last, he swiveled his eyes to Kay and put out his hand. "I'm Dermot." Kay shook his hand. He had a strong grip. "Great bike. Is it yours?"

"Yes," said Kay simply.

"Wow! Lucky lady." He seemed to remember Kay's question. "Little girl is it? I didn't see anyone at all. She might be playing in one of the cottages, but I'll watch out for her on the way back along. Now!" He changed the subject, "I'm here to fit the glass on the wood stove. Sean asked me to come over. Ah there ye are Sean," he said as the old man stuck his head out from under the hood. The two shook hands while Connor, hands busy under the hood of the car, merely nodded in his direction and turned back to his work.

Sean called after them as they entered the cottage. "Kay will show you the stove now Dermot. I've me hands full here with the fixing of the car so."

Pam came to the door of the cottage, tea towel in hand. She had tied a kerchief around her brown curls, from which one had already escaped to hang over her eyes. She pushed a hand up to catch the curl and in the same movement, swept the kerchief from her head, patting her hair self-consciously. "Dermot," she said. "I didn't expect to see you here."

Kay was surprised at the coy expression on Pam's face. She looked from Pam to Dermot and noted how tall he was and broad in the shoulders. He had a strong face, long like his body. His hazel eyes looked every which way but at Pam.

'Ah!' thought Kay, 'something going on there, or if there isn't, there should be.'

Dermot managed to raise his eyes to Pam's then and smiled. Kay glanced at Pam in time to see her eyelids flutter as she pushed her curls back from her forehead.

"Well," Kay gestured to Dermot to follow her into the cottage but then thought better of it. "Actually, I've something I need to do back there in the kitchen." She winked at Pam. "Pam could you show Dermot the wood stove." Kay walked quickly into the back of the cottage, leaving Dermot and Pam to inspect the stove. Kay stood behind the half-closed kitchen door, smiling to herself as she heard them talking carefully to each other.

Pam said, "I suppose Sean already told you the problem here. You see how the glass broke in two places so that now there are three pieces instead of one?"

Dermot answered, "He filled me in, so he did. And I've the glass here to fit, for I know the stove. It was written down in the book at the store. Liam bought it from me some years ago."

"It's er, a good stove I think." Pam ventured.

"Aye it is so."

"Why do you think the glass broke like that?"

Dermot glanced at Pam then quickly looked away. "Ah well now, it can happen when there's a change in temperature and the fire is still hot. Especially if it's not been tended. It happens more in winter mind, if the fire is left like that."

"So, it's been broken since Kay and Liam left here?"

"Likely so."

There was a silence. Kay hoped it meant the two were gazing into each other's eyes. She risked a peek through the crack of the door. Unfortunately, shy Dermot was already focused on taking out the remaining piece of glass, leaving Pam hanging about like she was forgotten. Pam looked at Dermot a moment longer then shrugged her shoulders and left him to his work. She made straight for the kitchen where Kay grabbed her and pulled her into the bathroom, closing the door behind them both.

"What's going on Pam?" she whispered urgently.

"Well, I like him." Pam's eyes were soft. "But he never makes a move."

"I'd say he's shy."

"Maybe so."

"Why don't you ask him out?"

"No way. I'm an old-fashioned girl when it comes to asking men out."

"Really Pam, I'd never have believed that."

"If he can't pull up his courage to ask me out, why would I want him in me life? I need a man with guts. You know, not afraid of anything, especially not of me."

"Pam!" Kay wanted to give Pam a little shake, but she refrained from doing so. "Some men are just shy around women. Maybe Dermot is one of those."

"I'll not make the first move. No, I will not!" Pam was firm. "Don't look at me like that Kay McKiernan. I'm a strong woman. I can't have a weak man in my life. Look what happened last time."

When Pam and Kay first met, six years earlier, Pam had gone through a breakup. Her boyfriend had gone back to Dublin, leaving her to manage the pub alone. She had found that she was good at the job and so she stayed and had great success. She'd expanded the business to take on tour buses for lunches, that were catered by women hired from the community. It worked out well and Pam had found her place again. It was a homecoming of sorts, as she had gone to school here in the village before taking off to the bright lights of Dublin in earlier years.

Kay watched the determined expression on her friend's face. She thought maybe Pam had erected an emotional wall around herself, determined to let no-one in. "But Pam, hasn't he built his business from nothing? That's determination at least?"

"Aye, well. I need more than that."

She felt sudden empathy for Pam and tried to fold her into a hug. But Pam was having none of it.

"I don't need comforting Kay. Not for this anyway. He has to prove himself before I'll think on him."

"In what way Pam? How d'you need him to prove himself?"

"I don't know," Pam was thoughtful. "I'll know it when I see it but right now, he can't even look me in the face."

Kay punched her friend lightly on the arm. "That's because he likes you so much, you silly."

"Hmm!" Pam threw a cloth over her shoulder and went to dust the back bedroom, thus ensuring she wouldn't bump into Dermot for the remainder of time he was in the cottage.

Frowning, Kay made a move to go to Dermot and give him her opinion on asking Pam out. But then she stopped, realizing her stubborn friend would not thank her.

Kay entered the room just as Dermot put the finishing touches to fitting the glass. He clipped it into place and tested its firmness by closing and opening the door several times.

"You've done a good job, Dermot." Kay said quietly, causing him to turn quickly.

"I didn't see you there, Kay."

"Sorry. You seemed lost in thought."

"Ah! I was after thinking about, thinking about …" his voice trailed off.

Unable to resist broaching the subject of him and Pam, Kay opened her mouth to speak. At that moment Sean clattered into the cottage followed by Connor wiping his oily hands on a rag.

"We're all done Kay," said Sean with pride in his voice as if he had done the work himself. "Connor's a fine lad to have around when things need attention and I was able to help him, wasn't I Connor?"

Connor smiled kindly at the older man. "Sure, ye were a great help Sean."

"Now Dermot," said Sean. "All done with the glass door are ye?"

"I am Sean and I'll be off now." Dermot turned to Kay who had opened her purse. "I'll send ye the bill Kay."

"Well if you prefer it," she began.

"Or you can pay me by credit card once I'm back at the store. Will that do ye?"

"That's great Dermot and thank you." Kay shook Dermot's hand warmly.

"I'll be away so," said Dermot in an unnecessarily loud voice. He walked toward the door but not without a glance in the direction Pam had taken. There was no sign of Pam, so Dermot had no choice but to exit the cottage and climb into his truck.

Kay remembered that Aoife was down the lane somewhere and ran after Dermot. She was about to call out to him when he rolled the window down and said "Don't ye worry now Kay. I haven't forgotten the little girl. I'll drive slow to be sure."

Kay smiled gratefully and watched as he drove away. Pam called from the kitchen, "Shall I put the kettle on? Will you have a cup Sean? What about you Connor?"

At the sound of Pam's voice, Kay walked back into the cottage. With hands on hips, she fixed her friend with an enquiring stare. Pam looked back at Kay and shrugged her shoulders before turning away to fill the kettle again.

CHAPTER 3 – OLD NELL

Left to her own devices, Aoife wandered along the leafy lane. She peered into hedgerows and looked under leaves, hoping to find a fairy or two. This was after all, Ireland. A precocious child, she had read several story books already. Some of the stories featured fairies and Ireland together in a single sentence.

Disappointed that no fairies were immediately evident, Aoife was surprised when a flash of red crossed her vision. Looking up, she saw a bird with a red tummy. It landed on the branch of a tree quite nearby.

The bird flew from tree to tree, resting briefly each time as if waiting for Aoifc, who skipped along in pursuit of it.

Sean came along the lane on his bicycle. He stopped to chat. "Well now Aoife," he greeted her.

A polite child, Aoife dragged her eyes away from the bird. "Hi Sean. Where are you going?"

"I'm off a little way down the lane there, to see my caves."

"Oh!" said Aoife, only half listening. She glanced back at the bird which seemed to be waiting for her. "That's nice."

"Aye well, I like to keep the caves in the pasture down at the end of the lane. But then I like to move them too, or them caves will get bored do ye see." He shook his head in wonder at the nature of his yearling calves.

"Hmm," said Aoife, focused on the bird.

"Now! I see you're exploring the village. Ye'll find a great many empty cottages so."

He finally had Aoife's attention. "Mommy said my great and my great-great, have gone the way of all things."

Sean's brow furrowed in concentration as he tried to follow Aoife's words. "The way of?" He stopped in mid-sentence as he grasped that she was referring to the passing of her grandmothers. "Ah, yes. Well, that is the way of it, yes. Hmm." Sean considered how to approach the turn the conversation had taken. He opted to change course instead.

"It was a grand little village in its time. Sure, when I was a boy I'd be stopping in at this cottage and that. I knew your grandmother and great-grandmother as a matter of fact, for they lived just along the lane here. Good people. Yes. good people." He ruminated for a moment. "I knew them all in this village. I knew where I'd get a welcome and a glass of sugar water or bit o' cake so I did." He smacked his lips at the memory. "Aye, there was Nell's cottage along the way there. She was always ready with a smile and slice o' cake. Delicious it was. They made their own in those days of course."

Aoife looked up at him, wishing she could try that cake.

"And then there were the Hannity's. They were just around the corner, down there before the bridge. They'd cows and they'd make their own cream and butter. Sure, me own mother would do the same, but the Hannity's butter…" His gaze drifted away as he recalled the memory. "Ah! It had a taste to it don't you know. I'm glad me mother cannot hear me say it, for the Hannity's butter was even more tasty than hers, god rest her soul."

Aoife brought his attention back to the present. "I know about souls. I mean," she amended, "I've heard about souls. I don't know what's a soul though. Do you?"

Sean adjusted his cap. "Ah! Well now. Everyone has a soul." He then scratched his ear as he searched his mind for an explanation Aoife might understand. "Ask yer mother about it so," he said at last.

"Grownups always say that when they don't want to talk about things."

"What's that now?"

"Grownups always say, 'ask your mother.'" Aoife was matter of fact. "But she never has a proper answer. Not really." Her face was glum.

The bright red breast of the bird fluttered its wings, ready to take flight.

"Look!" said Sean. "A robin."

"He's my friend." Aoife watched as the robin flew off. "Bye Sean. I have to go." She whirled after the robin, her conversation with Sean forgotten for now.

The old man watched her, nodding to himself. "Sure, it's good to have a child in the village again, so it is."

Aoife followed the robin. Aoife almost forgot to breathe in her excitement. The bird seemed to wait for her, holding itself in midair. Its wings fluttered swift and sure, making a whirring sound so that Aoife blinked in astonishment.

As she came closer, the robin sped away to another tree further along the lane, where it perched and sang its song.

Aoife crept forward carefully, head up, eyes bright, lips slightly parted in childish wonder. As she watched, the bird swooped from its perch to another tree across the lane, a little further along.

Aoife laughed delightedly as she and the bird resumed the game they had begun earlier. She watched the bird as it flew from tree to tree. She did not notice that she had passed by the cottage of her great and her great-great.

In this way, she arrived at a cottage beyond the end of the village.

The robin swept around a corner and out of sight. Aoife looked through the hedgerow as she tried to catch up. Partly obscured by an overgrowth of hedge and young alder trees, she could discern the dusty white of an old, tumbledown cottage that had only half a roof.

Aoife reached the end of the hedgerow and paused a moment, puffing with her efforts to keep up. The robin had turned into an open yard and was perched on the low branch of a hawthorn tree. She watched the bird, delighted by the pretty birdsong.

After a moment, her attention shifted to the cottage. To her surprise, the cottage which from the road had seemed old and ruined, was on closer inspection, fresh and white, its front door a glossy red. The cottage gleamed in the morning sun. To the right of the grass driveway, there was an impeccably well kempt garden, wildflowers all around its edges. Aoife noticed there was someone in the garden.

It was an old woman with white hair, long skirts and a kerchief tied around her head. She was cutting flowers with a pair of scissors and placing them in a wicker basket on the lawn beside her. She looked up as Aoife approached.

"Ah. Aoife bhi me ag suil agat." The old woman smiled, her rosy cheeks apple-like in her round face.

Aoife stared.

"Sure, ye don't speak the Irish yet. Ye will of course, in time. What I said was, Tis waiting for ye I have been."

"You have? I came after the robin. It was singing to me."

"Aye. Robins do that."

"I think it brought me here."

The old woman nodded her head. "They do that too."

"I don't know your name."

"Ye can call me Nell."

"Nell," repeated the child. "Are you the Nell that makes the cake?"

Nell smiled. "Cake is it yer after?"

"Well, if you've made a cake, I would like to taste it. Sean said you make really good cake."

"Hmph!" said Nell. "Maybe another day so."

Aoife looked at the house and back to Nell. "Is this your cottage Nell?"

"Once upon a time so."

"That's the beginning of a story."

"So tis now." Nell smiled again, her blue eyes twinkling. "Tis the beginning of yer own story Aoife.

"Hasn't my story already started?"

"Ah! But this is a new story within a bigger story and tis all about ye Aoife."

"Ohhh!" Aoife was captivated. She loved stories. "Will you tell it to me?"

"I will so, all in good time. But now, help me carry this basket of flowers inside the cottage there. Ye can help me find something to put them in. Brighten the place up so they will."

Without waiting for a reply, Nell turned and hobbled into the cottage leaving Aoife and the basket of flowers. Aoife looked around, shielding her eyes in search of the robin. The bird had flown away. Aoife looked uncertainly after Nell for a moment. Mommy had told her not to go off with strangers. But Nell can't be a stranger, she thought. She knew Aoife's name after all. She hesitated another moment, then picked up the basket and followed Nell into the cottage.

A fire burned brightly in an old-fashioned hearth. A black pot hung from a hook over the fire. Aoife saw that the hook was held by a handle which Nell now used to swing the pot towards her, away from the fire. Nell stirred the contents with a ladle, took a sip and smacked her lips together in appreciation. "Good. It tastes just right."

"Could I have some?" asked Aoife, remembering she'd had no breakfast that morning.

"Of course, ye can. In fact, I would like ye to drink a bit, for it will help ye to see."

"Oh, I can see all right," said Aoife nodding wisely. "Mommy says my eyes are too big and that I see too much already."

"Wisht now child. Tis a different kind of seeing."

"It is? How come?"

"Sure, and ye'll have the sight. Ye have it already but this will help ye develop the gift all the faster. And ye'll need it for to see the Folk when it pleases them to be seen. Ye'll like that well enough won't ye child?"

"I suppose so," Aoife agreed hesitantly. "Although I don't actually know who the Folk are."

"Well now, tis the Faerie Folk I am speaking of here."

"Fairies? Yes, I'd like to see fairies. I'd need help to see them wouldn't I because they're so small."

Nell laughed, a deep hearty sound.

"Why are you laughing? Is it funny what I said?"

"Sure, the Faerie are not little. They are big. Full grown like you and me."

"Like you and me." Aoife turned the idea over in her mind. "I didn't know that. I thought they were tiny, like Tinkerbell."

Nell laughed. "Well now and what is a Tinkerbell? Ah! Tis all right so," she dismissed the child's apparent confusion with a wave of her hand. "Tis Faerie Folk I speak of. Ye've not seen them yet, but ye will. Now can I tempt ye with a little soup?"

"I suppose so, if it will help me see fairies."

The old lady nodded at the child and grunted as if satisfied. She scooped a little of the mixture out of the pot and held the ladle toward Aoife.

"Will I have to drink a lot?" asked Aoife.

"No indeed, just a very little. A sip or two." Nell lifted the ladle to Aoife's lips.

"It smells good. Are there vegetables in it?"

"Aye vegetables to be sure. And other good things.

"What other good things?"

"Heather berries for one."

"Heather berries? I never heard of those."

"Some call them bilberries; small and dark blue they are."

"Oh! Like blueberries?"

Nell seemed to consider this. "Sweeter they are and a little darker in color."

"Better than blueberries then."

"Well, no. Just different. They are for to help ye see. And good eyesight ye will have too."

"Oh!"

"Will ye drink Aoife?"

"I will," Aoife tasted a little of the soup. The liquid dribbled down her chin and she wiped it away with the back of her hand. "I like it." She drank a bit more. "I can taste nuts. Does it have nuts in it?"

"Ah well, it's not that yer tasting nuts. No, that would be the secret ingredient. It tastes a bit like nuts, so it does."

"Why does it need a secret ingredient?"

"Why, to make it a seeing soup of course." Nell shook her head and smiled.

Aoife pondered this for a minute and then asked, "So, will you tell me the secret ingredient?"

"Ah me dear and why would I not tell ye? It's a particularly tiny mushroom do ye see?"

"A mushroom that tastes like nuts? Well, it must be very small. I can't see any in the soup." Aoife peered into her bowl just to make sure.

"Bless you child, tis all chopped up with the other vegetables and herbs."

"Where did you get it, the secret ingredient? From the store in Clonacool?"

The old woman laughed. "No indeed. I picked them myself from the hawthorn grove."

"It tastes good. Maybe I'll get some mushrooms from there and ask Mommy to make the soup at home."

"Well child, ye would have to be out and about under a full moon, up there in the circle, to find these mushrooms. And ye would have to know exactly where to look too."

"Oh!" said Aoife. She could see how that would a problem, especially if it was dark. She didn't think Mommy would let her go looking for mushrooms in the night, full moon or no. She finished drinking from the ladle.

"Tis a good girl ye are Aoife," said Nell. She placed the ladle back in the pot and pushed it into its cooking position over the fire.

Aoife looked about the room expectantly. "I don't see any fairies yet."

"Now, tis the Folk will not show themselves til they are ready to be seen."

Aoife asked anxiously. "Yes, but when will I see them?"

"When they are ready and not a moment before. Ye'll just have to wait child."

"Oh," said Aoife, a little disappointed. "Okay."

Aoife looked around, exploring the room. She saw that there wasn't much furniture, just one big wooden chair by the fire and a table with a straight-backed chair next to it. A dresser stood in one corner of the room. There were so many dishes, cups, mugs, teapots and jugs of all sizes on the dresser that Aoife told herself it surely could not take one more thing. In the far corner near the fire, there was a bed. "Do you sleep in here?"

"In my time I slept in here every night."

"Isn't this your time?"

"Sometimes," said the old lady mysteriously.

Aoife watched her, waiting for more of an explanation. As none was given, she left the subject alone. Instead she inspected the bed, touching her fingers to it. "Is this mattress made of straw?"

"It is so."

"Is it comfortable?"

"Tis warm on cold nights."

"That's good," said Aoife politely. Her attention was drawn to the open door where the sky seemed to darken suddenly, threatening rain. "I should probably go. Mommy won't want me to get wet."

"If ye must go, then ye must." Nell walked with her to the door.

Aoife had a thought and stopped to ask, "Mommy should see the fairies with me. Will I bring Mommy here to drink the soup?"

"Mayhap child. Mayhap. Go on wit' ye now, away to yer mother. Tis going to rain as ye say and ye will not want to get your pretty clothes full of water, now will ye."

Aoife laughed at the idea and looked up into the sky for the rain that would fill her pyjamas. There were dark clouds to be sure but no rain yet. As she turned into the lane, Aoife looked back to see Nell standing in her doorway. She waved. Nell waved back and then was lost to view as the hedgerow hid the cottage behind her.

When Aoife arrived at her own cottage, Pam was hauling a picnic basket onto the big wooden table under the alder trees. She and Kay looked up just as Aoife ran into the yard with the rain starting full pelt behind her.

"Damn!" said Pam and hauled the picnic basket off the table.

"You were a long time Aoife," said Kay. "Did you go to your great-grandmother's cottage?"

"No. I followed the robin."

"You did? That's nice and where did the robin lead you?"

"To Old Nell's cottage."

Kay and Aoife followed Pam, who had relocated to the long refectory table inside the cottage. Kay continued the conversation with her daughter. "You say you didn't go to your great-grandmother's cottage Aoife?"

"I forgot." Aoife sat down on the bench under the big mirror. "I met Sean. He went to see the caves."

Kay laughed. She'd had that conversation with Sean too. "Calves," she explained to Pam.

"What else would it be!" said Pam.

Aoife was soon busy with sliced apple, cheese and crusty bread spread with Irish butter. "This is good," she said, swinging her legs, as she did when she was happy.

Pam leaned forward, "And where is this Old Nell to be found Aoife?"

Aoife considered this. "I shouldn't call her Old Nell. She said I could call her Nell. But really," she lowered her voice, "she is very old."

"I see." Pam was amused. "Where does she live, this Nell?"

"Way, way down the lane, past the great-greats. All the way down."

"Hmm," said Pam. "I thought I knew everyone at this end. But sure, there are so many small villages scattered about the outskirts of Clonacool, I can't expect myself to know everyone. Sure enough if they don't come into the pub I'll hardly know them." Pam looked over at Kay. "I keep meaning to get out more and then I don't. I just get so busy in there you know. I can't say I've heard of Nell though. You'll have to show me where she lives Aoife."

"I can't walk back there now. It's raining," said the child reasonably.

"True for you," said Pam. "But you say it was past the great greats." Pam winked at Kay for she had explained Aoife's attempt at mastering the difficult concept of a grandmother, a great grandmother and a great-great grandmother. "What did Nell's cottage look like?"

"Well," began Aoife.

"Don't speak with your mouth full Aoife." Kay had strict rules about etiquette. "We don't want to see your half-masticated lunch. Finish what you have in your mouth and swallow. Then drink water and swallow again. And then you can talk."

"Sorry Mommy. Oops. I did it again." Aoife's hand flew to her mouth. "Sorry." Aoife chewed her food carefully, self-consciously aware that both her mother and Pam were watching. She swallowed an extra big gulp of water for effect, to show how seriously she took her mother's advice.

Kay tried to maintain a stern expression, while Pam smothered giggles behind her hand. Kay sent an admonishing glare in Pam's direction while Aoife had her glass of water upended, drinking obediently.

Pam mouthed 'Whaaat?' She turned back to the child. "Now! Aoife, tell us about Nell and her cottage," she smiled encouragingly.

Aoife began her story again. "She's very old and she has red cheeks like an apple."

CHAPTER 4 –LIAM

Kay strolled along the track that led through the bog. The bright sun of early spring warmed her back. Aoife ran ahead with Sean's collie which had tagged along for the outing. Felan had been a pup when Kay was last in Ireland but had grown into a sizeable animal.

As the child and the dog ran off the track onto the spongy bog surface, Kay's first thought was to call a warning. She drew back her raised hand in favor of a deeper instinct, that of allowing her child the freedom to roam at will. She told herself there were not many wet muddy areas left, where the child might sink her rubber boots. She smiled as she remembered Liam calling them wellies instead of rubber boots. She thought it funny how things were named so differently between here and back home.

Turning her attention back to the bog, she recalled Sean telling her the bog had been overworked in the past fifty years, so that there weren't many places a body might actually sink right in.

‘How terrible,’ she thought, ‘for those Celtic men and women of earlier centuries traversing the bog late at night, who may have been under the influence of alcohol or within dark moonless night, had wandered off this narrow track. The mud would have claimed them instantly, like a terrifying monster from the depths. The mud would suck at their bodies while they floundered and sank ever deeper. All that would be left was maybe a bit of Irish tartan to mark the place where their living breathing self, had moments before gasped in a terrible knowing that they were looking their last at the stars.

‘What thoughts did they have in those moments, as the truth of their destiny came upon them with full force? Did they think of the eternity that awaited them? Did they look their last on the beauty of the night? Were drunken senses restored to full clarity in those last moments? Did the stars never seem so bright nor the moon so full? And as the oozing, sucking mud claimed the very breath that separated them from their former selves, did they throw one arm up into the night, an intentional witness to the life they had lived?’

Such thoughts caused Kay to quickly look around for Aoife. Her sudden panic was restored by the laughter of the child and the playful barking of the dog. She thought to call Aoife back to the safety of her side, yet she subdued the instinct of the helicopter mother.

Kay had learned to favor a deeper awareness that Aoife was not like other children. It was as if a voice whispered inside her head that her daughter was of the Fae, aware of nature, knowing just where to place her feet.

The child of a mortal woman and a prince of the Sidhe. Kay reflected on this as she so often did. She recalled the moment when she made her decision not to go through the mist with Mac. He had urged her to recall who she was, a shape shifter, the mythical Caer of his dreams.

Until the very end she had resisted this concept but then at last, the memory of her former life had surfaced. Then and only then she had realized she could not go with him through the mist. If she had then all would be lost, as she could never return from there to her own time. She knew this with a surety that she could not even fathom. Yet know it she did.

And now, when she looked on Aoife, her heart swelled with a great love for the child. Had she entered the mist, she wondered now, would Aoife have been born? What would she herself have become in that place that was not a place? At least here in the world, which was for her the sole reality, Aoife lived and breathed as an ordinary child. If it came to pass that Aoife developed her own powers then it would be through the natural way of things, not because she was in another realm that was not of Kay's making. Here at least, Kay could control to some extent, the progress of Aoife's development, or so she preferred to believe.

That Aoife was Fae, there was no doubt. There had been times when she was around other children back home, that the power in her was recognized. When crossed by another child, Aoife would stand very still, her slanted green eyes glinting strangely. The other children said they felt compelled to look at Aoife, that they had seen something in Aoife's eyes that made them wary of her. This had resulted in Aoife missing out on some of the birthday parties, where all the children had in common the comfort of their ordinariness. But Aoife was no ordinary child.

This was one of the reasons why Kay had agreed with Liam's impetuous decision to give up their life back home and come to live in Ireland. Knowing that the child needed space to grow into herself was more important than Kay's own fear of returning here. That fear was born from her exquisite pain and yearning for Mac, for he had taken her heart along with him that night.

Even thinking on it now brought emotions surging throughout her body. With it came a memory of the overwhelming passion she had known with Mac at the edge of the mist. Kay could not risk that again.

She had purposely built a deep friendship with Liam where their lovemaking, while not of the visceral passion she had felt with Mac, was good and lasting and organic. By its very nature, the sex she experienced with Liam was carefully woven throughout the fabric of their daily lives, so that they were never far from the act of love itself. Kay practiced this at a conscious level. She encouraged it as a way of binding them together, through playfulness and spontaneity.

That had not always been the case, for Kay had been somewhat repressed prior to meeting Mac. It was as if the lovemaking between her and Mac had opened something within her, a deeper awareness of her true self. Between this awareness and the counseling, she was able to take in her stride Liam's natural obsessive tendencies. On occasion, this let to him being controlling. The woman she was back then was easily subdued by this, but not so anymore. She consciously allowed him to win now as the need arose, by curling him witch-like, around her finger or more precisely, around her tail.

And this was strange in itself, for when she was with Mac, she had known in those last moments that she was a mythical swan shape-shifter he had insisted she was. She had known this when she stretched herself out for him to take her in the soft mossy ground at the edge of the mist, her skin on fire for him.

There had been a sensation of feathery down about her rump and of a mist that gently tickled her tail feathers, of which she had previously been unaware.

It was in that moment of climax, that there was a joining with the moon and the stars and the mist that invaded her body. She recognized Mac then, knew him as the Maccan, prince of the Sidhe of the Tuatha de Danaan. Mythical creatures, they dwelled in the place beyond, accessed only through the mountains of western Ireland.

Kay had known too, that she was Caer, the shape-shifting swan, a descendant of Lir. She was the Caer that Mac had dreamed of and sought all those years. Swans mate for life. And so it was, as Mac emptied himself into her willing waiting womb that she not only knew she was pregnant, but knew she was his for all time. And yet, fearful that Mac would come for his child if he realized Kay was pregnant, she had left Ireland with Liam almost immediately.

Kay felt she was in a stronger position now. Liam and Aoife had attached as father and daughter. It was a strong bond that could not be denied. Aoife had enjoyed a normal childhood, that is until she had begun to exhibit signs of her Fae lineage. If Kay had entered the mist with Mac, she might not be in control of her own destiny and that of her child.

Aoife's laughter brought Kay's head up in search of her. The child ran, bouncing over the springy surface of the bog. A light breeze lifted her curls. Kay laughed, her own mood lightening as she looked on her daughter.

Suddenly Aoife paused as if listening. Seeing her, Kay listened too. They both turned their heads instinctively in the direction they had come. The distant rumble of an engine came to them on the breeze.

Aoife moved first. "Daddy!" she yelled and raced across the bog with Felan running and jumping beside her. Barking in excitement, the animal raced forward only to stop and wait for her to catch up before he raced off again.

Kay paused only to see the joy in the spring of her daughter's step as she ran to greet her father. Soon Kay was running too, as much as the stone and pebbles and unevenness of the track would allow.

Felan left them as they passed Sean's cottage. Kay and Aoife ran on down the lane until they reached their own home. A taxi could be seen jauntily receding in the billowing dust, away back to the airport road.

A tall man and well-muscled, Liam waited in the yard of the cottage, his chestnut hair gleaming in the sunlight. His suitcases were forgotten to one side of the driveway as Liam gazed in delight at the verdant garden, with its naturally growing wildflowers and the daffodils they had planted together years before. Birds called their welcome from the holly, larch and alder trees. He turned as Kay and Aoife approached, blue eyes intense against his ruddy complexion.

"Daddy! Daddy! You're home," Aoife cried as she raced into Liam's arms. He swung her up into the air and held her there, the two of them looking with delight into the eyes of the other, for all the world like a natural father and child.

Kay held back, enjoying their moment of reunion. She cherished such moments for the closeness that it brought between the two. She loved the solid reality that a man like Liam brought to fatherhood. Kay knew that he loved this child with his whole heart, loved her fiercely and without reservation. Kay was devoted to him for it. She felt strongly that Aoife needed the grounding that such a loving relationship could bring. This was after all, a child born to a destiny neither she nor her mother could even guess at.

Aoife scrambled down from Liam's arms and ran to her mother, arms outstretched. "Look Mommy. He's here. Daddy's here." Aoife grabbed Kay's hand and pulled her towards Liam. "Come and love him Mommy."

Kay laughed and locked eyes with Liam. She moved toward him, exuding a certain animalism in her walk. It was the unconsciously conscious way in which she tied him to her that he could never understand. He only knew that whenever he saw her, he wanted her.

As Kay walked into Liam's arms, it was Aoife's turn to watch them re-connect. It was as if in some deeper part of her, Aoife recognized and understood that in such embrace lay the safety of their very existence as a family unit. Kay glancing down, caught this expression on Aoife's face. She wondered if her daughter could possibly know such a thing, or even be aware that it was needed.

Chattering and laughing together, the three walked into the cottage. Liam carried the bigger of his two suitcases. Kay and Liam exchanged a look of amusement as Aoife brought up the rear. Struggling mightily with determination, she dragged Liam's smaller case along the dusty driveway.

"We've had mice Daddy," puffed Aoife as she finally abandoned the case just inside the door of the cottage.

Kay immediately rolled her eyes. "It's been terrible Liam. Sean tried to help us get rid of them, but the little creatures keep getting back in somehow."

At this, Aoife shifted uncomfortably. Liam caught the action and looked pointedly at Aoife who refused to meet his eyes.

"Well!" he said. "We shall have to take care of that, now won't we? Maybe Aoife can help." He gently poked her in the stomach and whispered in the child's ear, "And you can tell me why the mice keep coming back in, okay?" He tickled Aoife. Her sullen expression quickly turned to delight. Liam looked over and winked at Kay.

The three prepared lunch together of homemade soup and crusty bread rolls with Irish butter. As Kay passed Liam a bowl of soup, their fingers touched and lingered, eyes meeting with the promise of delights to follow.

"Are you tired Liam?" There was innuendo in Kay's voice. She raised an eyebrow for emphasis.

"Tired?" Aoife was incredulous. "He only just got here. Silly Mommy. How can he be tired?"

Kay and Liam laughed. "Well," explained her father. "It was a long flight." He looked to Kay for assistance.

"Don't you remember Aoife?" Kay prompted. "You were so tired on the plane, but you couldn't sleep for ages."

"I was excited, that's why. Were you excited Daddy?"

"Ha ha. Yes, I was." He yawned then. "I am quite tired actually."

"Oh," said Aoife. "I think I'll go for a walk in the village if you're going to sleep. I've been exploring Daddy, finding things. I'll take you around the village tomorrow when you've finished being tired."

"That sounds like a plan honey. That's what we'll do." Liam ruffled Aoife's curls.

"Well." Aiofe got down from her chair and gathered her dishes to take to the kitchen. "I have to go now." She wiped her mouth with the tea towel. "See you later," she called as she skipped out through the front door.

Kay and Liam watched her go, laughing at her childish antics. "So, how tired are you?" Kay fluttered her eyelids at Liam.

He smiled at her. "I am tired Kay," he stroked her hand. "But if you don't mind, I just want to go for a quick walk. I won't be long. I'll go on my own," he said as Kay got up from the table, prepared to go with him.

"On your own," said Kay. "Why?"

"I just," Liam appeared to grasp for words. "Want to clear my head that's all." He moved toward the kitchen door. "There's a big tree at the end of the field there. It might be suitable to hang a swing for Aoife."

"Can't it wait til tomorrow?" Kay was perplexed.

"It won't take but a minute or two. I'm too wound up to sleep right now."

"I have the cure for that." Kay caught up to him by the door and wound her arms around him.

Liam turned back and dropped a quick kiss on Kay's head. He gently disengaged her arms from his body. "I won't be long, I promise."

Kay watched him walk across the field through the reeds. "Well!" she muttered. "I must be losing my charms." She gathered up the lunch things from the dining table. When she returned to the kitchen window, there was no sign of Liam. She looked left and right but couldn't see him through the oak trees that edged the field. "Maybe Sean's in the meadow and they're chatting." She dismissed a little nagging voice at the back of her brain.

An hour later, Kay was unpacking Liam's suitcases, deciding which items could be put away in cupboards and which would go into the wash. It wasn't in her to leave Liam to unpack. She knew from experience that he wouldn't do it for several weeks. It would end up driving her crazy to see the still-packed suitcase sitting in the living room day after day. She didn't have the patience for it.

She came across a small red notebook at the bottom of the case and recognized it as one Liam had bought. His intention had been to use it as a sort of diary while he was away on vacation.

Picking up the notebook, Kay began to open it. She closed it again, not wanting to invade Liam's privacy. Unable to resist, she opened it and flicked through the pages. Mostly they were notes about sightseeing, sore calves from hiking, a reminder to ask about guided hikes in the mountains, more sightseeing notes. Then toward the back of the book, Kay realized some of the pages were well thumbed as if the same pages had been visited often. She flicked to one of these which opened on a series of markings, horizontal lines close together, one beneath the other. One or two of these lines had arrow markings at each end. Some of the markings looked like an H or half of a Z. She turned the book upside down, but it didn't make sense that way either.

Kay made a mental note to mention finding the notebook to Liam and ask him about the markings. She placed the book, along with Liam's clean clothing, inside the wardrobe where he would see it easily. As she became busy with other things, Kay forgot about the notebook.

When Liam returned, Kay was in the garden watering her plants with the hose. It had been unusually dry over the past week and she didn't want her newly planted flowers withering in the heat.

With the intention of reaching plants toward the back of the rockery, Kay held the hose in such a way as to create a more direct and harsher stream of water. She was so focused on this task, that she didn't notice Liam behind her until he grabbed her around the waist. She screamed and flung her hands up, still holding the hose which had the effect of splashing them both with water.

"Oh!" teased Liam. "Bath time is it?" He flapped his hand through the water so that it sprinkled Kay.

Her immediate reaction was to reach around him to push the hose down the back of his jeans. He yelled and sprinted away, but to no avail because she followed, spraying him from head to foot.

Just at that moment, Aoife came back from her walk clutching a bunch of wildflowers. When she saw her parents playing in the water, she ran to join the fun.

"Me too! Me too!" Aoife laughed with delight as Kay sprayed first her and then Liam. The wildflowers were abandoned as Aoife rubbed the water from her eyes.

"Come on Aoife," yelled Liam. "Let's get Mommy!" Kay screamed and dropping the hose as she tried to make a run for it.

Quickly Liam picked up the hose and went after Kay. He covered half of the hose with a finger so as to create a stronger jet of water just as Kay had done earlier. Aoife held her face up to catch the drops of water with her tongue. Liam held the hose on Kay and watched as she turned and turned, laughing and holding her long neck up to the sun, stunning in her golden beauty.

CHAPTER 5 – FIRE RITUAL

Kay lay in bed, listening to Liam as he went through his morning custom of lighting the fire. She had told Pam it was an example of Liam's obsessive nature. Yet, it was a ritual she held close to her heart.

She could hear the clang of the fire tongs and rustle of newspaper as Liam began the procedure. Next came the riddling of the grate, effected by jiggling a little knob on the side of the stove, to release the ashes into the pan below.

Liam didn't get to do this back home. With central heating there was no need, nor did he have time to enjoy such a pastime. He was usually up and out of the door to his job. But here in Ireland, the ritual of lighting the fire was the way of things in their cottage and in many other Irish cottages too. It was part of the rhythm of days, handed down through generations of Irish people and one that Liam loved. It was comforting to hear him. It gave Kay the feeling that all was right with the world.

She knew Liam secretly liked to have this time to himself. He enjoyed the quiet at the beginning of the day. It was an opportunity for him to gather his thoughts, while his hands went through the busy motions of recreating the heart of the home. It was almost a religious moment, a mirror image of the sun rising through the window beyond the cottage. In the lighting of the fire, Liam created his own sun within his home, an offering to the day.

She smiled as she imagined him carefully positioning the smallest piece of firelighter in the center of the grate. He had an ongoing bet with himself to see how small a piece he could use to light the fire. Kay heard the sound of newspaper being crumpled and then the snapping of twigs.

The fire would begin to draw quickly, because Liam would leave the door of the wood stove open just a little. Sitting back for a few minutes his eyes would focus on the flame, watching for the moment when he should feed the fire with more twigs and then add a log of wood.

Finally, Liam would add bricks of turf bought from local men who dug the turf out from the peat bog, just beyond Sean's cottage. The turf would then be stored in a barn for a year or so. Once it was dry enough for burning, it would be sold on to the likes of Liam.

The fire must have caught because Kay heard it begin to crackle, followed by the clanging of metal on metal as Liam shut the door of the stove. He would wait until it sent its heat into the room and then turn down the flue just a little.

She heard the squeak of the damper handle, as Liam turned it to vent the chimney, allowing the fire to build. This was her cue. It was time to get out of bed and join Liam in the living room.

Kicking the bedsheets away, Kay stretched, her body contorting in delicious abandon. Ignoring the unmade bed, she pulled on her pale blue robe and pushed her feet into cotton slippers of matching color.

She found Liam still seated in what he liked to call his fire-lighting chair. He had drawn the curtains back to give himself a view through the window. He liked to watch the birds coming and going. The very next day after he had arrived, he made a visit to the local store to buy food for the birds. A variety of feed now hung from the holly tree. She kissed the top of his head. "Where's Aoife?"

"She ran off to Sean's place to feed the lambs."

"Did she change out of her pyjamas?"

Liam shrugged. "Don't fuss Kay. Let her be."

Kay rolled her eyes. She liked things to be orderly but acknowledged that she'd have to be up really early to catch Aoife. The outdoors was like a magnet to the child.

She perched on the edge of Liam's chair and gazed at the fire, appreciating the visual comfort. Liam brought her attention to the scene beyond the window. "Look Kay, they love the sunflower seeds." They watched as birds flew on and off the bird feeders. "I always ask for the shelled seeds," he said. "I find there's no waste if they're shelled."

He pointed out the little coconut halves filled with suet. "They like the suet too." He smiled his boyish smile at her. She kissed him. "They do, really, and peanuts," he said, kissing and talking at the same time. "I like to strew peanuts along the wall. Look!" They looked back through the window. Birds hopped about the wall, a testament to Liam's choice of bird food.

With a contented sigh, Liam turned to scan the room. Kay followed his gaze as he looked from the high, barn shaped pinewood ceiling, to the joists where the ceiling overlapped the yellow walls and down to the wood floor. All of this, he had built himself. He had restored the two-hundred-year old cottage, making a comfortably modern home from an old dilapidated shell. Kay watched his gaze come back to the hearth.

"It's all come together a treat hasn't it?"

"It is lovely, yes," said Kay, knowing that he was talking about the wood surround of the fireplace.

"This tree was old you know, maybe three hundred years. It was my good luck that it was struck by lightning. It gave me this beautiful piece."

He reached out and ran his hand over the mantel and down the sides. "See how I was able to split it in half. It was so easy, like it was waiting for just this purpose, to sit here and grace our home. It took a lot of sanding and polishing. But you know, I enjoyed doing it, working with my hands like that." It was certainly a unique frame he had created for the fireplace.

With his large hands, Liam then inspected the stonework behind the wood burning stove, nodding with approval and maybe a little surprise that it had all come together so well.

Kay yawned, breaking the momentary spell. "Decaf," she said and propelled herself toward the kitchen.

Behind her, Liam laughed. "Decaf indeed!" he mocked.

"Works for me." Kay yawned again and walked into the kitchen. She heard a gasp from Liam and popped her head back through the door.

Liam gripped the sides of his chair, eyes popping, staring in disbelief. Kay followed his gaze to see a cat lurking in the ferns, waiting for the birds to come swooping down after the seeds. It would pounce if the birds were not quick enough.

"Where's the broom?" yelled Liam. Kay flattened herself against the door. She knew from experience that Liam in defense of his birds, became a force of nature. He rushed past her, grabbed the broom and ran out of the cottage yelling for the cat to "Get outa there before I catch ya, you little rascal."

The cat ran, leaving Liam in the yard, legs apart, broom held across his chest like an assault rifle. He looked for all the world like he was defending his property against the marauding hordes.

Kay shook her head and went about the business of making her decaf. When she returned to the living room mug in hand, Liam was standing in the doorway of the cottage, a sack of seed in his hands, ready for spreading along the wall. He turned to Kay explaining, “Sorry about that. I like cats. You know I do. But I don’t want to encourage them to do their hunting here.” He was distracted by the activity of the birds as they clustered around the suet balls. “Look at this Kay. Come here and look.”

She padded over to join him at the door. He indicated the balls of suet, which also hung from the holly trees. “They love those suet balls, the birds. They need the fat for energy. Look at them. Do you see how the birds hang from them while they eat?”

Just at that moment, a dog jumped onto the wall. It grabbed a suet ball right out of the tree with its teeth and made off with it.

Liam bellowed revenge at the dog and dropped the sack. Seed spilled out over Kay’s slippers, onto the step and into the cottage. Liam ran off down the lane after the dog. Her decaf slopped out of the mug, adding to the growing mess as Kay tried to step back from the spilled birdseed. There were seeds between her toes. She could hear Liam yelling in the distance as he went tearing away after the dog, which yelped with alarm in its efforts to escape Liam’s wrath.

It was a good half hour before Liam returned. Kay had mopped up the spilled coffee and swept the seed back into its sack. Liam’s expression was glum. “I gave the farmer a piece of me mind,” he said. “He should feed his dog better so it’s not coming here after me balls.”

Kay laughed at his unwitting play on words. “It’s Thursday.” She placed a hand on his broad chest. His heart was still beating fast, a result of his race after the dog. “Let’s go to the pub tonight. There’ll be a live band.”

"But er," he began. He looked towards the field out back of the cottage, then down at her face. "Okay," he relented. "Let's do that." He took her hand and nibbled her fingers. She grinned at him and sighed with happy content.

CHAPTER 6 – PUB NIGHT

"Will she go to sleep all right Kay? I'm thinking the noise from the pub will keep her awake." Pam ruffled Aoife's curls gently. "Will ye sleep Aoife? Will you?"

Aoife yawned in answer and smiled sleepily, long brown lashes closing over her green eyes.

"See." Pam whispered over her shoulder to Kay. "What did I tell you? She's out, like a light already." She stroked the Aoife's cheek. "You're a good girl for your Auntie Pam aren't you Aoife? Sleep well my little love."

Aoife's breathing was steady as the two women left the room. Carefully closing the door of the apartment where Pam lived above the pub, they headed down the stairs into the noise and general revelry. Pam slipped behind the bar where Eamon, a local lad, helped out on Thursdays. He looked grateful for her arrival, snowed under as he was by drinks orders being called to him across the bar.

Liam was standing off to one side, sipping a beer and lost in his own thoughts. Kay slipped her arm through his. She sighed, content that Liam was home at last, albeit had taken him several days to recover from his hiking vacation and the resulting jet lag of his flight.

"A penny for your thoughts." Kay smiled up at him.

Liam shook himself out of his reverie. "Ah … just glad to be back in Ireland." He put his arm around her shoulder and pulled her against his side. "I love all this, the music, the craic. There's nothing like it in the world."

"Yeah? So why aren't you in the middle of it?"

He followed her glance toward the bar. "Just taking it in, you know."

It was Thursday and that meant there were bigger takings for Pam than any other night of the week. Regulars crowded the bar elbow to elbow and a good meter out into the pub. If drinks were wanted, customers beyond this crowd were obliged to repeat "Excuse me," several times before reaching the bar to place their orders.

Most of those close to the bar knew each other. For generations each family were familiar with the history of the other. This extended to the point where their collective stories went back a hundred years and more. Repeated at intervals for a laugh or a cautionary tale, their stories were like those told by warriors around a campfire after a hunt or cottars after a day in the fields in the days before electric light and television.

There was one such story being told right then. Kay and Liam moved closer to the bar, the better to hear it.

"And young Eoin back in those day," Tom Kelly was just getting started on his story. "He was a holy terror for the drink, so he was." The listeners nodded their heads, not for the fact that they knew the young Eoin referred to, but because most of them knew of the story, passed down as it had been by word of mouth, mostly within the camaraderie of the pub.

The teller of tales continued. "Aye he was one for enjoying his pint. And so …"

At this point he was interrupted by John Egan, a newcomer to the area and therefore not privy to the history being disclosed.

"How long ago was this now Tom?"

“It was a long time ago John.” Tom answered patiently and then continued. “Now! Here it was that on that day of days, a stranger passed through the village and … “

“How do ye know his name was Eoin?”

“What?” Tom was slightly irritated at the repeated interruption.

“I said, how do ye know his name was Eoin? It could as well have been Donal or Colum so.”

Tom regarded John for a long moment before answering. “Well now John, it could as you say, have been a Donal or a Colum but we know for a fact that it was Eoin.”

“How?”

“What’s that now?” Tom bent his ear towards John, as if not believing his own hearing.

“How do ye know for a fact that his name was Eoin?”

“Look now John.” Tom was clearly irritated but still trying to maintain a modicum of self-control. “His name was Eoin. We know this because his people lived right here in the village. Some of them still do. Now, do ye want to hear this story or…?”

“I do but …”

“But what?” Tom’s face had turned puce.

“Where had he come from, this stranger?”

“What the feck does it matter where he came from? Isn’t it enough that he was here at all?”

“Well, I was just thinking …”

“Stop with the thinking so. Aren’t ye a blow-in yourself! Will ye be quiet now and let me get on with the story or tell it yerself if ye’ve a mind.” Tom glared at John and then extended his challenging eye to the group, who responded by shaking their heads at the foolishness of John for questioning the validity of a good story.

Cowed at last and a little unsteady on his feet with the drink, John buried his face in his glass by way of acquiescence.

Tom glared at him. “It’s bad ye are yerself for the drink tonight.” This broke the tension and drew a laugh from the listeners. Tom went on “You and young Eoin, you’re a pair. Now let’s be having silence from you or I’ll never get the tale told.” He extended his glare once again around the waiting group. At the sea of contained innocence on the waiting faces, he relaxed visibly and began again.

“Now, this stranger he was wantin’ a woman.” At that point he noticed Kay standing with Liam. Tom nodded in her direction. “Pardon me if ye will, but it’s an old story and a true one.”

Kay smiled encouragingly. Liam squeezed Kay’s shoulder and winked at Tom, who started in on his story again.

“So,” he repeated, lowering his voice considerably not to offend Kay, but having to repeat the line anyway for the sake of continuity. “This stranger, he was a wanting of a woman.”

John opened his mouth again but was quickly silenced by a vicious dart of fire from Tom’s eye.

“Now! Young Eoin was short of cash for a bit o’ the drink. He’d a little of the mischief in him and that is needed to spin a good yarn, so it is. He saw in it, an opportunity of sustaining his imbibing habit for the evening, so he said to the stranger,” and here Tom changed the tone of his voice to add a bit of wily calculation. “There’s a woman back at my cottage. She’s unattached and she’s a comely girl so she is. If ye’ve a mind, I could introduce ye and see if ye get along, so.”

Tom fixed his audience with a wink and a knowing expression as he went on. “Now, the stranger, he became enamored of the idea of the woman in question. He bought pint after pint for young Eoin throughout that long evening. Eoin the rascal, he led that man along until himself was full to the brim with beer.”

The crowd laughed quietly, in full knowledge of the outcome but enjoying the story anyway. Even John was listening intently now, although it was easy to see he wouldn’t be much longer on his feet, as the drink had a good hold on him.

"At the end of the evening, young Eoin, the worse for drink, something like our John here now." The group laughed and jostled John for effect. John laughed along with the others although he frowned briefly as though a little unsure what the joke was.

Tom brought the story to its close. "And when it was finally revealed that the only woman in young Eoin's cottage was his ole mother, the stranger was so incensed that he took out his disappointment on Eoin. Drinking glasses were smashed and a stool broken before the two of them were thrown outside."

There were guffaws all around. Tom laughed with them and clapped his hands together with an air of finality. "They say young Eoin scrambled off through the fields as fast as his drunken legs would carry him. The only thing that saved him, was the other fella was just as worse for drink and he didn't know the village. Eoin got clear away and I heard he had the good sense to stay away from the pub for nearly a week after."

At this point another round was ordered, with Tom earning a free pint for his story and the craic that was in it.

Against this background of happy camaraderie, all ten seating booths were crammed with locals and tourists mostly come to enjoy the live music.

The musicians themselves took turns in singing whatever they had prepared for the night. The musicians were not paid. They were rewarded with free beer and all they could drink. This wasn't very much considering they sang and played all through the evening.

They came to the pub each week to play their instruments in the company of like-minded musicians. Between them, they had several guitars, a bodhran drum, a fiddle and a flute. Just at that moment, they accompanied one of their group, as he sang and played his guitar to Gordon Lightfoot's 'Early Morning Rain.'

Between songs, the group of seven or eight smiled and laughed among themselves. Telling quick anecdotes in quiet voices heard only among their own circle, they encouraged and uplifted with gracious comments on each other's performance.

Padraic O'Hare one of the guitarists, ran the show. He brought the sound equipment and microphone. As a sideline, he recorded hymns for local people to order. He didn't charge for these but enjoyed doing it as a service. His customers were mostly Catholics who commissioned the hymns sung by Padraic, to be played at home for the edification of their dear departed ones.

Another guitarist, Brendan Nolan, ran the local bed and breakfast. Well-liked in the community, he was instrumental in getting the Sunday tearoom going in the church hall. Women throughout the village took turns contributing homemade cake. This gave people a place to congregate after mass. They could enjoy the craic along with a cup of tea and a slice of cake. After this, they would go off to their homes to enjoy a traditional Sunday dinner of roast potatoes, two veg and lamb or beef with thick brown gravy poured over the lot.

Aileen Brophy was part of the group this week. She joined them whenever she was home from university. She mostly kept her head down and played her flute. In between songs, she smiled shyly at the others as they gently included her in the banter.

People nearby swayed in their seats to the music, sipping their drinks in near silence or singing along. As for the musicians themselves, they ignored their audience completely until each of them had sung their individual offering of the week.

At this point, it was considered acceptable to invite a member of the audience to sing a song. This night was no exception. An older man was singled out at the bar and encouraged to 'Give us a song now Aidan." Inclined to resist, more for the sake of not wanting to appear too full of himself, Aiden shook his head and took a coy sip of his pint.

The encouragement grew louder until one of the musicians yelled "Aiden, will ye come up now! Have ye lost yer guts man?" At this the small crowd around Aiden widened their eyes and waited in amused silence for him to react.

Unable to resist a dare, Aiden knocked the remains of his pint down his throat and slammed the glass on the bar. The decision was made. As Aiden turned toward the musician's corner, his pals clapped him on the back and cheered him on.

Space was made for Aiden to sit and the mic was handed to him. After quick consultation as to what he might sing, a chord was struck.

Aiden cleared his throat, threw his head back theatrically and began a song that was based on an old story.

> "I knew Danny Farrell
> when his football was a can
> With his hand-me-downs
> and welliers
> and his sandwiches of bran"

Aiden's pals at the bar raised their glasses and gave him a cheer before turning back to their pints. They quickly re-engaged in an enthusiastic discussion of the latest soccer scores.

Well into it now, Aiden continued without their support.

> "But now that pavement peasant
> is a full-grown bitter man
> With all his trials and troubles,
> of his travelling people's clan"

Most of the musician's took a deep breath and accompanied Aiden for the chorus, joined by a few of the onlookers from the booths.

> "He's a loser a boozer,
> a me and you user
> A raider, a traitor,
> a people police hater
> So lonely and only,
> what you'd call a gurrier

Still now, Danny Farrell,
he's a man."

Pam stepped along behind the bar, her face all business. She waved at Kay who pushed through to the bar, ducking under elbows that were raising pints of beer to waiting mouths. Pam grabbed Kay's hand and yelled above the noise "Come back here and help me out Kay."

"I can't. Liam will be on his own."

"I've fixed that." Pam waved to Dermot at the end of the bar. He waved back and made his way towards them. "I've asked Dermot to babysit Liam. They can have a chat and get to know each other while we have fun behind the bar."

"Fun you call it?" Kay laughed but looked toward Dermot. "Do they know each other Pam?"

"Maybe. Probably not. Just introduce them and get back here okay." Pam patted Kay's arm and disappeared back to the beer pumps, customers calling orders to her as she went.

Kay put her hand out to welcome Dermot. "Hi Dermot. We meet again."

"Yes."

Dermot seemed a man of few words, but he seemed happy enough to comply with Pam's request.

"Let me introduce you to Liam." She smiled at Liam and nodded back towards Dermot. "This is Dermot. He's Pam's friend."

The two men shook hands. "Do I know you?" asked Liam.

"I believe so. I was at St. Mary's High School."

"Ah!" said Liam. "Me too."

Dermot nodded. "You were a year or so ahead of me, but I remember you for all that. You played football for the school, wasn't it?"

"I did, yes." He laughed. "They were the days."

"They were. I remember one of the matches you played against the Holy Cross School. You scored three goals and the crowd was wild for you."

Liam laughed, flattered and entertained. The two were soon deep in conversation. Kay smiled happily at the success of the introduction and made her excuses.

No sooner did she get herself behind the bar, than customers called on her immediately for their orders. It was as if she'd been there all night and not just arrived. She took a minute to look at the brand name on each beer tap handle and another to familiarize herself with the location of the beer glasses.

Kay told herself it was lucky she was only being asked to pull pints. She'd have been hard put to figure out cocktails right now, as it had been years since she'd helped Pam behind the bar.

She took a customer's order and grabbed a glass. Tongue sticking out of the side of her mouth in concentration, she held the glass at the correct angle beneath the tap. She pulled steadily so that the beer didn't froth up, creating a one-inch head on the top.

With a grin of satisfaction, she placed the full glass down on the counter. "That'll be, er … Oh wait! I don't know what the charge is for a beer." She turned to look for help but Pam was busy at the other end of the bar taking an order.

"It's five euro," said her customer helpfully.

"Thanks." Kay smiled and took the proffered five euro note. She then took another minute at the till trying to figure out how to register the sale. She had almost given up when Pam came to rescue her.

"It didn't take long to forget everything I taught you Kay." Pam laughed and gave her a quick lesson. As Kay still appeared confused, Pam amended. "Look, just concentrate on pouring the beer. It's too much for you to think about otherwise. I'll tell you what, I'll get young Eamon there to stand at the till and take care of the money. "

"That's a good idea." Kay was relieved. Working the till was a nightmare as she recalled. "If I could avoid that, I'd be happy."

Pam winked and retorted, "Sure we don't want you messing up the money now do we." She nodded at several arms waving for attention over the shoulders of those closest to the bar. "Looks like you've customers woman."

Kay laughed and attended to business. For the next few hours she dropped into a rhythm. She pulled beer and served, listened for the next order, grabbed a clean glass, pulled beer and served. Now and then Kay looked up to check on Liam. He and Dermot appeared to be engaged in animated conversation, arms waving and probably, she thought, demonstrating some intricate soccer pass. She smiled to herself, content that Liam seemed happy.

Pam nudged her arm. "Pass these out among the tables will you and make sure the musicians get their share."

Kay looked up in surprise. Pam held out two plates of sandwiches cut into quarters.

"What midnight already?" Kay took the plates.

"It is and did you have fun Kay? You looked as though you were."

Kay considered a moment. "I did and I can't believe the time went so fast."

Pam nodded in agreement. "Time certainly seems to fly when you're surrounded by this crowd."

Kay distributed plates piled high with sandwiches throughout the pub. There were cheese and tomato; ham and cucumber, along with plates of sliced cake for a bit of dessert. Pam followed her about with a tray of cups filled with hot sweet, milky tea.

With the arrival of the sandwiches, the musicians began to wind down with the last number of the night. The crowd about the bar thinned out as orders were stilled and people left for the night. Several circulated for a quick hello with friends.

Tom was halfway through another story, this time about the dangers of going anywhere near a Faerie circle when there was a full moon or if there was a mist. Even worse apparently was a combination of the two.

John was scathing of such tales and made his opinion known. “It’s a load of crap, all that ole stuff. I don’t believe a word of it.”

Some of the group raised their eyebrows while others frowned their disapproval. To a man, they all leaned in to hear what Tom might say in reply. They were not disappointed. Tom turned his full attention on John and with eyes blazing he told the miscreant, “I can see ye’re a holy terror for the mischief making aren’t ye!” It was not a question. “How will ye do if ye’re out there on such a night. Ye’re all blather and balls now but we’ll see then won’t we. And if ye want to prove yerself, turn left out of the pub and that’ll lead ye in the direction for a Faerie circle so.” He nodded firmly to emphasize his statement and then with a show of contempt, turned his back on John and helped himself to a ham and cucumber sandwich.

The last of the customers were leaving as Kay made her way around the pub, collecting plates as she went. Carrying these to the bar, she noticed the man called John, as he walked out of the pub. He was certainly the worse for drink and seemed undecided about which direction to take. He started off to the left but seemed to think better of it and veered off in a half circle away to the right instead.

Pam thanked the musicians. Each carried his own instrument and cheerfully helped Padraic get the sound equipment out to his van.

Pam closed the door behind them and turned back to Kay. “Wine time!” she announced with a big grin. Kay responded with a little dance and brought out two wine glasses. Pam fetched them a bottle from under the counter and joined Kay in a booth beside the open fire. She filled their glasses.

Kay nodded toward Eamon still working away behind the bar. Dermot was helping by collecting empty glasses around the pub and bringing them to the lad for loading in the dishwasher. "I see you have help now. Bit different from when I was here before. We slaved away for an hour or more after everyone left just to get the place ready for the next day.

Pam crossed one leg over the other and swung her foot mischievously. "Sure, it's nice to see a man working away so it is."

Just then Liam came down the stairs from the upstairs apartment. "I checked on Aoife. She's sound asleep." He sat down beside Kay. She offered him a drink of her wine, but he shook his head. "Wine and beer. Not a good mix for me thanks." He yawned. "We should go soon."

"Aw!" Kay pouted. "You'll have to throw me over your shoulder to get me out of here."

"That can be arranged." Liam tweaked her nose. Kay batted her eyelashes at him.

"Get a room you two." Pam rebuked them playfully just as Dermot approached them with half a beer still in his glass.

"Come join us Dermot." Liam moved along to accommodate him. The two immediately launched into another discussion of soccer. Pam rolled her eyes at Kay and poured more wine into their glasses. After twenty minutes of trying to hold a conversation under the increasingly animated voices of the two men, Kay began to yawn too and fell against Liam in mock sleep.

"Oh!" he said, pulling a flopsy Kay upright. "I guess we really should go."

Kay opened one eye and winked at Pam, closed it again and began to snore dramatically. Liam responded by reaching under her arms and hoisting her out of her seat and over his shoulder.

"Good night all." he said.

"Oi!" yelled Pam as Liam made off with a giggling Kay toward the door. "Don't forget yer kid."

"Oops!" Liam said in pretended surprise. "Almost forgot we have an Aoife." He smiled hopefully at Pam and waited.

"Oh, go on then." Pam shooed them away. "She can stay here. Lucky for you I like the kid." She added darkly, "Just don't forget to pick her up tomorrow, or I may keep her."

"Ha!" Kay retorted gleefully as Liam carried her through the doorway. "You'll soon give her back. I guarantee it."

Pam turned back to Dermot. He had ignored the leaving of Kay and Liam, preferring instead to watch Pam. As she turned her bright smile and piercing eyes back to him, he blushed right up to his fiery red hair.

"Well," he yawned, "I should be away home too." He made ready to go, his 6' 2" height towering over Pam, making her feel quite dainty as she sat there in the booth. Her gaze travelled up, over his slim hips and broad shoulders.

Softened by the wine, Pam pursed her lips at him coquettishly. Dermot unfortunately took this as mocking, which made him all the more uncomfortable. He headed for the door but stopped halfway, realizing he hadn't said goodnight. He turned momentarily. "Goodnight," he said and sped through the door. Once outside, he mentally chastised himself for yet again, missing an opportunity.

Pam rolled her eyes and sighed. She gathered the wine glasses she and Kay had used, along with the now empty wine bottle and Dermot's beer glass. She muttered under her breath about some men needing a jolt to get them going and hoped that didn't mean such men would be the same in bed. She slid the glasses and bottle into the sink behind the counter, secured the door, flipped off the lights and stomped upstairs to her apartment.

In the parking lot outside the pub, Dermot fired up his Trident motorcycle and paused a moment, debating whether to go back inside. As he looked over at the pub, he saw the lights go out. "Too late you idiot," he told himself ruefully. He let out the clutch and rode regretfully into the night, mentally punishing himself for being too timid to take on the woman he loved.

As Kay and Liam drove over the old stone bridge near the cottage, Liam stopped the car at the top of the rise. He opened the passenger door for Kay to step out. Together they leaned over the parapet to watch the water tumble over the stones in the half moonlight.

After a moment, he drew Kay close, lifted her chin in his hand and kissed her mouth, tasting her gently with his tongue.

Responding immediately Kay rose on her heels, the better to meet his kiss. Liam grabbed her butt, bringing her tight against him. Kay slid her hands about his neck and flicked her tongue into his mouth like a little lizard.

That was signal enough for Liam. He pushed her skirt up as his fingers found the soft wetness between her legs. Liam pulled her panties away from her hips. Kay let them slide to the ground and stepped out of them. She began to unfasten the belt on Liam's jeans.

"I can't do it," she laughed against his mouth. "You'll have to help me." She began again to loosen his belt. Liam didn't answer but his kisses grew more urgent. Kay's hands fell away from the forgotten belt as Liam's fingers probed gently inside her.

She sighed then as Liam hoisted her onto the first bar of the bridge and knelt down on the soft grass that grew there.

Kay's head fell back as Liam pushed his face against her thighs. Her legs parted in welcome. As she gazed up at the half moon, Liam's tongue swelled her clitoris and his big hands held her thighs apart. She pulled his face in against her, climaxing in waves of warm release as she cried out to the night.

For a long moment, she hung in his arms as the flood receded. But Liam was not done with her yet. Gently, he lowered her to the ground and turned her so that her face hung above the rushing water.

Probing the wetness, he had moments before helped to create, he held her firmly, pulling her naked buttocks as he entered her from the rear. Kay responded by raising herself to meet him.

Kay's body responded as Liam pounded her against the bridge. She was a wild thing rutting with its mate in the night. Her body shook from the welcome onslaught. She closed her eyes so that all she could hear was the rushing of the water and the soft thump of his loins against her uplifted rump.

CHAPTER 7 – KAY AND THE NINJA

Kay walked towards the shed, motorcycle helmet swinging from one hand. Liam stood in the doorway to wave her off, Aoife clinging onto his leg, happy to be with her Daddy.

As Kay opened the creaky, pine-battered door of the shed, a broad smile brightened her face. Her Kawasaki Ninja motorcycle was her little opportunity for escapism. A thrill bubbled through her spine and shoulders, making the hairs stand up on the back of her neck.

She recalled feeling the same way about her Raleigh bicycle, a birthday gift when she was twelve years old.

Back then, early summer mornings would find her sneaking quietly from the house so as not to wake anyone. She would ride her bicycle through country lanes all the way out to Bowring Park and back again before school. Reveling in the sunshine, she enjoyed the calm before the rush of the morning traffic. She was alone in the world with only the singing of birds and the whir of bicycle gears. A great sense of freedom seemed to burst from deep within her, like an expression of self-love and achievement.

Kay would push hard on the pedals going up Bowring Hill to the park, thrilling at the exertion. She rejoiced at the power of her legs that easily buoyed her up the steep incline to the very top of the hill. Poised there for a nanosecond, she was queen of the world, believing for that long moment, suspended in time, that she could be or do anything.

It was just such a feeling when she rode her motorcycle. She ran her hand lovingly over the chassis of the Ninja and recalled how she had fallen in love with the motorcycle through the window of a showroom.

Aoife had been three years old at the time and was attending a morning daycare. Liam had recently started a new job. His long commute to the city made him pretty tired when he came home late at night. He'd eat dinner and then collapse on the couch exhausted.

Feeling at a loose end, she wandered through town one morning after dropping Aoife at daycare. Kay had seen the Ninja. Memories of Mac had flooded into her mind. Not that he had a Ninja, but he certainly had a motorcycle. It was part of his persona. She had once referred to him jokingly as her shiny biker guy. Smiling at this memory, she became aware that the salesman inside the store was smiling back at her. She looked back at the Ninja and sighed longingly, wishing she could have a motorcycle of her own.

Making a snap decision, she had marched into the store. The salesman greeted her with open smiles. He knew a buyer when he saw one. Thirty minutes later, she was the proud owner of the Ninja.

"Now!" she said to the salesman, "Where do I learn to ride this thing?"

Over the next few weeks, she and Liam argued continuously. "What the hell Kay? What possessed you to purchase a Ninja? You can't even ride a motorcycle." He tried to put his foot down in the matter, but Kay was determined. She had her own money left over from the college fund her parents had provided for her. She and Liam had long agreed the money was Kay's to do with as she pleased. Kay had reminded Liam of this and they'd both sulked for several more days. Finally, Liam had given in. "Fine!" he'd said. "But I want you to be safe. I'll find you an instructor," he added grudgingly.

And that's where Old Jake the bike nut had come in. When the Ninja was delivered to Old Jake's workshop, he insisted on testing it before agreeing to teach Kay. He had driven it sedately out of the workshop, but Kay distinctly heard him throttle up as soon as he was out of sight. It was obvious he enjoyed the ride, because when he returned, his eyes were on fire and a broad grin was stuck onto his grizzled old face. One look at that face and she was determined to discover what she secretly named 'the grin factor' for herself.

True to his reputation as a fair but ornery instructor, Jake firmly waved away Kay's protestations as he pushed the Ninja to the back of the garage. There, he stowed it behind his collection of motorcycles, which included a Royal Enfield, a Matchless 500 and two Nortons.

Kay's eyes popped as he pushed aside storage chests and toolboxes, to reveal a dusty but intact 1967 Honda 90 step through. "Bought it from a kid who wanted the money," he explained. "Not my kind of motorcycle but you have to admire the Japs. It's the world's best-selling and most popular bike. Runs like a clock, completely reliable and does 190 miles to one gallon of gas." He studied the bike a long moment and gave it a fond pat on the seat. Jake looked Kay in the eye and said, "I'm saving you from destroying your new motorcycle while you learn to ride." He nodded toward a bucket of water. "Now take this and give the old girl a good scrub."

Kay began to protest but Jake would not back down. "You want me to teach you to ride?"

"Yes. Yes, I do."

"Then we'll do it my way. Now get to scrubbing. You'll pass your test on this old lady before you go anywhere near that Ninja of yours."

Kay wanted to pass her test for sure. On reflection, she decided Jake's way was practical. Learning on an old motorcycle, would save her own from the many scratches and scrapes she would likely give it, as an inexperienced rider. She gave in and followed the program.

The program consisted of cleaning the old lady, as Jake insisted on calling the motorcycle, until the paint gleamed, and the chrome shone. It was good practice she supposed, like grooming a horse and learning to care for it.

Throughout that summer, Kay spent her mornings practicing on the little Honda 90 cub. Jake told her he'd known a few people who had owned or ridden one of these old ladies. He'd said they soon developed a soft spot for the willing and trusty little gem of a machine. "She's quiet you see, but free-revving, a smooth little engine." He nodded his head as if in discussion with himself. "It's not just that, although that oughta be enough for anyone. But it also has a comfortable seat and riding position. Reliable electrics too!"

Kay was impressed and said so, which spurred Jake on to further commentary on the advantages of the Honda. "They're a revelation compared to other bikes of the 60s era. Bikes around that time had a lot of Lucas electrics."

Kay shook her head. "Lucas electrics?" She was confused and not a little overwhelmed by all the information.

Mistakenly thinking Kay was eager for further information on the Honda, Jake went on. "Advertisements of the time called them Lucas, King of the Road. Bikers nicknamed 'em Lucas Prince of Darkness." He spat as he said this and nodded at the bike.

Kay turned her head, quietly disgusted by this predominantly male habit. Not wishing to offend her mentor, she said nothing.

She wanted to ride and to ride well. There was no doubt that Old Jake was the best teacher, understanding but firm. He didn't allow her to shy away from the handling of the bike in all weathers but urged her gently on, to increase her speed as her confidence grew.

Under his patient tutoring, Kay took to the little Honda cub like a duck to water.

There was an initial panicked situation involving a minor collision with a wheelie bin, which Jake fortunately did not witness. It wasn't long before Kay developed a smooth riding style and mastered the art of making gear changes that didn't threaten the good health of the machine.

Soon enough, Kay took her learner's test and easily passed. Jake presented her with a new helmet to match the lime-green color of the motorcycle. A week after her test, true to his word, Jake wheeled the mean looking Kawasaki Ninja out of the shed. It gleamed in the sunlight from Jake's wax and polish of the day before.

It wasn't the first time she'd seen her bike since it arrived in Jake's workshop. Occasionally, the Ninja needed to be moved around or out of the garage to give Jake access to one of his bikes. On these occasions, Jake had insisted Kay push the Ninja off its center stand and maneuver it around the yard. It was a good idea, because she found the 173 kilos of machine heavy and awkward at first, after using the little Honda cub. There were a few muttered curses during off-balance episodes of nearly dropping the bike. Quickly however, she became accustomed to the feel and weight distribution of the Ninja and realized why Jake made her do this exercise repeatedly.

With the Ninja permanently out from the back of Jake's shed, Kay was encouraged to start it, warm it up and ride up and down the drive. Jake expected tight turns while she pivoted with one foot dabbing the road surface. He would not permit foot-dragging from the word go. She also learned throttle control and gentle braking on the long driveway.

When the big day arrived, Kay was armed with her new motorcycle license. She had been suitably drilled on how not to drop the gleaming Ninja. She was about to ride her first real motorcycle on the highway.

Kay had beamed from ear to ear, despite the hair prickling on the back of her neck. There was a gleam in her eye that matched the neon-brightness of the Ninja. She felt comfortable in her riding ability and the new, handmade leather riding boots she'd invested in. Easing the Ninja off the center stand, she positioned herself on the comfortable dual seat.

Having already checked the fuel and choke, she slid the key into the ignition, made sure the bike was in neutral and stabbed the starter button.

The Ninja burbled into life. Kay gently and lightly revved the engine to warm it up. Retracting the stand, she took a moment to balance the bike between her thighs while she adjusted the mirrors.

She was finally ready for her first foray onto the public road on her very own beautiful and long-awaited Ninja.

Jake made some muttered excuse about a work-relation mission and rode off on one of his own motorcycles. Kay smiled to herself, knowing he wanted her to enjoy this in total freedom, without his anxious, over-zealous presence spoiling her moment.

She pointed the Ninja to the open gateway, selected first gear and smoothly let out the clutch. Gently, she increased the revs just as Jake had taught her.

As soon as the bike was on the road, Kay experienced the joy of riding her motorcycle. The machine took a leap forward as she went through her first change-up through the six-speed gearbox. Quite rapidly, the motorcycle got up to 60 miles per hour. At this point, she considered it more than fast enough on the local side streets of the town.

Kay headed for the main road, to really see what her motorcycle was made of. She wanted above all, to feel what Jake felt when he came back from a fast ride with his eyes on fire and a broad grin on his face.

Opening the throttle, Kay aimed the Ninja down the empty, early morning highway. The Ninja responded beautifully, singing a race-bred yowl from its muted silencers.

New sensations assailed and enveloped Kay. The first was a joyous sense that it was just her alone, with her now beloved motorcycle, an empty road ahead and a world to explore in a new way. Then came the sensation of the wind with an occasional cross turbulence buffeting the bike and rider as if it were a small plane.

Next came a feeling not of being perched on the machine, but being part of it in symbiosis, especially now as she swooped through a series of bends. She mindfully followed Jake's instructions to go in wide, throttle back, pick a line through the bend, then lean and open up again on the apex for a rapid and smooth exit.

After the fourth bend she got it, a joyous feeling with the Ninja handling like a dream. She laughed out loud as she recalled Jake being as excited about the Ninja as she was herself. He had even taken off the original tires and fitted Pirelli racing covers to her wheels.

Free as a bird and filled with happiness, Kay raised her head and despite the wind buffeting her face and helmet, she gave a "Whoop! Whoop! Whoop!" of triumph. In that moment she thought of Mac, riding his motorcycle along the highways of Ireland.

*****

Kay was brought back into the present by the promise of her own first ride in the brilliant sunshine of the Irish morning. Maneuvering out of the shed, she pulled the Ninja onto its stand. She zipped up her black leather one-piece suit, considering it money well spent. The suit hugged her body. She looked sleek and she felt sexy.

Liam yelled from the doorway "A bit fine for round here aren't you?" He winked at her.

Kay laughed and straddled the bike. She pulled her helmet down over her head and tightened the fastener. Her blonde hair lay sleek and smooth on her shoulders below the helmet. Leaning forward, she pulled the bike off the stand and started the engine. Liam whistled appreciatively and Aoife clapped as Kay leaned her body along the bike, touching her helmet to the tank for luck. She kicked the biked into gear and waved to him before flipping her visor down.

She took it slow and steady as she drove carefully out of the yard. A quick glance in her rearview mirror showed that Liam had already closed the front door. He and Aoife were lost to view.

As she had not ridden her motorcycle in Ireland before, she concentrated on negotiating the dips and ruts of the lane as it meandered away from the cottage. It was different riding along familiar roads on a motorcycle rather than in a car. The roads seemed more winding, some of them quite tight.

After twenty minutes, she connected with the N17 highway. Kay turned the motorcycle in the direction of Galway, although she had no intention of going that far. She recalled that the last time she was on this road was with Mac, when they had visited Galway for the Christmas Fayre more than six years previously.

Kay's belly tightened suddenly as a longing for Mac ripped through her. She tried to fight off the emotion, but it just kept coming. Unexpectedly, she questioned her agreement to Liam's request of coming back to Ireland. How could she avoid thinking of Mac when every turn and bend in the road reminded her of him?

If she didn't know better, those weeks with Mac could be passed off as a holiday romance. As memories of the enchanted mist and Mac combined to press down on her senses, she experienced a moment of loss.

Tears threatened to block her sight, but she determinedly blinked them away. Looking up, she laughed at the sky, but her gaiety sounded false even to her own ears.

When she returned to the States with Liam, she had found peace for a time. She was happy with Liam, happier than she had been before. That Aoife was a constant reminder of Mac only made her love Aoife more, even while she determinedly pushed away thoughts of Mac.

What gifts the child might have from her true father, she could not imagine. What she did know and felt truly thankful for, was the down to earth, funny and loveable Irishman of a father that Aoife had in Liam. If he even suspected Aoife was not his own, he had never shown it in word or deed, and she loved him for it. Such devotion as Liam's, was worth its weight in gold and ensured Kay's love and loyalty.

Kay opened the throttle and let it rip, roaring along the highway in the direction of Galway until she felt the past blow from her mind like dying sparks from an open fire.

CHAPTER 8 – THE MENHIR

As Kay rode out of the yard, Liam closed the cottage door and headed to the kitchen. “Pancakes for breakfast?” He smiled at the gasp of approval from Aoife who still clung to his leg, riding along on his foot. “Is that a yes?” Aoife nodded happily up at him. “Well then, you’d better help me look for ingredients while I get you an apron. He pulled the stow-away kitchen steps from behind the door and opened them near the food cupboard for Aoife’s easy access. Aoife was soon on the top step, alarming in her efficiency at finding ingredients needed for the sweet and not particularly healthy breakfast.

It wasn’t long before Aoife, still perched on the steps, whisked the batter mix while she chattered and provided continuous advice on the art of making pancakes.

“Daddy, why do you make the batter so thick? Mommy makes it thin and runny. Look! Like this.” She added more almond milk before Liam could stop her.

“Woah there Aoife. What are you doing to Daddy’s pancake batter?”

“It’s okay Daddy. I’m making it better. You’ll see.”

To Liam, the batter mix was now compromised. He preferred thick pancakes. With a comic frown of surrender, he succumbed to his daughter's insistence. "Well, okay. You know Daddy likes thick pancakes, but we'll go with your mixture." He leaned down to her level and looked her in the eyes. "This time only!" he said and winked. Aoife winked both her eyes in return and then laughed as he produced a gooey finger covered in batter and popped it straight into his mouth.

"You're sneaky Daddy. I didn't see you dip your finger in the batter."

"That's because Daddy's a charmer. See that, I kept you focused on my eyes." He opened his eyes wide as they held hers. "While I secretly did this." He produced another fingerful of batter and popped it into his mouth.

"Wait!" said Aoife. "Let me try." She tried but failed to hold Liam's gaze and find the bowl of batter at the same time. Her gaze slipped off to the side as her finger missed the bowl entirely. "Aw!" She complained.

"Ha!" said Liam. "You'll have to practice a lot more if you're to become a charmer like Daddy."

Their happy banter continued until there was a fine stack of the golden treats. Aoife grabbed the syrup. Liam brought the pancakes and butter. They ate at the refectory table in chewy appreciation.

"So, Aoife, what are you doing this morning while Mommy's off joy-riding?"

"I want to watch cartoons. The Irish ones are better than the ones at home."

"They are? Why's that?"

"Because they all speak Irish of course. Silly Daddy."

"Oh! Silly Daddy is it?" He tickled her under the chin. Aoife's fork clattered onto her plate as she clutched his hand. "And do you understand Irish, Aoife?"

"Sometimes. Can you find the show for me?"

"What about all these dishes young lady?"

Aoife smiled so that all her teeth showed. "Can't we do them later?"

"Ah go on with you, little rogue that you are. I'll tell you what. Bring the dishes to me in the kitchen. I'll stack them in the dish washer, but you have to put them away after. Deal?" Liam held out his hand, palm up.

"Deal!" agreed Aoife and smacked his hand.

Once Aoife was installed in front of the tv, Liam filled the dishwasher and began to tidy the kitchen. He was distracted by a movement in the field beyond the kitchen window. A small flock of sheep were making their way up the field from the meadow. If they wandered passed the cottage, it would be all too easy for them to get out onto the lane and from there, disperse every which way through the village.

Despite gooey drops of pancake batter still decorating the counter tops, Liam dropped the dish cloth in the sink and went out to herd the sheep back to the meadow. He didn't need to do much to encourage the older sheep to leave. No sooner did they set eyes on Liam, than they all turned and ran. Waiting by the gate, two of the sheep 'baaed' loud and strong for their young to follow. Liam assisted by waving his arms in a shooing motion as he came close to the lambs until they too, sped off toward the gate. Offspring safely accounted for, the minders immediately ceased bleating and turned to follow the last of the lambs through the gate and back into the meadow.

Liam followed them with the intention of securing the gate. Once there, he stood for a moment watching the lambs gambol after the flock.

His attention was soon drawn to the left, where the great ash tree spread its branches like arms held out in protection of what lay beyond. It was at this moment that Liam forgot his enjoyment of the lambs and indeed, forgot about Aoife. He was drawn like a lamb himself, toward his destiny in the grove beyond the tree.

Liam opened the big farm gate he had just closed. In his haste to reach the grove, he paid no attention to the inviting display of buttercups, daisies and forget-me-nots interspersed among the grasses of the meadow.

A thick circle of hawthorn had created the grove that could only be comfortably accessed by stepping around the side of the great ash. There was a raised mound to one side of this tree, a space that created an open doorway to the circle beyond. Liam stepped up and then down over the mound until he was inside the circle.

The early spring breeze that swept naturally across the meadow was, inside the circle, strangely muted. Liam strode to the far end where a stone menhir stood upright. Such stones were known locally as long stones, although this one was shorter than most. It stood only four feet tall and was partly hidden by hawthorn bushes.

Growing up in the area, Liam had often used the circle to play his childhood games and always with the menhir as the focal point. He had long considered the circle his private place and so it was with excitement that he examined the runes etched deep in the surface of the stone.

He had seen menhirs in other fields, but they had been exposed to the weather. This meant that any markings they may have had at one time in the distant past, had often been obliterated by wind and rain. This particular stone was protected by hawthorn bushes, which draped themselves around the menhir like a curtain. Etched into the stone, were clearly defined linear strokes which he knew could be identified as Ogham inscriptions. According to historians, such markings were used by druids and travelers to relay messages. Some markings were said to be made a thousand years ago and some even further back than that.

He ran his fingers over the runes, marveling that until recently, he'd had no idea what these markings meant or how they were related to the stone, the circle or the greater world outside.

He pulled a folded scrap of paper from his pocket and dropped it in his haste. It lay in the grass, open and easy for anyone to see, had there been anyone near him. Reaching down, he grabbed the paper and brought it near to the runes on the menhir, where he carefully compared each stroke and line.

His breath came in short ragged busts as he confirmed what he already suspected. The scribblings on the paper matched the runes on the stone. He stood quickly and looked around, laughter bubbling against his lips. Fingers shaking, he raised the paper to his mouth and kissed it. "This is it," he whispered. "I knew it was."

Liam held the paper up in the air and waved it about. "I knew it!" He shouted exultantly. "Damn!" He chastised himself and quickly looked about, listening carefully. He did not want to be overheard by a farmer who might come over to investigate and at the very least to interfere, by chatting about cows, sheep and what was Liam doing in the circle anyway. In such a small community, news travelled fast. Even in his current enthusiastic state, Liam realized he did not want attention brought his way by inquisitive people, who might get wind of what he was doing. For one thing, he might never be able to enjoy a quiet pint again at the local pub, without some idiot nudging another and enquiring "Now Liam, have you found anything interesting in the Faerie circle so?" He could imagine the good natured but embarrassing guffaws that would follow.

So, it was not without trepidation that he looked around him now, peering through the hawthorn into the meadow, hopeful that he was not overlooked. All was quiet. There was only birdsong and a slight rush of leaves as the breeze increased slightly.

"Now my beauty," he said, addressing the menhir. "I believe you're the portal." He patted the silent stone. "And whatever you're hiding in there, I will have it."

He backed away carefully from the menhir, until he reached the moss-covered tree stump. As a child, he had used the stump as a castle and even as a throne, when he had been successful in storming the castle. Forgotten now were the times he had imagined himself as high king of all Ireland, giving out decrees and then fighting with imaginary knights against all who might try to topple him from his throne.

He sat down hard on the stump, crushing his childhood games. Liam stared at the menhir and waved the paper at it. "I'm going to open you, so I am and then I'll…"

"Open what Daddy?" came a bright voice behind him. Liam turned quickly. Aoife was perched at the top of the bank with one hand resting against the thick trunk of the ash tree. She was dressed in her favorite silver and blue striped tights and pink ballet tutu. Wildflowers hung haphazardly from her hair and her small hand clutched a bunch of brightly colored varieties. Liam's breath caught in his throat as he looked upon his daughter. In that moment he thought she looked like a Faerie creature. Her slanted green eyes glinted strangely in the shade of the grove, her curls lifting and falling in the breeze that swept up behind her from the meadow.

Liam got up and walked towards Aoife, his hand out to stop her. "Don't come in here Aoife," he commanded. He was not sure why he tried to stop her, for he had never considered this place out of bounds in his own childhood. Yet it was different in that moment when he saw Aoife. She looked both human and mystical together. He had the strangest feeling that the child belonged here in this place.

It was in vain that he tried to stop her, for she had already jumped down into the circle, gazing about her with eyes wide and mouth pursed into a rosebud.

"This is nice Daddy. I like it."

"You … you shouldn't be in here Aoife." Liam grabbed her hand and pulled her up the bank and down the other side.

"You're hurting me Daddy. Stop!"

Liam, surprised by his own reaction, let go of Aoife's hand immediately and knelt down in front of her. "I'm sorry honey. I didn't mean to hurt you or frighten you."

"I'm not frightened." Aoife rubbed her wrist. "Just it hurts here now."

"I'm sorry baby," Liam repeated. "Here, let me kiss it better." He kissed her wrist with a wet smacking sound so that Aoife laughed. Liam continued. "Please don't come this far from the cottage. Sometimes it's not safe."

"Why isn't it safe?"

"Well, farmers you know. They have tractors and things. And sometimes they can't see little girls when they're perched up high on their tractors. They're big machines so it can be dangerous if you get in their way."

"Like a car?"

"That's right. Like a car." He smiled reassuringly and held her shoulders as he smiled into her eyes. "Okay Aoife?"

"Daddy, you're naughty. You're doing that charming thing again."

"I am not!" he denied, trying to lighten the tension. He didn't want the child frightened, just cautious maybe. Perhaps it was his own fears, of what he might find when he opened the portal.

Aoife held her face away from Liam's and regarded him. "Well okay Daddy. But don't try to charm me okay? I can see when you do it, so I know."

"Oh, you know do you?" Liam tickled her tummy which made her laugh as she backed away. He caught her before she could escape and said gently but firmly. "So, I want you to stay away from here. Don't come out through that gate into the meadow at all. Promise?"

"Okay," agreed Aoife, one hand behind her back, fingers crossed.

"How about a piggyback?" Liam tempted.

Aoife nodded her head and laughed delightedly as Liam swung her up on his back. He jogged across the meadow, neighing like a horse with Aoife urging him on.

Behind them, a figure emerged from within the circle. As if aware of the movement, Aoife turned her head to look back. The figure stopped at the ash tree to watch them go.

*****

Two hours later, Kay turned back into the lane that led to the cottage. She throttled down gently and relaxed into a deep appreciation of the green freshness of the place. It so often rained in Ireland, but never failed to astonish in the lush growth of wildflowers that carpeted every hedgerow, field and meadow.

Coasting into the driveway of the cottage, Kay stilled the bike and turned the key. She pulled off her helmet and shook her hair loose. Tilting her face to the sun, she luxuriated in its heat. The pulse of the motorcycle still reverberated through her thighs, bringing a sense of satisfaction that only a release of tension could bring.

The door of the cottage flew open and Liam came rushing out.

Kay pulled off her helmet, her smiling greeting turning to surprise at the expression on his face. “What is it? Tell me quick!” she demanded, still straddling the motorcycle.

“I can’t find Aoife!” Liam was frantic.

“I left her with you Liam.”

“Yes, but I was busy with, with other things. I looked up and she was gone.”

“Where were you?”

“In the study. I …”

“You’re supposed to keep an eye on her, not bury yourself in the study.”

“She can’t have gone far. We’ll just have to find her. Come on.” Liam strode out of the driveway in the direction of Sean’s farm.

Kay pulled the bike back onto its stand and stepped off. She left her helmet swinging from the handlebars and hurried after her husband. "You think she's gone to Sean's?"

"I can't think where else she might be."

"It's not good enough Liam. If I leave Aoife with you, I expect you to watch her."

Liam didn't answer, just kept walking.

"This isn't over mister," Kay reiterated and followed until she caught up with him.

They strode along the lane, side by side, united in their mission. It occurred to Kay that she needn't worry about her daughter for one very good reason. Aoife was a wild and willful child, prone to adventure and wild antics, yet she also had an innate wisdom and seemed to know instinctively how to keep herself safe.

They found Sean coming out of his cow shed with a pitchfork full of hay. He waved his free arm when he saw them coming, the smile on his face as welcoming as the sun. "Isn't it a beautiful day for walking. Is that what you're after doing?" Seeing their grim faces, he amended his tone. "Ah no, I see ye are in no mood for the walking now. What can I do for ye both?"

"Is Aoife here Sean?"

"Well now let me see. It's been a few hours since I saw her." Here Kay gave Liam a quick sideways look that was anything but warm. "Ah yes, I was bringing the hay up there to my caves when I saw Aoife at the other end of the lane. I think she was headed for Old Nell's cottage. That's where she was headed the other day when I saw her. I think she might still be of the same mind. She was off exploring that day and I did see her turn in there, into Old Nell's place so I think ye should start thereabouts."

Kay and Liam glanced at each other.

Liam sighed. "Thanks Sean. We'll be off to find her."

"Ah sure, come back and chat another time. I'll be here so I will."

They hurried back along the lane to find Aoife coming out of Nell's cottage. "Where've you been Aoife? You mustn't go running off like that."

"Hi Mommy. I came to see Nell. You know," she lowered her voice in a conspiratorial way, "Old Nell."

Liam and Kay looked up at the derelict cottage with the front door hanging off its hinges. Grass grew from the eves and the windows were green with moss and with the rain that had seeped in through the half-collapsed roof.

"Old Nell?" asked Kay. "Who's Old Nell?"

"Shhhh! Don't call her Old Nell Mommy. I told you about her. I told you and Pam." Aoife was aggrieved.

"Yes but," Kay looked from Aoife to the cottage and back to the child again. "But Aoife," she began.

Liam interrupted, "Aoife, did you go inside Nell's cottage? It's too dangerous to do that, the state the cottage is in."

"See. Daddy knows her." Aoife told Kay. "She's nice Daddy and very clean." She leaned in toward Liam, lowered her voice and confided. "I left Cara the mouse with Nell. She doesn't mind having a mouse and I can visit her whenever I want. Isn't that nice?" Aoife skipped up the lane a bit, then turned to say. "And, she gave me seeing soup." She spread her hands. "Of course, I can't see yet, but I suppose it will happen when they're ready to be seen." Aoife smiled at them both and danced ahead up the lane.

Kay turned to Liam. "When what's ready to be seen?"

Liam stopped, rooted to the spot.

"What is it Liam?

"Nell," he said, shaking his head. "She was old when I was a kid. Nell died 25 years ago."

"Are you sure?"

"Of course, I'm sure."

Kay blinked. She glanced at Liam from the corner of her eye and said, "Aoife has such a vivid imagination."

"I guess so." Liam stroked his chin. "I wonder who told her about Old Nell?"

"Probably Sean. He just told us he saw Aoife the other day. He was telling her stories about the people who used to live here. Aoife told me about it." She shrugged her shoulders. "It probably stuck in her mind and she's made up a little story about Nell. Kids do that."

Liam appeared convinced. "I'll catch up with her," he said and ran after Aoife.

Kay watched as he reached Aoife and swept her laughing into his arms. She sighed. "The sooner I get that child into school, the better."

CHAPTER 9 – BELTANE

The biggest culprit of untidiness was surprisingly not Aoife, but Liam. Kay had long given up scolding him for this. Instead, she made a compromise with herself. She tidied up after him in the communal family areas, living room, kitchen and bathroom. However, on his side of the bedroom where he dropped his clothes or the miscellaneous items lying about on his side table and floor, she simply left alone for him to deal with. This method helped her keep an equilibrium of sanity in her innate need for orderliness against Liam's natural disregard of it.

Each night, Kay helped Aoife tidy her toys and put her room straight. She preferred to relax after that and enjoy the evening with Liam. Kay liked to tidy up at night after her family, so that the cottage looked clean and welcoming to her each morning.

On days such as this, when the sun shone invitingly and the rain was at bay for a time, Kay was free to simply stack the dishwasher with breakfast plates, wipe a cloth around the kitchen counters and pursue the happy pastime of bringing the wilderness of her garden into some semblance of order.

An enthusiastic gardener, Kay enjoyed pottering about. She had begun with the fun task of filling the baskets to be hung from the eves of the cottage. She and Aoife had visited a garden center, coming away with petunias, trailing begonia, silver mist and creeping jenny. They lined the baskets with compost and carefully arranged the plants into the potting soil. She continued her theme with carefully spaced baskets of pretty summer flowers and trailing ivy along the wall Liam had built. In the wall, he had placed some of the stones from his mother's old cottage with the old paint facing outwards. He said the wall reminded him of his mother and how he had loved to help her paint a fresh wash of color onto the old family cottage every summer. Behind the wall, a natural rockery had developed. This had come about from the soil and rocks dug up to prepare the wall and the driveway, back in the days when Liam worked on restoring the cottage. Already full of naturally growing holly, ivy and aspen, Liam had years ago planted montbretia, which now began to spread its fronds among the trees. The green of the rockery seemed complete in itself, so Kay did not disturb its natural beauty with extra plants. Liam had added to the prettiness of the scene by festooning the holly trees with bird feeders and fat balls that brought a wonderful variety of wild birds into the garden.

It was tending this garden that Kay discovered Irish midges. She had been surprised by the swarm of tiny mosquito like creatures that left her head, arms and legs itchy for days. She recalled trying to describe them to a friend back home as, unlike mosquitos because you don't feel the bite but they sure itch just like a mosquito bite.

Kay tried to counteract the draw she seemed to have for midges, by wearing light colored clothing that covered most of her skin and left no tasty extremities. She also sprayed her neck and clothing with an insect repellant. This was useful for keeping the tiresome little insects away, but the stuff clung to her skin all day with an oiliness she would rather not have.

The midges especially liked to attack around the eyes. This was unavoidable when she was constantly bending or kneeling close to the ground. In the early days she walked around with her face smeared in Penaten creme to cool the itch and help with the swelling from bites. She took to wearing sunglasses, and then goggles on occasion, which looked ridiculous but worked to keep the midges away from her eyes.

As a fun activity with Aoife, Kay decided to make a spring wreath. She knew that willow trees grew down by the river. Their young branches would be useful for making the base of a wreath. The river was accessible via the meadow but that would have taken her by the Faerie circle, and she was determined to go nowhere near it. Instead, she strolled down through Sean's fields while Aoife danced alongside her, exclaiming delightedly at the lambs. She ran about the field after them and scattered the flock.

It was peaceful next to the river, especially so when she and Aoife stood inside the willow branches and looked out at the world through its green fronds. "It's like a secret place Mommy. It's lovely."

"Yes, it is lovely." Kay looked at Aoife speculatively. "You must promise Mommy never to come here on your own."

The child smiled and nodded her head. Kay was wise to Aoife's tricks and pulled her hands from behind her back to ensure she had not crossed her fingers while making the promise. Aoife's smile dropped at being found out, for her fingers were crossed as Kay had suspected. She held her daughter's small hands in her own. "Promise me." Kay nodded her head at Aoife for emphasis. "That you will not come down to the river without Mommy or Daddy."

Aoife was glum. "I promise."

"Well done darling." Kay kissed Aoife's hands. "I just want you to be safe. You can come down here, but one of us has to be with you." She smiled. "Now, help me pick out the best branches, nice and thin so we can bend them easily."

*****

Back at the cottage, Kay sat in the old rocking chair Liam had rescued from his grandmother's cottage. As Kay rocked gently and bent the willow branches into a circle, she speculated that the old chair may have known the very activity she was engaged in, for it must surely be over a hundred years old. It may have rocked generations of women as they busied their hands with crafts, rocked their babies and told their stories. If only chairs and cottages could talk. What tales would they tell?

Kay's thoughts were interrupted by Aoife bringing heather and moss for her inspection, as decoration for the wreath. Together they added these and threaded a lilac colored ribbon that would look well against the purple front door.

Hanging the completed wreath on the door, she and Aoife stepped back to view their work. "We're clever Mommy," said Aoife, waving a hand across the cottage. "Look what we done."

"Did darling. It's 'look what we did', not look what we done."

"Did. Look what we done, did."

Kay let it go. There were more important things in this world, she decided, than dwelling on grammar and pronunciation on a fine morning like this.

The dark green of the moss and heather complimented the large pink Bantry Bay roses Liam had planted 10 years ago. The roses crowded around the doorway. Kay had been obliged to tie the branches back so she could enter the cottage without getting pricked by thorns each time.

As Kay and Aoife admired their work, Sean walked into the yard accompanied by Felan. Aoife immediately jumped off the wall to make a fuss of the animal. Felan responded by rolling over to display his tummy for tickling. Aoife obliged and the two held a conversation with the one giggling and the other making breathy barking sounds of delight.

"Ah good morning Kay. That's a fine piece of artwork if ever I saw one."

"Hi Sean. Thank you. How are you doing?"

"Sure, I'm fit as a fiddle so I am. Now Kay," Sean jerked his head toward the cottage. "It's Himself I am after. Is he at home?"

Kay opened the door of the cottage and called "Liam! Sean's here for you." When there was no reply, she called louder. "Liam are you there?"

Aoife paused in her antics to say "Daddy went down the field. He's gone to see the Faerie circle."

Kay stopped in mid call and turned slowly to Sean who looked back at her, eyebrows raised. The unspoken question was plain on his face. What business could Liam have in the Faerie circle? Keeping her voice steady, Kay said "I'm sorry Sean. It looks like he's not here at the moment. What was it you needed?"

"Ah well now, I'm in need of a drill bit, for I'm after getting the satellite in for more channels on the telly."

"Good idea," said Kay. "We could do with a few more tv channels ourselves. Look, I'll have Liam come over later okay. Oh, and let me know how you get on with the channels."

"I will Kay, I will." He glanced once more toward the back of the house in the direction of the circle and then turned his attention to his dog. "Come along now Felan," he called. The dog was still having fun with Aoife as they chased each other in circles. "Heel boy!"

Felan came to heel and trotted beside Sean with tongue lolling as they walked back along the lane. Kay and Aoife watched them go until they disappeared around the bend in the road that led to their cottage and beyond into the bog.

"We should get a puppy," said Aoife. "Or a cat. Or a rabbit maybe." She pranced around her mother like a rabbit then looked up into her face. "What's wrong Mommy?"

Kay certainly looked distracted. 'Why would Liam be in the circle,' she wondered. Aoife pulled at her arm, breaking her thoughts. She smiled brightly at her daughter. "Sorry darling. What is it?"

Reassured by the smile, Aoife danced away and clambered up the stone steps onto the wall.

Kay took off her gardening apron and draped it across the little table. "Back in a moment darling. Don't go out of the yard, okay?"

"Okay Mommy."

Kay hurried into the cottage "Liam is that you?" Kay called out as the kitchen door banged shut.

It was Liam. His face was smudged with mud and there were bits of leaves in his hair. He walked straight past Kay and into the little room they kept as a sort of study.

Kay was surprised to see Liam close the study door behind him. Whereas before, she might have accepted this rebuff, she had since trained herself not to allow such behavior. She marched up to the door. Raising her hand to knock, she thought better of it. Instead, she turned the handle and walked into the room.

Liam sat at the desk, hands on his lap, staring through the window. He did not turn his head or acknowledge her presence.

"Liam, what's going on?" Kay demanded. "You just walked right past me. Are you feeling ill? What's going on with you?"

There was still no response. Kay put her face in front of Liam's. "Hello!"

Liam blinked. "Sorry Kay. What was that again?"

Kay swung his chair away from the desk and dropped herself onto his lap. Sliding her arms around his neck, she kissed him full on the lips and said, "Penny for them. Come on, tell me what's going on in that head of yours." She tapped his forehead and dipped her chin, waiting.

"I, er. Well. Nothing. I just went for a walk that's all."

"Uh-uh! A walk means trudging off down the lane or through the bog. It does not mean crossing the meadow to the hawthorn grove."

Liam looked as though he were about to refute this but one look at Kay's expectant face and he knew that resistance to this particular question was futile. "Look Kay. It's nothing really. I just went over there to see, well to look at, I mean damn it Kay, why are you questioning me like this? I've done nothing wrong."

Kay leaned back from him, the better to see his face. "You've been acting strangely for days Liam. In fact, it's since you got back from your vacation."

Liam opened his mouth to speak, then thought again and closed it. He looked off to the side, away from Kay's determined stare.

"Liam!" She held his chin and turned his face back to hers. "You insist on renting out our home in the States and moving us back to Ireland. Fine! Then you go off on a hiking vacation without us. Fine! And then I find you wandering off to the circle for no apparent reason. But now you're being secretive about it and that is most definitely not fine! What's going on?"

"Nothing. There's nothing going on Kay. I'm just enjoying being back here. You know, getting to know the countryside again."

They looked at each other for a long moment. "Really, that's all." He shrugged his shoulders.

Kay looked at him through half closed eyes. "Well, all right then. But you'd tell me if there was anything wrong, wouldn't you?"

He smiled at her then. "Of course, I would." Kay suspected there was more. She decided to let it go for now, but she would keep a closer eye on him.

"Now," said Liam. "What to do about those mice."

Kay allowed him to change the subject. There had been no invasion of mice since Liam had arrived. He had set up a rodent repellent system, that emitted a high frequency signal, effectively deterring them from entering the cottage. But she played along and cried out, "Oh my goodness. Yes! We have to do something about them. Now! Today!"

For the remainder of the afternoon and most of the evening, Liam went about the cottage with a determined expression, sealing holes where mice may have entered.

Kay watched him carefully. She noticed as the time wore on, that Liam seemed to become more relaxed, concentrating as he was on the job at hand. It was several hours later, that Liam squirted a final blob of expanding foam, into the space around the pipes of the en-suite bathroom. "There!" He said with satisfaction, sitting back on his heels. "That should do it."

Kay asked anxiously, "Just promise me no mice will get in."

"Don't you worry now. I'll hang a sign outside the door. 'No mice allowed!' Sure, they'll stay far away from the place if they know they're not welcome." He grinned at her. "Do you remember the mouse when we rented that vacation cottage?"

Kay laughed. "How could I forget? We were half asleep in front of the fire. The little thing must have thought it was alone in the place, paused as it was in the doorway. I swear I could see its whiskers twitching and one of its little paws stretched forward ready to take the next step into the room."

Liam teased, "You jumped onto the back of the couch, shrieking. The mouse turned tail and ran off down the corridor as fast as its legs could carry it. By the time I got into the corridor, the mouse had long disappeared into its bolt hole."

"I couldn't get to sleep for ages after."

"Don't remind me," sighed Liam in exaggeration. "You insisted we leave the bedroom light on every night."

"You were awful Liam," she reprimanded him, "pretending to see mice in the corner just so I'd try to bury myself beneath you."

Liam guffawed with laughter and stood up, taking Kay into his arms. “No amount of caressing and sweet talk would calm you down.”

“I was too afraid of a mouse running up my leg.”

“And I thought I’d lost my Irish charm, so I did.”

Kay laughed and reached up to kiss him. Liam held her tight as he returned her kiss but suddenly released her, pointing at the corner of the bathroom. “How did that little beggar get in? Look out, I’ll grab it.”

Kay didn’t wait to confirm this information but ran shrieking into the living room, through the kitchen and out through the back door. Without thinking, she was across the field and at the gate that led into the meadow with Liam in hot pursuit and yelling, “I’m joking Kay, just kidding.”

They were both breathless when he caught up with her. Liam grabbed her about the waist and pulled her to him in the sunshine. At that moment, a sheep bleated in the meadow, so that they both looked in the direction it had come. The Faerie circle sat silent in the sunlight. Its thick tangle of hawthorn bushes hiding the secrets within. The view had an effect on each of them. Kay looked away and stepped back from Liam. He dropped his arms from her waist and left her there, opening the gate from the field to the meadow, neglecting to close it behind him.

“Liam, where are you going?” she asked in surprise. She began to follow him, then stopped before she walked through the gate.

Liam seemed to remember she was there. “Back soon,” he called over his shoulder.

“Liam, it’s almost dark. What could you possibly be doing at this time? Come back!”

“Something I have to do.”

Kay watched in disbelief as her husband crossed the meadow, completely ignoring her.

"We should stay away from there," she called but could not bring herself to follow him. Determination entered her voice. "This has gone on long enough!" Liam didn't seem to hear her.

Kay turned back to the cottage. Her anger built up steadily, simmering like the soup she was making for dinner. With a mutinous face, she grabbed a large turnip and hacked it into submission. In her experience, there was no other way with a turnip. Its skin was thick and uninviting. Perhaps it was the same with Liam. The only way to reach through his stubbornness was head on. Well, if that's the way it needed to be, then that's the way it would be. She'd have it out with him that very night. She hacked at the turnip again.

Kay waited up for Liam until after 10pm. At that point, she went to bed. She turned off the light and tried to sleep but was so angry, she could not settle. She could not understand why Liam was behaving so irrationally. Eventually, she calmed herself by deciding she would have it out with Liam as planned, but it could wait until the morning.

Kay woke when she heard Liam moving about the room. She peered at the clock on the bedside table. It was after midnight. "Are you just coming to bed Liam?" She couldn't keep the resentment out of her voice.

"Not just yet. No." Kay half sat up. Liam sounded strangely excited. He was rummaging through the cupboard in the dark. "Ah!" he said. "Yes!" He pushed something into his pocket and left the bedroom. Kay threw back the covers and followed him, catching up just as he opened the kitchen door.

"Where are you going Liam?" Kay grabbed his arm. "You've been gone all evening and now you're going out again. It's the middle of the night."

Liam's honest blue eyes glittered as if with a fever. His breathing was fast as he said "It's all right Kay. Look there's a full moon. I can see just fine."

Kay followed his gaze and looked through the window at the sky. When she looked back at Liam, his face appeared shadowy after the brightness of the moon. “But why are you going out at this time of night?” She was angry with him but holding back, trying to understand.

“I…” he began. “Never mind that. I’ll be back Kay and I’ll have something exciting to tell you.”

“You’re talking crazy Liam. You’ve been acting so strange lately. Please, come back to bed.”

“I won’t be long Kay.” He tried to disengage himself from her grasp, but she held on fast and pulled him toward the bedroom. “Come back to bed Liam. Please.”

Liam hesitated, looking out through the kitchen window as if considering. He turned to Kay and smiled. “All right. You’re right. Let’s go back to bed.” He allowed himself to be led back through the house. Kay held the bedroom door open as Liam paused in the living room to pull off his boots, trousers and sweater, draping them over the couch.

Kay sighed with relief. They lay on the bed. Moon rays streamed through the skylight. The room and Liam appeared half in shadow, half in light.

Liam pulled Kay to him and began to kiss her, but not with tenderness. It was as if it were a task he needed to accomplish.

Kay pulled back resisting, halting his rushed pace. Liam’s eyes were ghostly shadows. Kay’s heart lurched within her as a quiet premise of danger came and went within her breast. She held his face in her hands and kissed the contours of his cheeks and then his mouth, pale in the silvery light. Kay took Liam’s hand and kissed it, placing it on her breast. Her heart was full of compassion. She could not understand what his agitation meant. Her soul again cried danger. If she could just keep him by her until morning, perhaps the day would bring the opportunity to talk this through. But now she sought to calm him, to bring him back, her body claiming him instinctively as her own.

Kay stroked Liam's face, neck and shoulders. In this way, her hands made their way down his body, her mouth following until she took the fullness of him between her lips. She teased, kissed and licked until his body relaxed and then began to tense in the way of love. Quickly, she positioned herself over him, her own pleasure adding to his. He opened his eyes to see her there, a silvery nymph bathed in moonlight, riding him through the shadows of his mind.

They lay spent, not speaking, panting in glistening sweat. Liam waited for Kay to fall asleep. He held her close, her head on his chest. When her breathing was soft and measured, he carefully disentangled his arm, turning her sideways so that his body was behind hers. Carefully he moved backward, displacing his body with the warm covers that retained his heat.

Rising slowly from the bed, Liam paused a moment, listening to his wife snoring softly. Usually, he would make a mental note to tease her about it in the morning. She would solidly defend her belief that she never snored. Liam would then make a big fuss, telling her he thought elephants were invading, it was so loud. She would react by reaching up to slap him playfully, and he would wrap his arms around her, so that she giggled helplessly in his embrace.

But tonight, he had other things on his mind. He walked quietly to the bedroom door and looked back at Kay. She was fast asleep, her face in shadow, turned away from the moonlight.

Quickly, Liam pulled on the boots, trousers and sweater he had left in the living room. He carefully opened the kitchen door and just as carefully closed it.

Once clear of the cottage, his earlier excitement flooded through him again. He strode through the field to the gate. There were sheep in the meadow again tonight. They skittered away as Liam came close. Sean must have moved them from the field just beyond his own cottage. He did that every week, varied their feed by giving them fresh pastures to nibble on.

Careful not to clang the gate, Liam slid the bolt behind him and looked toward the hawthorn grove. The moon hung directly above the circle which seemed to glow within the mist that had settled low about it. The mist swirled, ebbing and flowing so that to Liam, the hawthorn grove appeared to float atop the meadow.

Liam glanced at his watch. It was after 3 a.m. He had meant to get back here for just after midnight, but Kay's anxiety had delayed him. Excitement filled his mind as he concluded that all the elements were present. Moonlight, mist and the hour that placed him inside the first of May.

"Beltane." He whispered and smiled.

He thought he heard laughter as he approached the grove. Peering through the mist, he could make out shapes, figures half hidden by the hawthorns, weaving in and out of each other, as if dancing around a maypole. There was a distinct odor of woodsmoke and a flicker of orange color denoting a fire.

Liam increased his pace, anxious to reach the grove. As he stepped up beside the ash tree, a silence fell. His view from the top of the bank revealed nothing. The figures had disappeared, the laughter had faded, the fire was extinguished. There was only a slight breeze and the warmth of slightly cooling air along with the tantalizing aroma of a turf fire lately in use.

The moonlight shone a path that swept in and around the hawthorn, whispering of the unknown that hid tantalizing within the shadows.

Stepping down into the circle, he crossed the grove warily. Hawthorns creaked in his wake. He paused to listen, hairs rising on his back. The grove waited with him, mocking in its silence. Liam squared his shoulders and advanced on the menhir. Leaves shivered in a sudden breeze as he walked by.

Standing beside the menhir, he pulled out the flashlight he had retrieved from the bedroom cupboard and took the notebook from his other pocket. He clipped the flashlight onto the notebook so he could easily see the writing. Placing his free hand on the cold stone of the menhir, Liam began to recite the words from the page. He was no expert but had consulted several books and hoped he had made a good job of translating the Ogham.

Liam made chant of the words but to his surprise, nothing happened. He repeated the process trying different ways of pronouncing the words as if this might make a difference.

In frustration, Liam turned away from the menhir. He circled through the grove, stumbling over reeds and glaring into the shadows as if daring, inviting yet abhorring what might come to him there. The breeze followed, sweeping through the branches behind him. Liam staggered back to the menhir and repeated the chant again and again. Time passed as he knelt before the object that hid the desire of his heart. The breeze became wind, stealing the words from his mouth so that they could not be heard above the rustling of leaves.

Branches bent crazily as the wind began to roar, ripping his words away into the night. Yet no chasm opened up. No cavern revealed itself. No portal made a path for him. The wind began to tear at him, beating him back. Branches whipped him from tree to tree until he found himself at the top of the bank beside the ash tree.

The wind died away as suddenly as it had begun, as if rebuking his invasion of this sacred place. He looked about angrily, a little afraid and unsure of how to proceed. He had failed. Was there a mistake in the translation? Very likely, he thought, for he was not a scholar. He glared at the grove, his mind working to grasp at a solution. That there must be one he was sure. He felt it deep in his gut. He waited for inspiration to come but nothing did. He sighed in frustration.

Beltane would continue for another five days. He told himself he had time. It was not over yet. He turned reluctantly away, stepped down the bank and was immediately outside the circle.

As he walked away from the grove, he felt exhausted as if he had taken part in a physical struggle. The moon was low in the sky, the mist beginning to clear. A robin trickled its early morning song.

Liam heard a distant rumbling sound. Looking back, he traced the sound not to the grove but to the distant line of mountains that were barely visible in the half light. Thunder, he wondered. He looked at the sky but could see no rain clouds yet.

His attention was caught by the fluty tones of the blackbird, quickly followed by the repeated phrasing of thrushes establishing their territory and calling for their mates.

He turned for home. His body leaned toward rest, yet the recesses of his mind remained lit by the desire to succeed.

As Liam stumbled across the meadow, a shadow stepped into his footsteps. It followed him across the meadow, up the hill, through the field and to the door of the kitchen.

Liam closed the kitchen door behind him and locked it. He walked through the cottage, retaining the presence of mind to leave his outer clothing draped over the couch as it was before he left the bed of his lover.

In the bedroom, the dawn light had begun to slip through the blinds. Kay was on her side still, one arm thrown out over the edge of the bed. Liam carefully lifted the duvet and slipped into bed behind his wife. She pushed back against him, murmuring softly. Thus spooned, Liam fell into an exhausted sleep.

CHAPTER 10 – LIAM COMES CLEAN

Kay woke to find Liam sprawled on the bed beside her. His face was spattered with dust and there were leaves in his hair that she had not noticed when they made love in the night.

She observed him for a moment. She would have it out with him this morning. She debated whether to wake him immediately or let him sleep. There were creases in his forehead that sleep had not relaxed. She would wait until he was rested.

Pulling on her robe, Kay walked through the living room on her way to the kitchen. She sighed as she picked up the clothing Liam had discarded in the living room and dropped it in the laundry basket. She went back for his boots and placed them near the front door. She must have order, at least in the communal areas they all used.

Kay spent her morning playing with Aoife, enjoying time in the garden together.

At midday, Kay walked Aoife along the lane to Sean's cottage where she had arranged for her daughter to help Sean feed one of the new lambs.

Kay then brewed an extra strong pot of coffee and brought a large mugful into the bedroom.

Avoiding Liam's side of the bed for fear of the various articles of clothing she might step on, she crossed to her side around the foot of the bed. Careful not to spill the coffee, she sat on the bed and waited for the strong aroma to wake him.

Soon enough, Liam grunted and turned over, blinking in the sunlight that now streamed unrelenting through the skylight. "I really must find blinds for those windows," he mumbled.

Kay waited, saying nothing.

Sensing her disapproval, Liam sat up. In silence Kay offered the mug of coffee. In silence Liam accepted it. He sipped, his head jerking back slightly at the strength of the brew. He glanced at Kay and sipped again.

Kay opened the conversation. "This is where you tell me exactly, and I mean exactly, what is going on Liam."

He looked at her, opened his mouth to speak and closed it again. He took another sip of coffee, needing the clarity it might bring.

"Now Liam." Kay was insistent.

Liam let out his breath in a huge sigh. He took another sip of coffee and contemplated the contents of the mug. Glancing at Kay, he could see from her expression that she would not be put off again. And so he began, "It was while I was in Greenland. We came to a little coastal village. It was old and quaint, folksy you know, incredibly attractive."

Liam reached over and placed his coffee mug on the side table. He sat up straighter, eager to talk now the subject was in the open between them. "As I said, there was something about the place Kay. I didn't want to leave there. I felt the need to just stay, at least for a few days."

Kay watched his face, his attempt to draw her into the story succeeding so far.

"The others had no interest in the place. They wanted to move on. We consulted the map and arranged to meet in a few days, further along the coast. I'd take a bus or get a ride.

"So, I stayed behind and was glad that I did. I wandered about the cliffs and the beach all day and looked around the little village. There was nothing that really caught my attention but, I don't know, I was still drawn to the place. There was something about it that reminded me of here, the west of Ireland, the people maybe, I'm not sure."

"Anyway, I was staying in this old hotel. It was quiet that evening, not many guests. The barman was bored. We got to talking. He noticed my Irish accent and started telling me a story."

Liam grabbed a second pillow and stuck it behind his back. It was a moment before he spoke again, as if he was trying to find the right words.

"It was an old story, he said, the barman. I listened happily enough because I was beginning to think I'd made a mistake in staying behind on my own. That whatever it was I'd felt about the place, I was not going to figure out. Have you ever had that feeling?" Liam looked into Kay's eyes, hoping to draw a similar experience from her.

"No?" he answered his own question. "Well anyway this man, the tale he told, I just about fell off me bar stool." Liam became excited here and took a breath.

"The story was about some Dutch navigator who had found an island just off the coast of Greenland about 800 years ago. The account of his story said the place was protected by potent witchcraft and anyone who tried to approach was pushed off course so that their boats would overturn, and they'd drown in the sea. I was really only listening with half an ear until the barman said the name of the island."

Liam laughed nervously, wanting Kay to catch the thrill of it. "Tir na Nog he called it."

"Tir na Nog?" Kay was astonished. "But that's an Irish legend isn't it. Land of Eternal Youth. I don't understand the connection to Greenland?"

"I know," said Liam. He grabbed Kay's hands. "Of course, I sat up straight at that point and paid close attention. Bearing in mind Kay, this place I was in, it was at least fifteen hundred miles away from Ireland. Why would it have such a name?"

She shook her head, unable to hazard a guess.

"That's what I thought." He agreed with her unspoken words. "But then I recalled one of our teachers in primary school. She'd tell us stories of Irish myths. One of the stories was about Mannan Mac Lir. He's the Irish sea god, a bit like Poseidon only he was young and strong you know, like most Irish heroes." Liam winked at her and raised her hand to his lips.

"Anyway, it was Mannan's job to protect Tir na Nog. In the legend, there was something about Mannan protecting the ocean boundaries, so you can see how my interest was piqued. I mean, I hadn't thought of it before but if it was the job of the sea god to protect Tir na Nog, then it had to have been an island, right? Right!" He answered his own question.

Liam released her hands in his excitement, grabbed them again, released them. "Of course, I questioned the barman, disputed the name. Tir na Nog? I kept repeating. He said he could show me proof and he would do it, if I'd be up and about by 9am the next morning.

"Well I bought him a drink and we toasted Tir na Nog. The barman, his name was Mati by the way. He went on to talk of other things and I nodded along, saying yes and no here and there but Kay, I was entranced and excited. I could hardly wait to go to bed just so I could wake up the next morning and meet with the guy again.

"I'm telling you; my heart beat so fast all night. I could barely eat breakfast. I went outside to meet Mati as arranged. I half expected him to have forgotten or maybe he'd made up the story just to amuse himself and pass the time. But there he was, hiking boots on his feet and a smile on his face.

"He led me out of the village, up the side of the cliffs and along a track that kept to the sea line. There was no one about. It was quite a stretch of deserted coastline. We walked for about an hour, with him talking non-stop about nothing I can even recall now. I don't think I listened to him at the time, I was just so eager you know.

"Anyway Mati, he finally turned off the cliff road, to follow a path down the side of the cliff toward the beach. It was crumbling and stony. I was worried about falling and more than once I wondered if the guy meant to do away with me or some other dark deed."

Kay watched Liam carefully. He looked boyish. Excitement flushed his face as he relived the experience.

"Before we reached the shore, we came to an opening in the rocks. It was a cave." Liam stopped a moment and laughed. "It was dark in there." He stroked his chin reflectively.

"Mati took a flashlight and headed into the cave. Well that was when I decided I was going no further. I mean, I didn't know this man and wasn't about to go into a cave with him. We were miles from anywhere and no one had any idea where I was." Liam paused again, lost in the moment.

"Mati looked back and saw me hesitate. He waved me forward, but I didn't budge." Liam re-focused into the room and looked at Kay. "Then he said the strangest thing Kay. It was a quote. He said it was from the runes he was going to show me. I knew when I heard the words that he couldn't have made them up because they're from our own Irish mythology. They're nothing to do with Greenland. The words he recited to me were these …" Liam took a deep breath.

"In the time that is not a time
In a place that is not a place
On a day that is not a day
Between the worlds and beyond"

"Oh!" said Kay, recognizing the words. "It's about the—"

"The Tuatha de Danaan," Liam finished the sentence for her and went on with his story. "You can see how excited I was. I mean, at that point, I was hooked. I'd have followed him anywhere just to see for myself. He led me into this cave. It wasn't too far back. But then he walked around a little curve in the rock so that he was out of sight."

Liam took a breath and, half laughing in his enthusiasm to get the story out, he swallowed, took a breath and began again. "The runes, that's what Mati called them. The runes had been protected from the worst of the weather because they were around this bend in the rock, protected from the salt air and ocean winds. Runes… markings they'd call them here in Ireland."

He stopped talking briefly and looked at her again, as if holding onto a punch line. "Kay it was Ogham. You've heard of Ogham markings? No? Well up to eight hundred years ago, some say way back, much further than that. Druids and other people left markings on stones and menhirs throughout the country as they travelled. It was to leave messages or show where they were headed and such. But Kay, the thing is, I recognized the markings."

"Recognized them?"

"I did Kay. They were the same as the markings here in the grove."

"In the grove? This grove here in the meadow?" Kay was lost. "I don't understand."

"Kay, I played in that grove just about every day when I was a kid. There's a stone there, it's called a menhir. There are markings on it. I know they're Ogham markings because we learned about them at school. The thing is, I know the markings on that stone like the lines on the palm of my left hand. When I saw the markings Kay, I knew. I recognized them."

Kay shook her head. "I'm still in shock at the idea of you walking into a cave with someone you didn't know, miles from anywhere."

"Yes, yes!" Liam waved her concerns away. "But you can imagine how excited I was right?" He looked at her for encouragement.

She nodded, wary now that he had brought the hawthorn grove into the story, wanting him to continue.

"I had a notebook with me, always carried it, useful for jotting directions about tourist places and such. I pulled out the notebook, but I kept dropping it, Kay. I was so excited. I told him to hold the flashlight steady. I got the runes copied and then I remembered my phone."

"You made a call?"

"No. I took out my phone and snapped a pic. Look," he said grabbing his phone from the floor where he'd dropped it. He scrolled quickly through the photos. "Here it is."

And there it was. A flash lit photo of markings scratched deep into a rock face.

Kay looked from Liam's face to the photo and back again to Liam's face.

"But Liam, you were just talking about an island. The cave where these markings were found were on the mainland. How d'you explain that?"

"I don't know Kay but if the magic was so potent that the island could hardly be found, it makes sense the markings would be on the mainland but close to where the island might have been."

Kay watched him carefully. He certainly believed what he was telling her. She decided to let that go. "And you've compared these runes with the markings on the stone here, in our circle?"

"Yes. Yes, that's it. Do you see?"

"Well! Okay! I get that, I do." She was still perplexed. "But Liam I don't see what it all means, what it has to do with anything."

Liam laughed, the sound was erratic and half-crazy in its obsessive quality. "Don't you see, that for Irish writing to be found on the other side of Europe is an amazing thing. And then there's the myth of Tir na Nog, right!"

Kay nodded, trying to follow his logic.

Liam continued, his words coming fast now. "Who would have gone all that way to write Irish Ogham on the walls of a cave? Druids? The Tuatha de Danaan themselves?"

"You believe this?" Kay was skeptical, not of the existence of the Tuatha de Danaan for she knew only too well they existed. But Liam taking such things seriously, this was new.

Liam waved away her comments. "Yes, yes! And look. It's the writing along with the words that Mati recited to me. I believe it's the way in. Through the portal, I mean. It's the way in to where the Sidhe live, the Tuatha de Danaan. And I'm going to open the portal and, and …." Liam's voice trailed off as he became aware of Kay's face. Shock and revulsion ran one after the other across her features, her eyes and mouth grown round in horror.

Kay grabbed the notebook from the bed and began ripping it to pieces. Liam reached for it and tried to grab it from her. "What are you doing. Here, give me that. Stop it Kay!"

Kay turned in a fury and grabbed his phone. She threw it to the floor and stomped on it. Then she grabbed it up again and flipped through, searching for the photo so she could erase it.

Liam wrenched the phone from her with a suddenness that unnerved them both. He threw the covers back and half fell out of the bed, staggered to his feet and backed away from her, the phone held tight in his hand. "What the hell are you doing?"

"No Liam. What are you doing? You have no idea what you're messing with. Open a portal indeed. Over my dead body!"

"What the feck! You're acting like a crazy person!"

"Me? You think I'm acting crazy? Seriously Liam? Have you listened to yourself? Some crazy story about accessing a portal to the underworld and you're calling me crazy!" Kay was terrified. After all she had done to put distance between herself and Mac, to put distance between the Sidhe and her child, here was Liam going full tilt at opening a portal.

She could not reveal what she knew. It was imperative to their marriage that Liam know nothing about her affair with a man of the Sidhe. It was a Pandora's box that must remain closed.

If a portal were to be opened, it was feasible that Liam could discover more than he bargained for. He might even meet Mac. Such an event could cost her not only her own relationship with Liam, but maybe even Aoife's relationship with Liam as her father. This was especially true if Mac were to learn that Aoife was his and come to claim her.

Kay's face was white with the shock of it, that Liam could unwittingly put their little world in danger. It was unthinkable. She wished fervently at that moment, that she had not listened to Liam in his desire for them to return to Ireland. If only they had stayed in the States, none of this would be happening right now. Kay's mind worked at speed. She must put Liam off, stop him from pursuing this foolishness.

Liam interrupted her whirlwind thoughts. "Look Kay, I know it may sound crazy but …"

"Yes Liam! It does sound crazy and I need you to stop and think about what you're doing. First of all, you don't mess with things like this."

Liam opened his mouth to speak, but Kay didn't give him time to form words. she went on. "I'm surprised you even believe in all of this …. Stuff!"

"Kay!"

"Second of all!" She held up a finger. "You've no idea what you're getting into if you do manage to, what did you say, open a portal? To where Liam? What do you think will be on the other side of that portal? What if it's something terrible?"

"I don't think there could be anything terrible," he said. But the expression on his face told Kay it was something that had crossed his mind.

She pursued this thought to her advantage. "And if it is something terrible Liam, you'd release that, bring it into our home where our child sleeps."

Liam blinked at that but still he could not let it go. "Look at it as an interesting excavation then, a hobby if you like. I'll be careful okay?"

"Stop!" Kay became relentless in her need to make Liam listen. "If you don't stop this foolishness, I'm, I'm going to, to take Aoife and fly home. And if I do that Liam, I'm telling you right now, I will never, hear me, *never* return here to Ireland!"

"What? Kay! Don't you think you're overreacting?"

For answer, Kay pulled her suitcase from the top of the wardrobe and flung it on the bed. She began pulling clothing from hangers and dropping them into the suitcase.

Astonished at Kay's reaction, Liam alternately pleaded with her and grabbed clothing from the suitcase. He tried and failed to return dresses to the wardrobe as Kay pulled them out of his grasping hands. "Kay! Kay!" His anger turned to fear as Kay determinedly resisted his attempts to undo her actions. "I'll do it!" he cried in panic. "I'll stop!"

Kay paused in her frantic efforts to make her point. She glared at him.

"Please Kay. Don't leave. Don't take Aoife away from me." Liam grabbed her hands. "Please!" His voice broke.

Kay softened. She hated to see the hurt in his face, but she was adamant that she must make her point. She must save what they had. "Promise me Liam. I need a solemn promise."

"I promise Kay." Liam grabbed her and held her to his chest. "What the feck! If it means that much to you."

"It does mean that much Liam, it really does." Kay slumped against him in her relief.

CHAPTER 11 – THE GUIDE

Aoife sat on a kitchen stool. An oversized apron was tied about her middle. Solemn with concentration, tongue held between her lips, Aoife carefully pounded a mixture in a bowl. Cara the mouse, sat on Aoife's right shoulder, observing the process with interest.

Nell peered over Aoife's left shoulder, intent on giving her effective advice on the correct way of making a charcoal poultice.

"Now!" Nell instructed. "Tis important that ye do not add too much water for it must spread on the hurt part easily enough, do ye see?"

"Mmm!" Aoife nodded her head.

"And then, ye wash off the paste with a damp cloth. Look, I will show ye."

The two practiced the application and removal of the herbal remedy until Nell was content that Aoife knew the process.

"Where will I get the charcoal stuff?" asked Aoife. She pushed out her lips in satisfaction as her hands squeezed the mixture through her fingers.

"Well now, ye do not need to worry about such a thing just yet."

"But if someone gets hurted, then I need to know how to fix them."

"Be that as it may mo stor, I am after teaching you about the herbal remedies so that when ye're a woman, ye will be having the knowledge of it at yer fingertips so."

"That's a long time away. Will I remember?"

"Sure, and ye will. Are ye not the clever one now and tis why I'm teaching ye."

"It's fun Nell. Look!" Aoife held up hands black with charcoal. She pulled her fingers along her cheeks and laughed. "Where's the mirror? I want to see."

"Tch! Tch! Child. There is no mirror in this house. Come here and let me wipe ye clean so."

Nell produced a washcloth and applied it to Aoife's hands and face. Aoife pursed her lips and tried to speak as the cloth passed over her mouth. Cara gave a squeak and jumped off Aoife's shoulder, narrowly missing the poultice mixture in her evident haste to escape the washcloth.

"No mirror?" exclaimed Aoife. "But, how do you see yourself?"

"Sure, and do I not know what I look like, without a mirror to tell me. Stop talking now so I can finish the cleaning of ye."

Aoife was quiet, her eyes studying Nell's face to see what Nell might see if she looked into a mirror. "Your face is always clean Nell."

"Is it now?" Nell rinsed the cloth under the tap water and hung it to dry.

"I'll tell you if your face gets smudged okay. That way you'll know. Or I could bring you a mirror. Shall I bring you a mirror?"

"No indeed. Ye shall not bring a mirror into this cottage. There will be no more nor less than already belongs here."

"But that's silly. I'm here Nell and I don't belong here."

"Sure, and ye do. Why would ye be here otherwise. "Struth! Ye do say such things." Nell shook her head and patted Aoife's cheek.

"Nell," began Aoife. "Can I tell you something?"

"Ye can of course."

"Daddy went to the fairy circle. He tried to open something. I don't know what it was, and he wouldn't tell me." Aoife looked up at Nell. "He doesn't want me to go there, to the circle."

"Hmm!" said Nell. "Quite right he is too. Ye should not go near that place."

"But." Aoife twisted her mouth to one side before speaking again. "I want to go there."

"I know ye do." Nell waited.

"He made me promise. But I had my fingers crossed and I think I will go back."

The old woman nodded her head sagely. "I know ye will Aoife. I know ye will."

Aoife waited for Nell to say something else, maybe to tell her not to go to the circle. As Nell said nothing, Aoife concluded it wasn't such a terrible thing if she did go.

As if she had read Aoife's mind, Nell said "Ha!" as if something had been decided. Then the old woman straightened up and said, "Now I must get on with the work of the day."

Aoife blinked thoughtfully and wondered at the strangeness of grownups. She watched as Nell began to pursue her daily routine of sweeping, dusting and polishing.

Aoife followed Nell around, interested in all she did. "You do a lot of cleaning. More than Mommy does."

"Do I now?" asked Nell, interested, leaning on the stick of her broom while she listened to Aoife.

"Well, you don't have a robovac. It rolls around the carpet and sucks up the dust. Mommy says it does the work for you. We have a robovac. Well, we had one in the States but here, we just have a vacuum."

"Well, I cannot speak to that now, but I can tell ye a good sweep does the job as well as anything. That and a bit of work with the elbow do ye see?" She demonstrated, sweeping energetically and working her elbows.

"But you have to work so hard. You should get a robovac. Why don't you get one?"

"Ye have to appreciate the ordinary work, so ye do Aoife. For tis in the doing of it and doing it well, that ye practice being closer to God do ye see?"

"Mommy doesn't talk about God except she says oh my god sometimes. You know, when she breaks a fingernail or something."

"Does she now? Godstruth!"

"Godstruth? That's a good word. I'm going to use it."

Nell looked hard at her. "Hmph!" she said.

"Are you my friend Nell?"

"I am Aoife. I am that."

"It's nice to have a friend. I haven't met any friends in Ireland yet, except for Sean but he's always too busy going to see his caves. Mommy says that's because he's a farmer."

"Ah! Yes, I can see how that would be."

"You're very old Nell."

"Bless you child."

"You won't die, will you? People die when they get old. Sean's wife died. I think she was probably old."

"Well now, is it that, worrying ye child? Me dying? Hah!" The old woman seemed amused.

"Ye do not have to worry about that, for tis a different sort of friend that I am to ye."

"Oh?"

"I will always be with ye Aoife. I am your anamchara."

"Onum, onum what?" Aoife couldn't get her lips around the word.

Nell pronounced the word slowly. "Anamchara. It means I am your guide, your soul friend."

"Anumkara. My soul-friend. What's a soul-friend?"

"It means that I am here whenever you need me. I will help ye make sense of the world so I will. Mind, I may not always be kind about it, for there may be times when you need a good telling off and I will be here to give it ye. But you can depend on me being here for you every day of yer life."

"Til I die?"

"Yes indeed. Until ye die." Nell tucked in her chin and blinked as she regarded her ward.

Aoife regarded her mentor in return. "Wow! That's a really long time."

"Longer than ye can imagine Aoife." Nell's smile was kind. "Now!" she said, changing the subject. "There are eggs in the hen house that will not collect themselves. Be off outside with me now and I will show ye how to do it without disturbing the hens."

The bright day bathed the little backyard in a happy golden light. Aoife's laughter rang through the yard adding to the general melee of hens clucking, donkey braying, cows mooing and sheep baaing. Aoife ran about the backyard of Nell's cottage, exploring every nook and cranny.

In the henhouse, Nell instructed Aoife on how to collect eggs. This was simple enough if the hens were already outside in the yard scratching for feed, as she could simply pluck them from the straw.

Some hens still nestled on their eggs. The old woman carefully lifted these hens, crooning to them all the while to keep them calm, while Aoife removed the eggs from beneath.

The basket of newly gathered eggs sat by the scullery door. Aoife had no patience for putting them away tidily inside the cottage while the sun beckoned, birds called to each other and the green grass spread like a carpet across the yard.

She trotted after the hens who spread their wings and clucked their displeasure as they ran away from her. She hung off the gate calling to the donkey, tempting him by waggling a carrot provided by Nell.

Up in the storage room with its large aperture looking out onto the yard, Nell forked hay down into the cow shed below and laughed at the antics of the child.

"He likes me," cried Aoife as the donkey ate from her hand, which she held flat with the carrot displayed there just as Nell had instructed.

"Of course, he does child. All creatures will like ye if ye show them respect so."

"I love this place," said Aoife with her back to the gate. The donkey nibbled her hair. She reached up to pat his neck. "And I love you Nell."

"Ah go on wit ye. Here ye are, full of the nonsense now." But it was plain to see from the smile on her face, that Nell was pleased.

CHAPTER 12 – MAC EXPELLED

Hidden from mortal view within the mounds, the Sidhe messenger traversed the ancient route, passing beneath torches of smokeless fire, set into silver sconces of intricate workmanship. She spared no pause to marvel, as tunnels opened into great caverns sparkling with rose quartz and citrus colored sapphire. Filled with purpose, she raced on through the labyrinth of sparkling stone, that led deep into the mountains within the realms of the underworld, into the time that is not a time.

At last the path began to rise. She felt the familiar breeze on her face that lifted her spirit, despite the dreadful news she carried. Soon enough, she passed through the inner portal between the worlds that led to the place beyond.

The pupils of her eyes quickly adjusted to the sunlight that poured into a central meadow. Vast and green on this day that was not a day, it was alive with all the varieties of wildflower that could be imagined.

The messenger was swift of foot and dedicated to her task. Yet even in her haste, she could not help but admire the beauty laid out before her. Coming as she was from the mortal world, the scene was dazzling, as she beheld the home of the Tuatha de Danaan, a city of loveliness, warmth and welcome.

A great tree towered over the center of the plain, its spreading branches littered with birds trilling their music to the blue sky. Fountains sparkled with crystal clear waters from which salmon leaped and splashed. Hazel trees twelve feet tall boasted of their ripeness with clusters of flowers. Fruit trees crammed and heavy with blossom, dripped a carpet of petals from every bough. Golden apples hung in clusters from a silver-branched tree. The air was sweet with the perfume of orchids and roses.

Pretty cottages were dotted about the edges of the plain. Some were built of warm Connemara stone fitted together with great skill and accuracy, so that no joint or mortar was evident. The door posts were of carved yew, ornamented with gold or bronze. Other homes were fashioned from hardwood, their lintels edged with silver and adorned with precious gems. Roofs throughout the community were of feathered thatch, some brightly colored and others laced with white bird's wings.

Her way led through paths of glittering stone, edged with the greenest grass. A multitude of people sauntered in the sunshine. Many were red-haired, some blonde and others black. All had similarly slanted eyes of brilliant green or sparkling blue.

They were dressed in purple and gold, silver and blue, yellow and white with flowers woven through their hair or glittering metal decorations to hold back their long tresses.

Couples danced to the music of flute and harp. Others toasted each other with goblets of amethyst filled with red wine.

Racing games were underway, contestants vying against each other for favors.

Some gathered on a hillside with bows of yew and hickory, their arrows flying straight and true to the target. Onlookers clapped their approval.

Still others gathered about a riddle maker, bantering back and forth to guess the meaning of the puzzle on offer.

Blacksmiths worked their anvils on fires of charcoal, their bellows blowing to bend and blend silver and other precious metals. Swords of fine workmanship hung from the eves of the smith's domain, along with exquisite breastplates and accessories. High-stepping horses pranced and galloped freely across the great plain, their manes flying, their tails streaming.

Everywhere there was laughter and joyful merriment, that on another day would make the messenger slow her haste in favor of less urgent pursuits.

Yet this was not that day and as the messenger passed through the merrymakers, her presence was seen and acknowledged. They began to nudge each other and to follow. Soon there were great numbers of the people, trailing her course.

At the great throne of Ruadh Rofhessa, the messenger knelt on one knee before her king. Her chest heaved from the exertion of her journey. She waited for permission to speak.

The people gathered behind her, a murmur of questions filling the air like the busy buzz of a thousand bees. The great Ruadh Rofhessa held up his hand for silence. He nodded permission to the messenger who half turned to speak her words, torn as she was between reveling in her moment of fame against the serious import of her news.

Relaying her tale of the man known as Liam McKierney with his scribbled page of runes, she told how he had tried to gain access to the portal that lay within the circle near his home. She reminded those present that such portals were sacred to the Tuatha de Danaan, hidden from mortals for thousands of years except by particular invitation to a chosen few. Unable to hide her pride, she told of the great wind she had summoned to push Liam McKierney back from the menhir.

Her message being delivered, she added her own view of the situation. “Sire, Beltane is upon us. The portal is open if the man Liam McKierney were able to pronounce the words he has found in the land beyond the sea.” Here she gulped before completing the words she had prepared. “It is possible sire, if he were to enter, that he would accomplish what cannot be permitted.” The crowd gasped and turned to each other, a steady buzz of commentary rising once again.

Ruadh Rofhessa turned his ear to the two druids who sat either side of him. The first druid stood and waited for silence.

As one, the folk looked to her, their breathing shallow and anxious.

She spoke clearly so that all could hear. “It is well known among our people that on the moon of moons, in the hour of hours, at Beltane or Samhain, a portal may be accessed between the worlds.” She indicated the messenger. “It is the very reason our portals are guarded at such events.”

All nodded as a buzz of agreement rippled through the crowd. This was general knowledge, yet it must be spoken as if to remind them of the clear danger facing them.

The second druid now stood. Again, the people became silent as he began to speak. “This man Liam McKierney, if he gained entry through the portal on this night of nights, he could become a walker between the worlds.”

A momentary hush was followed by gasps of shock from all quarters, inspiring a sudden rush of wind that spread through the trees as the leaves sighed their disapproval.

The messenger signaled she had more to tell. The great king nodded slightly, giving her leave to speak.

The messenger added that she had witnessed through the window of the cottage, the moment when Kay confronted Liam. “The woman Kay McKierney, extracted a promise from her mate that he would not pursue the opening of the portal.”

As the people clapped their hands at this news and began to smile again and laugh, the king spoke, “The issue has been resolved?” Ruadh Rofhessa looked keenly at the messenger, waiting for her response.

“Great King, I watched most carefully. I saw it in the eyes of Liam McKierney, that he would not keep the promise made to his mate.”

A murmur ran across the crowd in a wave of disapproval. Ruadh Rofhessa held up his hand for silence yet again.

“That very evening as the dusk of the day passed into night, I observed Liam McKierney with his child. At a pause in their play, he walked to the gate and looked across the meadow to the hawthorn circle. I saw decision in his eyes. He will return to the grove while it is yet Beltane.”

The breeze sighed again through the trees, wafting a fragrance of rose, lavender and spikenard about the silent heads of the people. A shiver of regret passed through every member of the Tuatha de Danaan. They knew from experience the events that must now unfold.

Among this great and noble people, there was an aversion to doing real harm among the mortals who populated the lands beyond this place. Such ignoble tendencies were left to lesser beings that lived above ground but who were not of the Tuatha de Danaan.

And so, it was that on this day of days, not a sound could be heard, not a rustle of silk or a swirl of skirts or the clink of silver nor whisper of voice.

There was a shaking of heads and a furrow of brows. Even the youngest of the folk were impressed by the gravity of the situation and kept their high spirits in check, without need of admonishing by caring parents and elders.

The council had listened thoughtfully to the messenger and now they turned as one body to their leader. The great Ruadh Rofhessa was quiet for a long moment, the sea of eyes quietly troubled but respectful in their waiting.

At last, he spoke. His mane of red gold hair fell thick and long down his back, glinting in the sunlight as he looked upon his people. As one they focused their energy on him.

"This," he boomed, his voice seeming to reach to the very ends of the great plain, "cannot be permitted. One must be chosen to go from this place with a warning to the man Liam McKierney, that he must cease his quest forthwith. We did not cause the druid monks to carry the runes to the land beyond the sea, only to have it found before its time. Such a great and perilous sea journey was taken purposely in order to hide and secure the secret of the portal. It was done for the benefit of mankind, for they cannot come here and expect to return to their own time and place. It is true there have been some who traversed the worlds, only to find that when they returned home, all their loved ones had long passed on. A few of their minutes spent here, becomes seven lost years back there. It must be said that if this Liam McKierney, opens a portal and makes it known to others, it will cause pain and suffering to those who come here, only to find they soon yearn for a home they can never achieve in the time and place where they left it. We cannot permit such irresponsible conduct.

There was a murmuring that passed through all those present.

"Silence my people, children of Danaan." Ruadh Rofhessa waited for quiet among the folk.

The king turned to the messenger who knelt again on one knee before him. "How close is Liam McKierney to accessing the portal?"

"I believe he is close," responded the messenger. "He works feverishly at the runes and sees it as a challenge. Furthermore, he is not without intelligence and courage."

"Then we must send an envoy to convince him of his foolishness. We cannot risk a walker between the worlds coming among us. He must be told to turn away from his quest. Only we know how it might impact the world if the portal were opened before its time."

The messenger raised her hand and asked the question all were quietly wondering, "Who shall go to meet with this mortal?"

The first druid leaned forward and whispered a name into the ear of the great one. They quickly conferred with the second druid who likewise nodded gravely.

The king and his druids turned their green slanted eyes toward the waiting throng. They sought out a figure strong and tall, dressed in midnight blue and silver, who stood off to one side of the crowd.

"Maccan. Come forward," commanded Ruadh Rofhessa.

Maccan, reluctant but loyal, detached himself from an ivy-wrapped marble pillar and moved through the crowd toward the high platform. The folk parted to allow him through. Reverence was evident in the expression of the folk as he passed, for they knew the sacrifice that must be made if The Maccan were unable to persuade the McKierney to give up his quest.

"Maccan, Sidhe prince of the Tuatha de Danaan." Ruadh Rofhessa smiled with empathy at his strong and beautiful son. "You have brought about this dilemma. And so you have been chosen for this quest."

Here, The Maccan made to interrupt but Ruadh Rofhessa silenced him with an uplifted hand. "I know your sadness my son." He nodded in empathy. "You sought to find Caer."

Maccan could not hold back. "I did find her father. She yet lives." Maccan waved a hand as if Caer were close by.

"Hush my boy." Ruadh Rofhessa would not be interrupted. "You left your post to seek this woman. You should have come to me first. Do I not have the wisdom to guide you?"

Maccan nodded his head briefly but remained silent.

"But that is not all. It is possible that because of the love you hold for this woman, it could be the very reason she has returned here with Liam McKierney and her child."

The messenger spoke again. "Sire, I observed the child. She is of the Sidhe."

"Ahhhh!" The crowd nodded their heads, understanding the further dilemma. Several turned to look at The Maccan who was visibly startled by the words of the messenger.

Ruadh Rofhessa paused. He looked out over the gathering as if to relay a warning. "The child!" His voice raised sharply as he fixed his gaze on The Maccan. "The child is one of us! And now she is here! And with the gifts she no doubt possesses, she may unearth us yet, in rctaliation for the penalty her father may now pay for his impertinence."

A great sigh passed through the folk, echoed by the breeze as it swept again through the trees. The Maccan was unable to look into the face of his father.

"Look at me now." The voice of the great king was gentle. "I cannot blame you entirely my boy." He smiled. "It is the nature of the god of love to follow his destiny. But now you must make amends. It falls upon you to turn this McKierney away from his quest, to warn him off before it is too late."

The Maccan raised his head, his eyes mournful and pleading. "No father. Please. Do not let me be the one to do this."

But Ruadh Rofhessa went on, "And if you cannot deter him, then you know what must be done."

A collective sigh of pain came from the people. Anguish was plain upon the face of The Maccan, for he clearly knew what this would mean. If he were unable to persuade Liam McKierney away from his quest, there would be only one solution.

Ruadh Rofhessa placed a hand firmly upon the shoulder of his son. "You brought this tragedy upon your own head. You must be the one to bring it to its end."

The Maccan swallowed, the enormity of such an act even greater than the pain of never returning to his people and the presence of his father.

"Persuade this man with all the powers you are blessed with. Cause him to turn away from his quest and all will be well. But if you cannot do this before the end of Beltane, within five of their days, then there is but one alternative. Do you understand?"

"I do father." The voice of his son rang hollow even to his own ears. A human should not be killed by one of the Tuatha de Danaan. Such a deed sealed the fate of its executioner, who's fate would be to exist beyond the realms of this place forever.

Satisfied that the unspoken rule was understood, Ruadh Rofhessa pronounced. "It is so ordered. Go now!"

Maccan looked one last time into the eyes of his father which shone with love and empathy. He straightened his back and with head high, he turned and strode through the folk who parted to create a passage, their faces sad for the loss of their brother and friend.

When the footfall of Maccan receded from the great chamber, the eagle eyes of Ruadh Rofhessa turned again to look for and alight on the form of a most beautiful woman. Honey colored hair wound around her head and fell into lengths of loveliness down her back. "Eiru!" commanded Ruadh Rofhessa. "Come forward!"

Again, the crowd parted and waited expectantly. She of the laughing eyes and flirtatious demeanor did not hesitate but came forward to the platform and stood before her leader.

"Eiru, goddess of the earth and keeper of the Beltane fires. It falls to you to reach out to the child of Maccan and the woman he believes is Caer. It is your quest to friend this child and teach her the ways of our people, ever guiding her toward realizing her own power and how she may use it for the benefit of our folk. Bring her to us. Train her to be a light bringer to both our peoples."

Eiru bowed her beautiful head. Glittering blue eyes shone with love for her leader and with dedication to her task. "I will do this and gladly Ruadh Rofhessa."

The great red-haired man placed a hand upon Eiru's head and gave his final blessing to the quest. "And may this child, this future walker between the worlds, come to realize her true place in the order of things past, present and future."

Eiru departed from the presence of the king, in the direction The Maccan had taken. Preoccupied as the folk were in watching Eiru's departure, most did not notice Ruadh Rofhessa beckon to the messenger, who ran lightly up the steps and knelt before her king.

CHAPTER 13 – AOIFE AND THE LADY

Kay and Aoife were in the kitchen. Kay peeled vegetables while Aoife stood on the kitchen steps beside her. They wore matching green and white striped aprons.

"We're like real chefs aren't we Mommy, just like on tv."

"That's right darling, real chefs."

Kay sliced carrots and passed them to Aoife to drop into the pot.

"And I love the music Mommy. It's so pretty."

"What music is that?" Kay smiled at her daughter.

"The music from over there." Aoife gestured with a carrot toward the field behind them.

Kay paused a moment to listen, then said "I don't hear anything. It might be the pub down in the village. Sometimes I can hear music coming from there. Is it nice music?"

"It makes me want to dance." Aoife swayed back and forth on the step.

"Well that's good. Dancing is therapeutic. We should all dance more often."

"Thera … What's that Mommy?"

"Therapeutic? It means beneficial."

Aoife's face was questioning.

"It means something that makes us feel happy."

"Oh! Well this music makes me feel happy and I want to dance."

With that Aoife jumped off the step ladder and began to sway and twirl to unseen music.

Kay stopped to admire her pretty child. Aoife had a far-away look on her face as she spread her arms and dipped her head.

"That's a lovely dance darling."

"I'm a swan Mommy."

Kay looked at Aoife with a strange expression. Did her daughter know about her shape-shifting incident? But no, how could she? It was before she was born. It was, Kay reminded herself, the moment of Aoife's conception when Kay had briefly shape-shifted into a swan. Could she instinctively know about her mother's experience at some deep cellular level or was it yet another display of the power of Aoife's budding powers. She tucked her thoughts away for later contemplation. "You are a beautiful little swan."

"And you're the Mommy swan. Come dance with me."

Once again, Kay looked sharply at her child and once again, she saw nothing in her daughter's innocent eyes to alarm her. Tentatively, she said, "But I don't hear the music."

"Just do what I do," commanded Aoife. "It's easy. Look." She pirouetted.

Kay laughed, put down the carrots and joined her daughter, dancing and laughing as they twirled together around the little kitchen.

"I should get the tambourines." Kay began to leave the room, intending to use the little hand drums to add rhythm to their dancing.

But Aoife had paused in mid-twirl and was listening intently. "I have to go now Mommy. I'll be back soon."

"Oh!" said Kay. "I was going to …" But Aoife was gone. Kay was used to Aoife's flights of fancy and watched her daughter as she ran out of the kitchen door. "Wellies!" yelled Kay. "It's wet out there." There was a scuffling sound and then Aoife appeared in the field. She was wearing her pink rubber wellies.

"Don't go too far," she called after her daughter. "Daddy should be home from town soon."

"I promise." And the child was gone, hidden from view by a patch of blackberry bushes that had grown wide and tall during Kay and Liam's six-year absence.

Aoife followed the music to the end of the field. Here, she climbed through the bars of the farm gate, twisting her body and allowing herself to fall to the ground in a lump. She picked herself up and ran across the meadow, reaching the ash tree with pink cheeks and puffing breath.

The music stopped as Aoife approached but she was certain this was where it had come from. Feeling very daring that she was about to enter the circle alone. Aoife pursed her lips with determination. She told herself that the time when she saw Daddy in the circle didn't count because she didn't get to explore.

At the great tree, Aoife paused. Nell had said the ash tree guarded the entry to the fairy circle that was formed by the hawthorn trees. She said the ash tree was very old, probably four hundred years or so. Aoife thought it must be exceedingly old to have so many branches and leaves that they almost blocked the entrance to the fairy circle.

She wondered if the tree had guarded the fairy circle for all that time. Her pink lips in a perfect circle of wonder, Aoife looked up into its heavy-leafed branches. A gentle breeze stirred the leaves so that they sighed in its passing, seeming to whisper a greeting to the little girl. Satisfied that she was welcome, Aoife turned her attention to the hawthorn trees beyond.

With a thickness of intertwining branches, each hawthorn was interlocked with the next so that the grove seemed impenetrable. The entrance into the fairy circle was effectively hidden from view if you didn't know where to look. Luckily, Nell had told her precisely how to gain entry. That was how she had found Daddy there last week. There was a break in the hawthorn Nell had told her. She'd said it was wide enough for an adult to pass through if they turned sideways and that it would be even easier for a child such as Aoife.

Carefully stepping between the exposed roots, Aoife climbed around the ash tree, her stubby little hands making a grip of the nobbly bits of the trunk. Pleased with herself at having gained entry to the grove, Aoife paused just inside to take stock of her surroundings. The hawthorn formed an almost perfect circle, a secret place that she imagined only she knew of. Well, Daddy knew too as did Nell, but they didn't count because they were grownups.

The silence in the grove was broken only by the singing of birds. There was a wide tree stump in the center of the circle, big enough for several people to sit.

It had rained earlier that morning so that it was too wet to try out the tree stump. Instead, Aoife walked slowly around the grove, her rubber boots making a swishing sound in the rain kissed grass. Aoife noted the tufts of reeds dotted about. She saw that the reeds created a circle, separated from each other like crowns that only needed lids of some kind and they would become stools. Aoife said out loud. "Fairy stools that make a circle inside a circle."

The reeds were quite thick. Aoife wondered if sheep were ever allowed in here to munch on them and keep the place tidy. She supposed they hadn't found the secret way into the grove and that pleased her.

Her exploration of the circle brought her to the far end where two hawthorns leaned towards each other, perfectly framing a view of the fields that led down the hill to the river.

An unexpected rush of wind rustled the leaves. She turned to follow the sound as it flowed through the grove and moved out through the gap in the hawthorn.

Aoife turned back toward the center of the circle and headed for the tree stump. What was left of its roots were covered in moss that had begun to encroach on the seating area of the trunk. Aoife decided it would be her throne. Ignoring the fact that its surface was wet, she sat down on her throne so that she faced the view of the fields.

Crossing one leg over the other, she leaned forward, chin in hand, elbow on knee, to survey her kingdom.

"Hello," said a voice right next to her.

Aoife jumped in surprise and turned to see a beautiful lady sitting beside her. She was framed by the sun that shone from behind, lighting the ends of her honey-colored hair like golden fire. She wore a long dress that was white and gold and silver all at the same time.

Unable to speak, Aoife blinked at the vision and wondered how the lady had gotten into the circle without her noticing.

"That's because I was already here." The woman smiled a smile that reached all the way from her wide red lips to her slanted blue eyes. "You just didn't notice me."

"I didn't say anything. Did you read my mind?" asked Aoife.

"Not really," said the woman. "I knew what you must be thinking from the expression on your face." She laughed, a lovely tinkling sound that seemed to suit her. "I am the Lady Eiru."

"I'm Aoife." She reached out shyly and touched Eiru's hands. "I like your rings. They're pretty." A Celtic ring with a three-looped figure nestled on Eiru's forefinger.

"I am glad you noticed." Eiru held out her hand for Aoife to examine. "Do you see the three rings. They symbolize the ever changing, yet recurring cycle of life."

"What does that mean?"

Eiru laughed. “It means life changes all the time, yet it remains the same. Have you noticed that Aoife?”

“I think so. I used to live in America and now I live here but everything’s still the same because Mommy and Daddy are here. And so am I.”

“Well that’s a good start to understanding the meaning.

“I like your laugh. It sounds like bells.”

“You are very sweet Aoife. “

Aoife frowned. “Are you real?”

“Yes” said the woman, “And I am also one of the Fae people.”

“I see!” said Aoife, not seeing at all.

“And you are Fae also,” said Eiru.

“I am?”

“Of course. We are never just one thing, are we? And you can see me can you not? Not everyone can. That is how I know you are Fae, for that is what Fae means.”

Aoife gasped with pleasure at being included as one of the Fae, although her expression showed that she still did not understand. She asked, “Does Fae mean fairy and are you a fairy? Because if you are, you’re too big.”

“Am I now?” Eiru laughed down at Aoife, who put out a hand and lightly touched Eiru’s arm.

“You feel real,” said the little girl.

“I am as real as you.”

“I always thought fairies were tiny but then a friend told me they’re big, not like Tinkerbell at all.” Aoife wore a sad expression, a lifetime belief in tiny fairies shattered.

“I am not a fairy. I am of the Faerie. There is a difference.”

“I see,” said Aoife again, trying to appear more mature than her years.

“I am of the Sidhe,” explained Eiru mysteriously.

“The Shee? What’s the Shee?”

"Well, to put it simply, we come from an ancient people called the Tuatha De Danaan. We have lived in Ireland for a long time, almost since the very beginning."

"I didn't know that."

"Of course, you did not." Eiru reached out and stroked the child's soft cheek. "You are too young to know these things." She caught Aoife's chin and titled her head up until they looked into each other's eyes.

"But you will know my dear. In fact, these things are already in you to be discovered when the time is right, and you are ready to be chosen. That time is almost here."

Aoife was pleased to be sought out by such a gorgeous creature. Her green eyes were wide with the glamour of it all. She shivered with anticipation, certain that magic must be about to happen.

"Have I been chosen?"

"Yes, indeed my little one."

"What am I chosen for?"

"Well. First of all, you and I will be great friends. Later will come the choosing."

Aoife thought the lady looked like a fairy or at least a princess anyway. She suddenly remembered the music and opened her mouth to ask the lady about it. But then she forgot again as she thought how glad she was to have two friends. One friend was old but very nice and one friend was young and very beautiful. Aoife kicked her heels against the tree stump and smiled up at the lady.

CHAPTER 14 – DREAMS

"Caer..."

"Mmm" mumbled Kay. She lay on her side, covers kicked away to cool her in the warm night.

The voice in her ear whispered again. "Caer." A mist curled through the open window, stretching long fingers towards her, stroking the back of her thighs. Kay rolled onto her stomach, exposing naked buttocks. Her legs opened slightly to the persistent caress. She sighed as unseen fingers slid into the crevice between her thighs. Desire caused a moist reaction that waiting fingers slid into, pushing, exploring, delighting. Kay shivered with anticipation, moaning as her hips began to move up, and then down, a slow, gentle motion.

"Caer ... Ah Caer."

Kay opened her eyes. She blinked in the dark room. The clock showed 1:23 am. The window was open. The night had cooled, bringing a slight breeze that wafted into the room. Her legs were cold, but her belly was warm with desire. "Mac?" she whispered. But all was quiet except for Liam's soft snores beside her.

Pulling the covers up and over her shoulders, she reflected that she had not dreamed of Mac since Aoife was born. His voice just now had seemed so real, as if he were right here in the room with her. She glanced around. There was no other presence besides her and Liam. She rolled over and put her arm about Liam's waist, as if to remind herself who she was married to. Loyal to her relationship, she shrugged off thoughts of Mac as something she must not allow. Pushing her body against Liam's back, she took comfort in his solid form. She closed her eyes again.

The dream came immediately. She was on a road. There were tall trees. It was dark. There was a sudden movement from the left. A large brown wolf sprang onto the road and ran towards her, jumping up at the last moment. Her body recoiled and she cried out, waking with a start. She rolled onto her back and turned her head to the side. The clock showed 1:25 am. Surely it was only a minute since she had fallen asleep.

The wolf dream had been so alarming that she was afraid to go back to sleep. Kay felt around on the carpet for her phone, which was charging by the bedside. Clicking it on, she googled brown wolf dreams.

"A messenger," she read, whispering the words so as not to wake Liam. "A brown wolf symbolizes the guardian in your life. Huh!" She scrolled down to another interpretation. "A brown wolf attacking can symbolize danger, a warning from your guardian. Hmm!" Kay believed in dreams. She tapped her phone as she considered the information. No helpful ideas came to mind. She returned the phone to the floor and snuggled down into her pillow again, closing her eyes.

Immediately she found herself standing outside the hawthorn grove. Liam stood a little way ahead, his back to her. Mac stood facing Liam. His hand was up, palm forward against Liam's chest. "Stop!" He commanded.

Kay jerked awake again, her heart beating fast. She spun round, looking for Liam. He was snoring gently beside her. Kay put a hand over her heart and let out her breath in a whoosh! She looked at the clock, 1:45 am.

She got out of bed and pulled on her robe. Picking up her phone, she went quietly to the kitchen and set a pan of organic rice milk on the stove, to heat for hot chocolate.

Her cell phone rang. She looked at it for a moment. Who could be calling her at this hour? It was Pam. Kay tapped the green button. "Hello! Pam?" she whispered. "Do you know what time it is?"

"Yes. Sorry. I just had a feeling you'd be awake. Tch! I should have left it til morning."

"I was awake as it happens. What's up?"

"Kay, I had this dream."

Kay was suddenly wide awake. "What dream?"

"It was Liam."

Kay took the pan of milk from the stove and turned off the burner. "What about Liam?"

"Look, this is crazy, but I dreamed …"

Kay interrupted. "Was there a wolf?"

"What? No! Just listen okay."

"Okay!"

"Liam was at the grove, not in it, just outside it."

Kay blinked, astounded. "Go on."

"Mac was there," said Pam. "He tried to prevent Liam from going in. But he, Liam wouldn't listen."

"Wow! What happened then?"

"Well, that was it," said Pam.

Kay processed this information.

Pam became impatient. "Kay, are you there?"

"Yes, I'm here," said Kay at last. "I just had the same dream Pam except there was no pushing. There was just Mac yelling at Liam to stop."

There was silence again as they both thought it through.

"I googled it," said Kay. "When a brown wolf attacks in a dream."

"What brown wolf?" Pam was confused.

Kay told her about the two dreams she'd had along with her interpretation of them.

"Well it's got to mean something real, a warning maybe, since we had the same dream." Pam paused to think. "You know, I haven't given Mac a thought, well not very often anyway since that night when you nearly walked off with him into wherever it was that he was taking you. And now this. Both of us having the same dream and at the same time." There was silence while Pam's mind worked. "What are you not telling me Kay?"

Kay sighed. "Liam's been messing about in the grove. He thinks he's found a way through the portal."

"What portal?"

"There's a menhir in the circle," explained Kay. "You know, a stone thing with markings on it. Liam's convinced it's a portal to the otherworld."

Pam had studied Irish mythology and folklore at college. She was knowledgeable but pragmatic. If anyone asked why she had studied such ethereal subjects and then chosen to run a pub in the west of Ireland, she would respond, "Taking those courses seemed the right thing to do." That was all she would say, except for one time when Kay asked Pam if she was a witch. Pam had considered the question and then responded, "If I am, then I'm an extremely practical witch." So now when Pam responded to Kay's statement about Liam and the portal by asking, "But why would he even try?" it seemed a perfectly reasonable response.

Kay quickly told Pam the tale of Liam's discovery of runes in Greenland and his obsession with the hawthorn grove and how she had made him promise to give it up.

"Well," said Pam. "Since we both had this dream, I'd say we're being warned that Liam has no intention of giving it up. You're going to have to talk to him."

"I will."

"Want me to be there when you do Kay?"

"No, I can handle it. I'll speak to him first thing in the morning."

"Yeah! Sounds like it should be done as soon as possible."

"I wonder why he's so insistent on getting into the portal right now?" Kay mused.

"It's Beltane," Pam offered. "The portals between the mortal world and the otherworld are said to be thin right now, easily opened if you have the right words."

"But Beltane is passed already."

"Nope," said Pam. "Beltane is five days long, until May 5th ish."

"It's the 3rd today."

"Yep," Pam said. "Not much time."

They were silent again.

"Well …" said Kay.

"Well …" agreed Pam.

"I'm going back to bed."

"Me too. Talk tomorrow."

"Night Pam."

"First thing in the morning Kay!"

"For sure."

Kay put her phone on the kitchen counter and tip-toed into the bedroom. Climbing into bed, she cuddled up against her husband, who had turned towards her side of the bed in his sleep. Pulling his arm around her, she held his hand in hers. Kay spooned into Liam's protective embrace until sleep relaxed her body so that their hands fell apart.

CHAPTER 15 – WARNING

A turf fire burned gently in the cool of the spring morning. Liam was busy with pencil and paper, quietly designing a practical cupboard with shelving. Kay watched him in silence from the doorway. His head was bowed as he concentrated on his task. Kay held this peaceful vision in her heart, wishing it could remain this way. She did not want to break the spellbound moment and yet she must. She took a deep breath, walked into the room and sat beside him on the gray leather couch beneath the window.

"Liam." Kay placed her hand on Liam's arm. Her heart was filled with empathy for him. He was such a good man, a kind man. Yet for all that, if her dream was to be believed, he would not give up his obsession to find a way in through the portal. She wondered what she could say that might dissuade him.

Without looking up from his work, Liam lifted Kay's hand and kissed her fingers. Her hand fell gently down as he released it and continued to draw, brow furrowed in concentration.

"Liam." Kay said again.

"Mmm," Liam turned the drawing sideways for a better perspective.

"I have to talk to you babe." Kay waited. "Liam."

"Look at this." He showed her his drawing. "I'm making a cupboard at the end of the utility room. It's for sheets and towels you know, somewhere to keep them. Nice and tidy you said you wanted them. Well, this will do it I think." Liam looked up at her face at last. Seeing her expression, his voice faltered. "What's wrong honey? Don't you like it?" He looked down again. "I can make a different design if you'd prefer?"

"Liam it's not that." She put a hand over his. "I love the design. Of course I do. I love how you always think of me and try to make things easier, except of course when you leave your stuff lying around in the bedroom." They both laughed at this, Liam's untidiness an ongoing quibble between them.

"What then?" he asked.

"It's about the hawthorn grove."

He blinked. "The Faerie circle? What about it?"

"We agreed. You agreed Liam, that you wouldn't go near it again. I have to know I can trust you to do that. I mean, not to go there."

The clock ticked for several seconds in the silence between them. Aoife could be heard in the yard, talking to the birds.

"I promised, didn't I?" Liam said at last. He seemed irritated, defensive.

"Yes, you did promise. I'm reminding you of that promise."

"Well I don't know why," he grumbled. "You asked me not to go there and I haven't gone there. What more d'you want Kay?"

"Nothing I suppose. I'm just making sure it's a firm promise."

Liam pulled her close, so that her head rested against his chest. "Sure, what other kind of promise is there?"

It seemed to Kay that his words held a question within a question, yet she could hardly continue the discussion when he'd clearly said he wouldn't go to the hawthorn grove. She forced herself to relax into Liam's arms. For his part, Liam held his wife and gazed out through the window, watching the freedom of the birds as they swooped in and out from the trees.

That night when the cottage was quiet and his women were sleeping soundly, the moon trickled its light across Liam's face as it peeped through the skylight. Liam became restless and could not seem to find a comfortable position. With a sigh he sat up, swung his feet to the floor and rested his head in his hands as if debating with himself. After some minutes he glanced at his wife's sleeping form, then stood and left the room, carefully closing the bedroom door behind him.

At the kitchen door, he looked through the window across the field, nibbling his knuckles thoughtfully. Suddenly decisive, he pulled on his wellies and opened the kitchen door.

At the gate leading to the meadow, Liam looked across at the hawthorn grove. It was still Beltane for this night and one more. He opened the gate and walked through.

He was almost at the Faerie circle when a shadow stepped out from behind the ash tree. Surprised, Liam stopped in his tracks, heart pounding. The moon chose this moment to hide behind clouds so that the sky became dark.

"Liam!" said the figure. Having thought he had encountered a spiritual being, Liam was both relieved and alarmed that the figure was human, a man by the size of him and the timbre of his voice. Had this person come to do him harm and how did he know Liam's name?

"Who are you?" demanded Liam in the most challenging voice he could muster. This was his meadow damn it. Well, it was Sean's meadow but the field behind was his own. "Hey! I asked you a question. Who are you? What the hell are you doing here in the middle of the night?"

"Liam. Please go back." The voice seemed disembodied for the face was still in shadow.

"How d'you know my name. And who are you dammit!"

"Liam, there is nothing here for you. There is real danger if you keep pursuing your course."

"What the feck?" Liam was shaken but he was a man in his prime and not afraid of a bit of rough and tumble if the occasion demanded. "Get out of my way you crazy. Get away off this land and don't come back here. Go on now, away with yer." Liam positioned himself for a fight if need be. He expected it. He even wanted it, tired as he was at being stopped so many times from accessing the portal. First it was Kay, then that blasted wind the other night, and then Kay again this morning and now this idiot.

The shadowy figure walked directly up to Liam and placed a hand none too gently on Liam's chest. "Go Liam, while you still can."

Liam grabbed the man's arm with his left and let go a right punch directly into the man's face. The man recovered quickly and wrapped one arm around Liam's neck and then twisted his right arm up against his back.

The man spoke quietly into Liam's ear. "I advise you most strongly to leave this place. If you cannot trust yourself to stop this foolish quest, then take your wife and your child and go from here. Get as far from here as possible. This is a warning Liam. Take it at face value. Take it very seriously." The man shoved Liam's arm further up his back. "Do I make myself clear Liam?"

Liam tried to move but found he couldn't. He had no choice. He nodded his head. The man twisted his arm higher up his back for effect and then just as suddenly let go, spinning Liam to the ground as he did so.

Liam lay for several moments where he fell. He lay on his side until his breathing righted itself and he could feel the strength return to his arm. Rolling onto his knees, he looked around. There was no one in sight and no noise of footsteps leaving. There was only the breeze, sighing through the hawthorn bushes, silhouetted against the dark sky.

Standing at last, Liam held his clenched fists by his sides. His face was contorted in a mask of sheer bull-headed determination. He advanced on the grove.

To his utter surprise, he could find no way into the circle. The moon was still hiding itself behind the clouds so that it was very dark. The entryway beside the ash tree could not be identified. Liam peered and tried to feel his way forward, but it was impenetrable. Frustrated, he explored all the way around the circle, until after many minutes he found himself back at the ash tree. There truly seemed no way in.

In a fit of temper, Liam kicked the ash tree hard. He fell down from the force he had exerted against the solid trunk. Brambles stuck into his back, pulling at him as he tried to stand. His face like thunder, he staggered away from the hawthorns, from the ash tree, from the circle.

At a safe distance, Liam turned and raised his fist. "Don't think I'm giving up!" he yelled. "Because I'm not! I'll be back here tomorrow night and I'll bring a spotlight and a chainsaw." For good measure he added, quite unreasonably, "And then we'll see who wins."

CHAPTER 16 – PRINCESS

Aoife sat on her moss-covered throne. She watched, entranced as Eiru twirled in a wide circle around the grove. Eiru tantalized Aoife with her slanted eyes and merry laughter, as she moved her arms and body in a lovely dance.

It seemed to Aoife that the hawthorn trees danced with Eiru. Their leaves rustled in the breeze as she passed by, creating a strange but delightful music as branches swayed and bent to the dance of the beautiful woman. Even the grass seemed to sparkle. For a long moment, Aoife could not quite distinguish Eiru from the trees or the grass. All three seemed as one in the sunlight.

As she watched, Aoife could be still no longer. She climbed to her feet on the trunk, careful not to slip on the moss. Holding out her arms she cried "Me too! Me too!"

Eiru's red lips pealed with laughter as she swung Aoife up in the air. The little girl squealed with delight.

Aoife thought Eiru's breath was like the sweetest of flowers. She breathed deeply.

Eiru's voice was enticingly low. "The time is coming Aoife, and I must tell you stories of wonder to prepare you." She swung the child up in the air yet again. "Yes. Stories of wonder and delight."

Aoife giggled and cried "Stories! Tell me stories!"

Eiru collapsed in a graceful heap on the tree trunk, her warm arms still holding Aoife close. Her dress felt like silk against Aoife's cheek as Eiru leaned down to speak softly into the little ear. "Many years ago," she began.

"No! No!" Protested Aoife. "You have to start it like this." Her face was solemn, a small finger held up in admonition. "Once upon a time. That's how to start a story."

"Well then," laughed Eiru. "So, it shall be." She paused for dramatic effect. "Once upon a time … "

Aoife sighed contentedly and leaned against Eiru's softness, content to listen as she idly watched butterflies flutter about in the grove.

A family of sheep paused just beyond the circle and looked in, baaing inquisitively.

"There was a little girl. And her name was …" Eiru paused.

"Aoife of course!" said Aoife with a smile.

"Of course!" agreed Eiru. "And this little girl … "

"Aoife" interrupted the child.

"And this little girl, her name was Aoife," amended Eiru. "She was a Faerie princess. But she did not know that she was."

"Ohhh!" Aoife was captivated.

"Yes," confirmed Eiru. "And on the day, she found out she was a princess, she learned that there was a condition."

"What's a condition?"

"Well it is a rule, you see?"

"A rule about her being a princess?"

"Absolutely. A rule about her being a princess. She was to follow the rule otherwise she could not be a princess. Do you think that is fair?"

"I suppose it is. It's a good idea anyway to make a rule." Aoife was quite solemn. "especially for being a princess."

"That would be important would it not? Do you think you could follow a rule Aoife, if you could be a princess?"

"Will you tell me the rule today?"

Eiru held the gaze of the little girl. The two were still for a long moment as they contemplated each other. Then Eiru said in measured tones, “I will tell you the rule Aoife, on the day that is not a day, in the place that is not a place.”

Aoife screwed up her face in thought. She decided that although she couldn’t quite see what Eiru meant, she very much wanted to know more about being a princess.

“I could follow a rule if I got to be a princess.”

“Well that is very good to hear.” Eiru leaped up with the child in her arms and twirled them both in a circle. Aoife tipped her head back and laughed up at the sky. In doing this, she didn’t see the expression of satisfaction on Eiru’s face.

CHAPTER 17 – THE MEET

Dermot regretted that he still hadn't summoned the courage to ask Pam out. He longed for the moment where he imagined them both encased in leather with Pam's thighs wrapped around him on the back of his motorcycle.

Dermot wished he wasn't so shy. He would have asked Pam out already, but he felt at a loss around her, especially when she seemed to him, so very self-assured. He supposed it was self-confidence that gave her the ability to run the local pub. You'd have to have confidence to do that as well as being efficient and organized, which she obviously was.

It was just that whenever he summoned up the courage to ask her out, she was usually busy serving behind the bar. "Yes?" she would say, with her mouth in that fixed smile that she always wore when serving customers. The bar was usually busy too, with people calling over his shoulder for their orders so that it seemed he just couldn't find the chance to talk to her. He'd always give up and just ask for another pint. Then he'd sit at the bar moodily nursing his beer and wait for a more opportune moment. He'd even taken to waiting behind after the bar closed, for the chance to talk to her. But when those chances came, he'd lose his nerve and leave and then kick himself for being so shy. What could she say after all? She could say no, that's what. Or she could say yes.

Unfortunately, Dermot's brain would always get stuck on the bit about her saying no and that was enough to stop him from asking her out.

As he rode his motorcycle along the country lane, he mulled over a dream he had. It was his hope that Pam might agree to accompany him on a trip he was planning to the Northwest 200 up in Northern Ireland. That's where the annual motorcycle races were held. For Dermot to consider inviting Pam to this event, showed that his preoccupation with her as the object of his desire, was at least as important as his love of motorcycles. He regarded this annual event as not so much a road trip in his mind, but in more reverent terms, as a pilgrimage.

Lost in this hopeful dream, Dermot gently flicked the Triumph Trident from corner to corner on the uphill lane leading out of the village. He enjoyed the sense of calm and near meditation the activity brought.

When he was in this mood, he tended to avoid highways unless by necessity or on a long trip. He had once fallen asleep while riding a motorcycle along a highway. Waking up as he ran into the grass verge on the edge of the road, he had come back to himself with a fright. His heart had jumped into his throat as he wrestled his about-to-crash, motorcycle back onto the tarmac. He was only just in time to avoid a crippling disaster with an oncoming truck.

On this day however, he was in easy cruising mode, a gentle 60 to 70 mph glide along country roads.

*****

Ahead of him, Mac's ears pricked up when he heard the angry beat of a three-cylinder engine. The sound rapidly closed to where he waited at the crossroads on his Norton. He glanced behind to confirm that it was the Triumph Trident he had been waiting for.

Dermot was surprised but thrilled to see the Norton paused at the corner. It was only a few years ago in the Isle of Man, that a bike just like his three-cylinder Triumph had beaten a Norton in the production model TT. Some said the Trident had won by default, because the Norton ran out of petrol a few miles before the finish and had to do a fill up. But win the Trident did. As far as Dermot was concerned, every time a Norton was encountered, it was time to prove the score yet again and without the shame of possibly winning on a foul.

Mac faced forward as the whine of the three-cylinder bike rapidly approached. It was not often that two motorcycles met on these roads, so it was an easy bet for Mac that Dermot would idle his bike beside the Norton.

At the crossroads, the two riders turned their helmets toward each other. Dermot nodded, quietly admiring the jet-black Norton Commando with its combat 850cc twin cylinder engine.

Mac nodded too, but before Dermot could react and take off his helmet for a chit-chat, the Norton rider changed down a gear. Its throttle opened wide, so that the Norton shot off along the road.

Dermot, surprised but excited, responded to the unspoken challenge by hunching down and leaping forward directly behind the Norton, striving hard to come abreast of it.

In Mac's very capable hands, the race-bred Norton heeled over to the limit. His boot scraped the tar, flick, straight into a right hander at 90 mph.

The Trident was at full chat, its noise level high as it tried to catch up. Dermot laughed with delight at the unexpected competition. He was close enough now to pick up the slip stream of the Norton so that they were one behind the other. But then the Norton rider suddenly wound the throttle fully open for the long straight road ahead.

At a lethal bend in the road that Dermot knew only too well had caused several accidents in the past, he changed down rapidly, which caused him to slow into the bend.

Mac had no such caution. He whipped through the curve at racing speed, as if the road was still on the straight. Then he shot ahead into the distance.

The Trident rounded the corner and seeing the Norton so far ahead, changed down through the gearbox and throttled back to a crawl. Idling the engine, he straddled the bike and tugged off his helmet. The hair on his head was flat and wet with sweat from the thrill of the chase. The expression on his face was incredulous and full of admiration for the Norton and its leather-clad rider. He wanted a re-run that was for sure and this time on the track of his choice.

CHAPTER 18 – PUB CHALLENGE

Dermot was on his way to see Pam. Determination glinted in his eye for he intended to ask her on a date.

As he rode up to the pub on his Trident, his attention was caught by a parked motorcycle. He recognized it as the Norton he had competed against earlier that evening.

Pulling his motorcycle in beside the Norton, Dermot admired its fine racing lines. Feeling a little guilty, what with his own bike sitting beneath him in silent reproval, he patted the Trident, placating it for not inspiring quite such a love as Norton bikers had for their steeds.

From what Dermot knew, it wasn't just the performance of the machine that held the attention of Norton riders, it was the classiness of the bike. Since the badly neglected Norton factory was taken over in the 1950s, technicians and mechanics had worked for decades to overhaul and improve its engine. This had brought the machine to world class standing in its handling and steering.

Entranced as he was by the Norton, it finally occurred to Dermot that its owner was probably inside the pub. All thoughts of Pam forgotten for the moment, Dermot quickly entered the pub and stood in the doorway as he looked around for the Norton's rider.

Mac sat at a table leaning back in black-leathered splendor, looking for all the world like the king of the bikers. His broad shoulders were straight as his black hair which was almost but not quite at an untidy length. The two-day stubble on his face only added to the mystery of the man. He appeared relaxed, one leg stretched out as he sipped a beer and gazed off into the distance.

Dermot, feeling a little outclassed, pushed a hand through his hair which had again been flattened somewhat by the helmet he had just removed. Squaring his shoulders in his leather jacket, he approached the biker's table. "Join you?"

The biker turned to Dermot. His slanted green eyes gave a flicker of recognition. He nodded casually at an empty chair.

Dermot pulled out the chair, noisily scraping its legs along the floor. "I'm Dermot," he said.

"Mac." They shook hands.

Mac was in no hurry to speak. Dermot felt like a vassal and Mac his king. He shook himself and broke the silence.

"Buy you a drink?"

"Sure."

Dermot caught the eye of the bartender and gestured for a round of drinks. As a regular, Dermot's drink was known. The bartender glanced at Mac's drink and pushed a fresh beer glass under the pump.

"Great bike." Dermot began.

Mac took a sip of his beer and nodded his head. "She is."

"You left me behind in the dust today."

Mac smiled. "The Norton has been known to do that."

"Any chance of a re-run?"

"I am not sure I will be around long enough." Mac was nonchalant. "I am just passing through really."

Dermot, alive to a discussion of motorcycles as he might never be when around Pam, pushed for a re-run. "It was the bend that slowed me down. Too many accidents on that particular road. I know a better place though, a straight run with only one double bend right at the end. Want to have another go?"

"It would have to be soon."

"How about tomorrow?" pushed Dermot.

Mac seemed to consider this. "If as you say, there is a double bend at the end of the road, it might be advisable to have a flagman beyond there, as a warning to oncoming drivers." He looked at Dermot and waited.

"Great idea," said Dermot. "I think I know just the man."

Mac listened intently.

"Name of Liam. I'll ask him. He's the only guy I know who'll not be working tomorrow. Yes, I'll ask Liam."

At this, Mac leaned back, apparently satisfied. He nodded his approval. "Then it is agreed."

They discussed the time and place. Mac finished his beer and left the bar. Dermot stayed on thinking about the race. He was still there nursing the same beer, when Pam and Kay arrived back from their Sligo shopping trip. Dermot hadn't realized how much time had passed til he heard Pam giving orders to the staff. The bar had filled up and the group of musicians were just settling down to their first song of the night.

It was to be a special event, for Aiden Doyle had agreed to an appearance. Not only was Aiden a musician, he was also a Seanacai, a storyteller. His style was to tell stories interspersed with fiddle music. It was a time-honored tradition that went back hundreds of years.

The crowd was silent, including those huddled around the bar, for this was a story they all knew well and welcomed as their own. Aiden opened his mouth and began to speak the myth of the ancient hunter-warrior clans, in a sing-song rhythm.

It was the day of all the days.
It was the hour of all the hours.
That Finn McCool and his share of men
Went hunting in the mountains of Donegal.
They followed a doe deep out into the mountains.
A patch of mist fell down on their vision.
Without a house within their vision and she gave them the slip

Here the storyteller brought his fiddle up to his chin. He launched into a wild fiddling that sounded just like the doe running through the mountains, away from the hunters.

Dermot had Liam pinned to a corner of the bar, intent on involving him as flagman for the race the following day.

"Have you an interest in motorcycle racing yourself Liam?"

Liam took a sip of the beer Dermot had pressed upon him. "None at all Dermot, no."

I'm surprised at that now. Isn't Kay one for the motorcycles herself?"

"She is, that's true. But I've no interest in it."

"None yerself is it?"

"None Dermot. It leaves me cold."

"Hm." Realizing this might take a bit of persuasion, Dermot considered how he might gain Liam's attention in the peculiarities of motorcycle racing.

Liam watched Kay as she bustled about. Thursdays at the bar were becoming a regular occurrence. Kay seemed to enjoy helping her friend and Liam was glad of it. He hoped it would help her settle down in Ireland. It was good for Kay and him to have an evening out too, especially with Aoife safely asleep in Pam's small apartment over the pub.

His thoughts strayed to the hawthorn grove. He had one more day to open the portal before Beltane would be over. He hadn't wanted to come out to the pub tonight, but Kay had insisted. He knew he was lying to Kay, by continuing with what he considered to be his quest to breach the portal, yet he couldn't help himself.

Realizing that Dermot was still talking to him, he focused on the man's face. "Sorry Dermot, what were you saying?"

"I said you should see it. Maybe we should all go. You, me and the two girls?"

"What was that now?"

Dermot blinked in happy reflection. "The Northwest 200. It's only the biggest motorcycle race in Ireland. Up north they hold it. In Portrush. Attracts entries from some of the fastest and most fearless riders ever. Joey Dunlop's half lap record still holds at the event and it's long after his death so."

"Joey Dunlop?" Liam mildly resented the intrusion on his thoughts, especially when he preferred to sit quietly and consider his options for gaining entry into the portal. He wished Dermot would stop talking. He glanced at the clock over the bar. Too early to leave yet. What was it Dermot was going on about? He tried to take an interest. "He's a racer is he, Joey Dunlop?"

Dermot was warming to his subject. "He's only one of the fastest riders out there. The way he went around those turns, his knee out for balance, you know to help him lean the bike further into the angle."

Liam was bored. He began to look around for Kay. He said, "I think I need another drink." He made to pull away from Dermot and his endless chatter about motorcycles.

"I'll get it don't worry." Dermot signaled the bartender who gave him a thumbs up in recognition of his order. Turning back to Liam, Dermot leaned in to make himself heard above the noise of the bar, effectively cutting off Liam's retreat. "Road racing's big in Ireland, bigger than people would think. Joey had his 13th win at the 200. He held the record for more than a decade."

"Is that so?" Liam looked at Dermot with a sigh. No one was coming to rescue him. He resigned himself to his fate.

"Oh yeah!" Dermot continued. "And they race in terrible conditions. The roads are full of you know, cow shit. So many twists and turns too and of course the mud's bad because it's so often raining. Have you been there lately, up north?"

"I haven't. You know, I've been abroad."

"Oh right." Dermot's eyes began to sparkle even as Liam's clouded over. "You know what gets me? It's the whine of the motorcycles at the starter line when they all leap off in a clump."

"Right," agreed Liam half-heartedly.

"It's seeing the bikes close up with the sounds and the smells. It's just ..." Dermot searched for the right words. "It's an exciting build up, to a crescendo, you know!" Dermot's eyes were bright with the vision of it.

"Of course."

Colin Rafferty, leaning on the bar with his drink, overheard their conversation. He was also a motorcycle enthusiast and chipped in. "It's a fine sport so tis."

"Right?" Dermot was pleased to welcome the reinforcement. "And then there's the high-octane whine as each motorcycle zooms past in a rush of gas." Dermot closed his eyes and inhaled, as if the smell assailed his nose at that very moment."

Liam looked at Dermot's entranced face and couldn't help but smile at the sheer enthusiasm of the man. He began to take an interest in what Dermot was saying.

Dermot's drink threatened to cascade from his glass as his excitement mounted. "You hear the ground rumbling." He turned from one to the other of his listeners. "It's like a panzer division coming down the hill when a clump of them are coming along together.

"Ow-er! So, it is! So, it is!" agreed Colin, although neither of them had ever experienced the sound of a panzer division coming at them.

"Think about it now," said Dermot. "How can you train for a sport where if you make one wrong move, you can die."

Liam considered this. "They don't care about that. They do it for the excitement."

"Right!" Dermot's eyes blazed with enthusiasm. "The big challenge is the need to win. To let out the clutch and enjoy the circuit. And they've to learn the track. They have to do their homework. It gets inside them, the knowing of the track." Dermot put his glass on the bar with a thwack to make his point. "Ah but they can never be complacent with it." He stabbed the air with a finger. "They've to treat it with respect. They can't come to the 200 thinking in a complacent way."

"True for you," said Colin. They have to come at it with an attitude of constant learning.

This remark set Liam to thinking. He needed to go at the hawthorn grove with that same attitude. He could let nothing dissuade him. He had to learn from the mistakes he made so that he could overcome each obstacle. The man he had met there came to his mind. It had been such a strange experience. He had since decided the man must have been trespassing and yet how could he have known about the portal? He shook his head to push these thoughts away. He couldn't allow anything to stop him. There would be no going to the grove tonight because Kay was watching him too carefully. But tomorrow, he'd go back there and be ready for anything. He scratched under his chin thoughtfully. He'd need to do something to throw Kay off her guard, make her think he'd forgotten about the grove, so that she wouldn't be worried about his sneaking off.

Again, Dermot brought him out of his reverie.

"Every year they say it can't get any faster, yet every year it does get faster and it's not just the motorcycles, it's the skill of the riders."

"Ah tis true." put in Colin. "There's nothing like a race between riders who know their stuff."

"What do you think Liam?" asked Dermot.

"Well er," Liam didn't want to appear rude by appearing too engrossed in his own thoughts. "I think it takes more than the rider's skill. Doesn't the quality of the bikes come into it too?"

"That it does Liam. That it does."

At that moment, Colin turned away from Liam and Dermot to join in the loud round of applause for the beauty of the old Irish myth and the fiddle playing of Aiden. It was a song-poem that never failed to bring a patriotic gleam into the eye of everyone there, who had ever aspired to be a great hunter or warrior such as Finn McCool.

With Colin distracted, Dermot saw his opportunity and leaned in. "I'm glad you said that now Liam. For tomorrow it's meself is in a race with another rider, not far from here. It just so happens we'll be in need of a flagman, to ensure the traffic coming up from around the bend is warned to wait there til the race is done.

Around them there were loud cheers of "More! More!" Aiden bowed his head to popular demand, announcing "In the spirit of the great storytellers of long ago, I'll tell ye the tale of the fiddle player."

All of the visitors and most of the regulars were quiet, listening intently, enjoying this for what it was, an authentic re-telling of an old story from the turn of the century.

Dermot pressed his advantage. "Will ye do it Liam? Will ye?"

Liam quickly considered the invitation. It was exactly what he needed to throw Kay off the scent, make her think he'd forgotten about the grove. "I'll do it," he said.

"Good man yerself!" Dermot sat back with a happy sigh. The race was on!

Over in the musician's corner Aiden was beginning the main story of the night. "Now," began Aiden. "There was a young man. He lived with his mother and they didn't have much in the way of money. Now, this young man, he took a notion about buying a fiddle. His mother said, ye're too old to play the fiddle. You're 20 years of age and you'll never learn to play the fiddle, ye will not.

But away he went to town that young man and bought himself a fiddle. He brought it home under his coat.

His mother on seeing her son with the fiddle, told him son, ye'll never learn to play that fiddle. Ye might as well put it away for all the good it will do ye.

Ah, said the young man. If that's the way of it, I'll put the fiddle on the wall and let it hang there for as long as it likes.

Well, a fella came that night to ask the young man to come play the fiddle at the dance.

Ah says the young man, I have no tunes. I have a fiddle surely, but I can't play it.

Don't worry said the fella, just bring yourself and the fiddle. They'll be glad to see you and the fiddle. There'll be someone there can play it so.

Well the young man said I'll do it. Now the road to the dance led up and around the hill and over the moor through a very lonely place. As the young man walked the road that evening, he came upon a man with hair of red fire that was there before him on the road. And what was it but a Faerie and the young man didn't know it.

Where are you going? asked the Faerie.

I'm away to play the fiddle at the dance there but I've no tunes in me.

Show me the fiddle now says the Faerie.

So, he showed him the fiddle and the Faerie took it and looked at it and strummed it three times.

The Faerie gave the fiddle back to the young man and told him, now go away on there. You'll play the fiddle like no one else can. Ah, you'll be the best fiddle player in the land.

So away went the young man to the dance. When they saw him coming with the fiddle, they all jumped to the floor ready for the music. What are you going to play? they asked him.

Well, I don't know if I've anything in me, but I'll try so I will. The young man put the fiddle to his shoulder and such a happy reel came from it and he called it the Faerie Reel.

From that time on, he was called the best fiddle player in all Ireland and he still kept his fiddle hanging on the wall there in his home to bring it down whenever he was called on to play.

But then at 85, he departed from this world. Now at the moment of his parting, the fiddle disappeared like a shot and it was never seen again. And that's because it was a Faerie fiddle do ye see."

At this point, Aiden took up his fiddle and played a jolly tune that set the feet of all the people in the pub to moving, whether they were sat in their seats or stood at the bar. It was almost as if they couldn't help themselves or that maybe their feet had minds of their own.

As the bow struck the last chord across the fiddle, there was a fine round of applause for Aiden. Such stories with the fine fiddle playing set everyone's spirits to lifting. This was displayed by a healthy call for drinks so that Pam, Kay and their helpers behind the bar hardly had time to get all the drinks poured before more orders were coming in.

After the bar cleared out that night, Dermot stayed behind to talk to Pam. He was buoyed by thoughts of the race the next day and the success of his conversation with Liam that evening. The fiddle playing of the Faerie Reel had given him a further jolt of self-confidence.

Thinking to sweep her off her feet, Dermot began by regaling Pam with stories of the North West 200.

Pam didn't seem too impressed, so Dermot launched into a further explanation intended to sell her on the idea.

"Come with me Pam. It'll be an outing for you, for us both. It's one of the top three events of its kind in the world. You have to see it to truly appreciate the scale of the thing. It runs from Portrush up north there, through Port Stewart and Coleraine, over almost 9 miles. Riders get up to speeds of 200 miles an hour. All the wives and girlfriends go with, for the day that's in it."

Pam looked at him in astonishment. "A bit of a nail-biting ordeal for the wives and girlfriends!"

Dermot blinked and began again. "You'd love it Pam and there's miles and miles of sandy beaches."

"Haven't we our own sandy beaches not a good hour from here?" Pam retorted.

"Well sure that's so, but there's also the Giant's Causeway to see up there."

"Hmpf!" Pam was dismissive. "Don't we have the Dingle ourselves and the Cliffs of Moher indeed!"

"Ah Pam! Can't ye just enjoy it for the day that's in it?"

Pam was silent a moment as she considered the purpose of his sudden loss of shyness. "Are you after asking me on a date Dermot?"

Dermot stroked the table, realizing the moment had come upon him without him realizing it. "I am." Dermot sat straight and said it again. "I am. Yes, I'm after asking you out."

Pam half smiled at him. "And when is this race?"

"Next week it is."

"Will we go for the day?"

"Ah well, I was thinking we'd go for the weekend so."

"The weekend?" Pam laughed. "You're a bit fast, aren't you?"

Dermot was suddenly lost for words. "Oh, I didn't mean. That is, I er."

"Well," said Pam. "If you can find a nice hotel maybe I will."

"You will?"

"Maybe."

Dermot's registered his relief as a smile spread across his face, which was quickly followed by a frown. "Ah! But I've a van."

She tried to follow his train of thought. "A van is it, to tow the motorcycle? I didn't know you were competing."

"Eh? No, I'm not competing."

"So, why do you need a van? We could take my car. It would be way more comfortable for a journey like that."

"Well no. I thought we'd take the van you know, to sleep in."

"Sleep in the van?"

"Sure, well it's part of the fun isn't it? We won't be the only ones either. The trailer parks will be full of sleeper vans."

"Is that what you're thinking now is it? That I'll be sleeping in a van with you?"

"Er, well." Dermot looked confused.

"You can drop me at the nearest hotel or a B&B at the very least."

"Ah! No! But Pam you're not thinking this through so."

"Am I not?" Her expression was dangerous, but Dermot hadn't realized it yet.

"Well sure it's the buzz, the camaraderie of the experience, the van, the camping …"

Pam interrupted. "The lining up to pee in smelly port-a-potties." She wrinkled her nose. "No thank you!" she declared emphatically. "I'll join you at the campfire, but I'll not be sleeping the night in a tin can with the midges nibbling at my ears all night long."

Dermot smiled then and seemed to find his sense of humor at last. "Ah now, they won't get near you for won't I be nibbling at your ears meself!"

She laughed at him then. “Ah! Go on with you, silly man. Get over here and kiss me.” A slow smile spread across Dermot’s face. He got up from his chair and pulled Pam to her feet. He proceeded to kiss her gently, his arms around her slim figure, her breasts firmly pulled against his body.

When Dermot finally released her, Pam murmured, “Well, that was worth waiting for. Let’s do it again.” So, they did, and this time Pam allowed Dermot to gently explore her mouth with his tongue. She found she liked it.

Dermot, over the moon because he had finally made his move on Pam, told her, “I want ye to love it like I do Pam. The motorcycle racing. Do ye think ye can?”

“I don’t know Dermot. Probably not. But I’ll come with you and we’ll see how it goes.”

“Well I’m excited about it and I know you will be too once we get down there. I was thinking Liam and Kay might come too.”

Pam thought this a good idea because if she became bored with the racing and she probably would, then it would be well to have a girlfriend around to talk about other things besides the racing. Dermot interrupted her thoughts.

“Kay has her own motorcycle. She probably doesn’t know about the event so it will be a treat for her.”

“Oh right. I forgot about that.” Pam was reflective. “Liam’s been distracted since he got back from his hiking trip. It would probably be good for him to get away.” She made up her mind. “I’m not sleeping in the van mind.” She shook her finger at him.

Dermot held up his hands in surrender. “But will you come visit me in the van?”

“If you play your cards right, I might let you visit me in the B&B.”

“Ah but won’t we be making too much of a ruckus for a respectable B&B what with you making pretty little noises and the two us thumping the bed so the springs will be likely to split.”

"Go on with you, boyo. Who said anything about you joining me in bed? And where did you suddenly get your cheeky talk from? Hiding it from me you've been is it?" Pam seemed pleased and gave him a coy look. "Not that I'm saying it'll happen mind, but d'you think we'll be less noticeable, making a load of noise in a van, down in the trailer park?"

"Well the advantage of that, is there'll be so much noise going on with everyone partying all night that no one will be likely to hear us."

"Say no more! I don't get enough rest as it is. I'll not be putting my night's sleep at risk, surrounded by all-night revelers."

He pulled her to him again. "And what makes you think ye'll be getting any sleep at all."

She laughed up at him and pulled his head down to hers.

CHAPTER 19 – FLAGMAN

"So today," began Liam as he loaded the breakfast dishes into the dishwasher.

"What's going on?" demanded Kay.

"What d'you mean?" Liam paused with a bowl in his hand, looking confused.

"You're filling the dishwasher!"

Liam became defensive. "Can't a man help around the house without his wife being suspicious of his motives?"

"Ah! So, there is a motive?"

"Stop putting words in me mouth. I'm just helping out is all."

"Good. That's good." Kay was not convinced. She settled herself on a stool at the breakfast bar. She didn't have to wait long.

Liam had barely closed the dishwasher on the stacked dishes before he began again. "So, I thought, today I might hang out with Dermot for a bit."

"Oh yeah?" said Kay.

"Yeah, well he's got a bit of a race on with some guy he met. He's asked me to be the flagman, you know at the finish line. That, and stop traffic while the race is on because it's a bit of a bend just before the finish there."

"Ah!" said Kay. "So that's it."

"What?"

"You're trying to get out of babysitting is it? You know it's your turn. I'd planned to go into the village for a look round."

Liam appeared nonchalant. "I thought you'd be glad to see me doing other things besides…" He gestured toward the field. "Besides er …"

Kay caught on immediately. "Ah!"

"But that's fine. If you'd rather go off to the village, I'm happy to stay here."

Kay's eyelashes flickered. She had momentarily forgotten the pull that the circle might have on Liam, despite his promise to keep away from it. "No. No. I can go another day. Tomorrow maybe. We could all go together."

"If you'd rather," said Liam.

"Yeah! That's fine. You go be a flagman today. Tomorrow we'll go into the village." She smiled. "Deal?"

"Deal!" agreed Liam.

CHAPTER 20 – FURY ROAD

Dermot had heard road racing described as a tough sport loved by equally tough men who embrace danger. Not that he considered himself particularly tough, but he acknowledged that he'd like to be. He had raced a bit in his younger days, but his near road accident had given him pause so that he became a more practical man, no longer taking the same chances that had once appealed to him. He viewed today's race as an opportunity to prove to himself that he could, even a little bit, still be that tough guy, who in the face of danger would not be afraid to embrace it.

He thought of Fury Road in the North 200 race. It was aptly named, for the bikers flew around the curves on their motorcycles, shifting from one extreme angle of the track to the equally extreme angle of the other. Many-a-biker had gone flying off their motorcycles there. During a final lap one year, a motorcycle had rolled over twice, sending its rider in one direction and the bike, now twisted, in the other. The other riders in the race just barreled on, for at the last lap, they all knew it was necessarily an attitude that no prisoners would be taken. It was every rider for themselves.

For today's race, Dermot had specifically chosen an out of the way country lane where he wouldn't feel obliged to watch out for oncoming vehicles. There was a good straight before a series of sharp bends in the road. Dermot hoped that by positioning Liam around the corner to prevent oncoming traffic for the duration of the race, that this would allay his caution about unexpected vehicles appearing on the road. When Dermot explained the race venue, Mac had quickly approved it.

Dermot's smile was involuntary as his eyes swept from this Trident's upper curves and lower slimline frame, to the alloy rimmed wheels with the Dunlop racing tires.

He couldn't help but think back to when he first saw the Trident in its highly polished showroom appearance. It looked like it was capable of doing 100 mph parked.

The pleasure of that memory came flooding back before had he even caressed the highly polished red tank that gleamed now in the sunlight, glittering like the prized jewel that it was.

Dermot threw his right leg over the motorcycle, holding both bars as he leaned forward and nudged the beautifully balanced weight of the Trident off the center stand. It retracted with a satisfying dull thud.

Nerves tingling for the upcoming race, he leaned forward on the motorcycle and turned on the petrol tap. His hand felt for the tiny button which he gently pushed and released 5 times to tickle the petrol and prime the engine. It fired up hot and ready as Dermot himself was.

On the far side of the lane, Mac flipped his helmet visor down, pulled on the chrome choke lever, twisted open the throttle slightly and found compression with the kickstart lever. With a well-practiced swing and thrust of his leg, he booted the Norton's 750 cc twin cylinder engine into life.

He listened to its offbeat burble on full choke and started to gently rev while gradually taking the choke off.

On the other side of the tarmac, Mac's face was grim. He frowned with the intensity of the commission that lay ahead of him. Snicking the bike into first gear, he gently fed in the clutch with his left hand and pointed her to the road.

The two men eased their bikes to the agreed start position at the corner of two intersecting country lanes. With half an eye on each other, they revved their engines into a roar. Mac had been aware the other day that tight bends caused Dermot some hesitation. The man was afraid of death. Such thoughts need not be considered by one of Sidhe, Mac considered this a drawback of being mortal. Because of this, he held back now until Dermot made his start.

As Dermot took off along the road on his Trident, Mac fed in the clutch of the Norton and opened the throttle. He sped from a standing start to around 20 mph in first gear. Smoothing into higher gear, he rapidly accelerated along the stretch of road.

Motorcycles aside and with the best will in the world, Dermot was no match for Mac. Frustrated with himself as he realized this, Dermot marveled nevertheless, at the clean resonant satisfying bellow now coming up behind him, from the twin exhaust pipes and silencers of the Norton.

Mac soon overtook and left behind the distinctive howl of the Trident's three-cylinders and pushed on, changing into top gear to give the Norton engine her head. A quick look behind showed Dermot far in the distance on his Trident as he predictably slowed in anticipation of the unseen bends ahead. Mac leaned into the first bend. He dangled a leg into a high-speed airstream. This resulted in significant force on his leg, which became like a small parachute. It created a turning moment by pulling the rider's leg around. This encouraged a pull on the outside handlebar, further helping to turn the bike thorough counter-steering. Taking the racing line, he accelerated at the Apex to rocket up to 80mph with the arm stretching power that was his.

The Norton now in its element, he flicked it with ease from corner to corner, using engine gears and throttle to control speed. Using only the lightest of touch on the brakes at the tight right hander before opening the throttle, he changed into top gear, giving the thoroughbred its head at 110 mph as he adopted a racing crouch to cheat the strong headwind.

Mac approached the designated finish line where Liam stood in the center of the road. Liam dutifully waved the black and white checkered flag that Dermot had dug out of his garage. As expected, there was no traffic on the little used country lane.

Mac's heart leapt in his breast at the deed he was about to carry out. Murder! his heart cried. Assignment! his brain insisted. It was the decision of Ruadh Rofhessa that this must be done. Gritting his teeth, he prepared for impact.

Liam's eyes opened wide with horror at the speed of the Norton as it roared toward him. He was like a deer caught in the headlights, mesmerized and unable to move. The flag drooped in his hand. At the last moment, Mac twisted the handlebars to avoid Liam. The Norton wind-whipped past, causing Liam to spin around.

Mac could not bring himself to commit murder. Direct order or not, he knew it to be morally wrong. His people would have to take their chances at Liam finding a way into the portal. Mac would make Liam listen, warn him that another would be sent in his place. He would talk sense into Liam.

Dermot rounded the bend looking for the Norton. Liam had his back to Dermot, the flag trailing on the tarmac as he watched Mac roar away up the road.

Suddenly a third motorcycle shot out from a gap in the hedge, Liam directly in its path. Dermot tried to call out, but his helmet impeded his warning cry. He watched helplessly as the new rider impacted Liam, throwing him high into the air so that he turned twice before hitting the ground with a thudding smack.

Mac screeched to a halt, flipped up his helmet and looked back in time to see the rider go through the hedge on the other side of the road, leaving her victim lying in the dust. He recognized the rider. It was the King's messenger.

Dermot barely skidded to a halt, before he was off his motorcycle and at Liam's side. With shaking hands, he pulled out his phone and stabbed in the number to call for help. Yelling at Liam to hold on, he sickened as he looked from Liam's bleeding head to the twisted limbs that lay at odd angles like a broken doll.

A voice from the phone captured his attention. "Hello! Hello!" yelled Dermot. "There's been an accident. We need help." He dropped the phone as he saw Liam's eyes begin to glaze over. "Hold on mate." He implored Liam. "Help's coming. Hold on." But it was too late. Even as he begged Liam to stay, he could only watch helplessly as the life left the body of his new friend.

Mac pulled up beside Liam and jumped off his motorcycle. It fell on its side, wheels spinning. The two men knelt in silence beside Liam's body, each wracked with guilt for their part in the death of this good man.

"He came out of nowhere," muttered Dermot. "Smacked right into him and didn't even stop. What the hell was that? Some kind of cross-country madness …" Words failed him at the senseless act. He looked up at Mac. "Did you see him?"

Mac nodded, his mouth in a straight, tight line. "I know her," he said.

Dermot looked surprised. "Her?"

Mac stood up. "I can do nothing here. I'm going after her." He grabbed his motorcycle, not bothering to put on his helmet. Black eyes glaring, he rode his motorcycle through the hedge in pursuit. He chastised himself as he rode after the messenger, that he should never have agreed to this. He should have tried harder, revealed his identity to Liam and taken him into his confidence, explained the repercussions if Liam were to unlock the portal, somehow made him understand. Somehow!

Dermot listened as the sound of the Norton receded into the distance, until the ensuing silence was replaced by the faint sound of emergency response vehicles approaching.

Five miles on, Mac stopped his motorcycle and let it fall. He stepped away from it and staggered until he too fell to the ground. He sank his head into his hands as tears flew from the corners of his eyes and sobs wracked his body at the horrors of this day.

The messenger was now the one who could not return to the place beyond, for she and not Mac, had committed the unpardonable crime of executing a mortal man. He realized now that the messenger was a backup, in case Mac could not carry out the assignment. The messenger would have taken on the task because her king demanded it, as had Mac. Yet, it was recognized among the folk, that such a deed damaged the purity of the soul, rendering it impossible for such a person to return to live among them. For Mac, the disgrace of not carrying out his assignment would be severe punishment, probably also banishment. Right now, he cared nothing for that. He mourned only the loss of the good man he had at the last minute hoped to spare. He thought of the pain Caer would now face and of his own failed moral fortitude.

CHAPTER 21 – COURAGE

Red apple cheeks stretched tight in a knowing grimace; Nell flung wide her cottage door as Aoife rushed up the grassy, daisy-dotted driveway.

Tears ran down Aoife's face as she ran into the warm fresh-baked bread aroma of Nell's embrace.

"My poor child. My poor child." The old woman rubbed Aoife's back with comforting hands, broadened from a lifetime of hard work.

"He's gone. My Daddy's gone. A-and he's not c-coming back."

Aoife pressed her face into Nell's full-bosomed chest. "I told Mommy to do the charcoal poultice to fix Daddy. But she wouldn't listen a-and I didn't know where to find the charcoal and Mommy said it was t-too late." Sobbing, Aoife reached her arms around Nell, as far as she could, holding onto the old woman's pinafore for support.

"So tis happening is it?" Nell's face was grim now. "It's terrible news for ye so it is."

Aoife looked up, "Did you know Nell? Did you know my Daddy was going to, going to…" She continued to sob as her eyes met Nell's. "How did you know?"

Nell took hold of Aoife's arms and bent down until their faces were level. "It doesn't matter how I knew Aoife. Tis only important that I did know. And now I can help you in what must happen next." She fished a big white handkerchief from a pocket in her apron and wiped Aoife's nose. "Blow!" She commanded.

Aoife hiccupped and blew into the handkerchief. "Wh-what happens next?"

"Come away in child. I've made a special soup that will help to strengthen ye. And it is strength ye will need now.

Aoife bent her arm as she'd seen Liam do when he flexed his muscles. "How strong do I need to be?" She looked doubtfully at the little muscle on her arm.

"Get away with ye child. It's not that kind of strength. It's the courage that ye'll need. Aye, I should have said courage. For the time has come so it has and ye'll need a great deal of courage when they come for you."

"Who's c-coming for me Nell?" Aoife looked about with wild eyes, as if expecting someone to jump out of the shadows and carry her off.

"Not here mo stor. Ye will always be safe in this cottage. Ye will find out soon enough child about the other thing. Now! Let's get on with the serving of the soup. It will tell ye all ye need to know when the time comes."

"Aoife allowed herself to be soothed. She settled herself among the plump red cushions, gazing sad and sorrowful into the fire. Nell fussed about among the gleaming brass poker and tongs to stir the fire. The large black pot simmered as usual. Nell pulled the pot towards her and lifted the lid. The aroma of a fine vegetable soup wafted through the air. A good-sized bowl was ladled out for Aoife. Nell cut a thick slice of homemade bread and spread butter from her very own cows on the top.

Despite herself, Aoife's mouth watered, as she realized she had not eaten since dinner the night before. The bread was light and fluffy. It tasted unlike any her mother usually bought at the store in Clonacool.

Cara sat on Aoife's shoulder, her long nose twitching in appreciation of the aroma. Aoife took a little piece of bread, dipped it into the soup and placed it to her shoulder for Cara. As the mouse nibbled at the bread held between her paws, Aoife finished off the delicious food, using the last of the bread to mop up the soup from the bottom of the bowl.

Satisfied at last, Aoife sat back among the cushions, the couch so deep that her legs stuck straight out beyond the seat. Patting her tummy with one hand Aoife sighed. By way of thanks she gave Nell a watery half-smile and said, "I'm so full now, I could probably throw up." She yawned. "I feel so sleepy, I think I have to just …. "The little girl's eyes closed, and her head lolled to one side. Cara appeared satisfied too, for she slept where she had dined, on Aoife's shoulder with her tail wrapped around her body.

Old Nell smiled gently, took a knitted wrap from the arm of the couch and tucked it around Aoife's limp body. "Aye little Darlin' you will need all the comfort you can get for what is coming your way. But never fear, that soup will give ye courage. Aye and ye will have wisdom too, such as never should be needed in such a small child as yourself. And I am here to help ye see the coming of things, that ye will not be surprised so." Patting Aoife's chestnut curls, Nell left her to sleep and the soup to do its work.

CHAPTER 22 – ALL LAID OUT

The roses that hung sweet and heavy around the trellised doorway had been severely reduced in number by an overnight storm. Petals were strewn in a carpet from the door of the cottage all along the driveway. The petals lifted gently in the breeze and danced like couples waltzing in circles around a ballroom.

Pam walked in with Dermot trailing behind. The day promised warmth and sun flooded in, lighting up the sleepy look of the place.

Kay was crumpled in one corner of the purple couch. She had obviously slept there. The jumble of pillows and duvet attested to this.

Dark circles under her eyes from crying, she looked up at Pam and said, "It's too bloody tidy Pam. Without Liam here, there's no shoes and junk to pick up. Even the floor on his side of the bed is tidy. I can walk there without tripping over stuff." Her voice shook then. "It's terrible Pam." The tears rolled fresh down her face.

Pam sat beside her and opened her arms. Kay flopped against her friend who wrapped her arms about her protectively.

Pam looked up at Dermot and nodded toward the kitchen. Dermot responded with, "I'll put the kettle on." He walked out to the kitchen and closed the door behind him.

"What will I do Pam?" Kay sobbed into her friend's shoulder.

Pam wisely offered no advice, just held Kay for long minutes, stroked her hair and made comforting noises.

Dermot could be heard banging about in the kitchen as he searched out crockery and filled the kettle from the tap. He glanced at the two women through the glass door, as he mulled over the last few days. The Police had found him at the scene. He had explained about the race between himself and Mac, of how they had asked Liam to act as flagman and then a third rider coming out of nowhere. The paramedics had exchanged glances. Dermot could see from their faces how foolish they thought him. And they were right, Dermot admonished himself. Grown men acting like kids. He was deeply ashamed of his part in Liam's death. And what had happened to Mac, he wondered. The police wondered too and wanted to talk to him, to find out all he knew about the third rider. Dermot had no information except that Mac said he knew the rider. A woman, he'd said. How did he know her? Where from? And why hadn't Mac been seen since? Surely, he could have come to the pub in the expectation of finding Dermot, or someone that knew of him. It was all such a mystery. And then there was Kay's face when he'd said a guy named Mac was the other rider. Her face had gone completely white. She had turned to Pam with eyes as huge as the moon. The two of them seemed to know the name but Pam had reassured Kay. No, she'd said. It couldn't be the same guy. It wasn't possible. He wasn't like that, Pam had said. Whatever that was about, Kay had believed her. She had calmed right down. He wondered what they were talking about now. With the electric kettle beginning to whistle, it was impossible to know.

Pam asked, "Is it okay for Dermot to be here Kay? I mean, after all that's happened."

"I don't blame Dermot if that's what you mean. I blame myself. I should never have allowed Liam to do it. But how was I to know? And who does that, murders a man and rides off?" she looked at Pam's face, as if she expected to find the answer there. "Who does that Pam?"

"I don't know Kay. I don't know." She held her friend closer. "But you can be sure they will catch them."

"But that won't bring him back." A fresh flood of tears streamed down Kay's face. Pam said nothing more, just held her until at last, the sobs subsided into the occasional hiccup. "I don't think I can do today Pam."

"Yes, you can." Pam encouraged her gently. "I'll be right here beside you. Every step of the way. We'll do it together. All right?"

"All right." Kay was like a child in a dark corner and Pam a mother figure leading her out into the light.

They sat quietly as Kay gathered her strength and listened to the sounds from outside. Birds could be heard calling to each other in the trees, still pecking away at the abundance of food in the hanging feeders.

Pam looked through the window over Kay's head. A cat lurked on the wall, keeping perfectly still. Unsuspecting birds swooped down to scoop up seed left sprinkled along the wall by Liam in his final feeding of them.

The cat's eyes suddenly opened wide. He pounced but missed as a bird flew up in a rush of wings. The cat swiveled its head up, following the bird as it flew away. After a moment, the cat settled down and feigned disinterest once more.

Pam cocked her head toward the bedroom door. "I'm glad you decided to go with some of the Irish customs of holding a wake. Who's with Liam right now, Kay?"

"It's Sean just now. He's been here since before dawn. I set up a chair beside the coffin. It was kind of him to offer."

Pam nodded. “This is a bit different to the way you would do things back in the States I’m thinking.”

Kay agreed. “Yes. But I wanted Liam to have an Irish funeral. Well, as much as I could handle. I wanted him to know I’d given him a good send off. Done the best I can you know.”

Pam reached out and placed her warm hand over Kay’s cold fingers. “I’m sure he’d be happy about that.”

“And all his friends from when he grew up here. They’ll want to see him again, I think. Although none have come to the house, except for Sean. You and Dermot too of course.”

“Ah, they’ll be here Kay. Don’t you waste time thinking on that one. They’ll be here. And it’s out of respect that they haven’t been here before now. The men especially won’t come into the house of a young widow just like that. It’s not respectful you see.” She wanted Kay to understand. “It’s different with Sean. He’s an established friend of the family that’s been in and out of the house.”

“I suppose so.” Kay was doubtful but had nothing to base her knowledge on, only that she had wanted to give Liam an Irish wake and funeral. She had sought the advice of the local catholic priest. Not that Liam was a practicing catholic, but it was where he was brought up, so here she was, doing it.

“Where’s Aoife?” Pam thought to ask.

“She’s playing about here somewhere.” Kay sat up. She pulled an unused tissue from the pocket of her jeans. She dried her eyes and then blew her nose but seemed unconcerned about Aoife. “I think she helped herself to breakfast. She said was full anyway when I asked her. I just felt it best to let her do what she wanted today. I tried you know, but I’m in no fit state to be cheerful for her.”

Remembering all the preparation this day had required of Pam, she said “Thanks for doing the food for the wake Pam and helping me with organizing the wake. I couldn’t have dealt with it. Not that as well as everything else, you know.”

The two women looked toward the bedroom door, behind which Liam was laid in his coffin ready for the wake and the viewing of those who would want to pay their respects.

Pam intentionally brought Kay's focus back to the living room with a dismissive. "Ah sure, I've people working at it, the food. It will all be delivered here when we're ready for it." She smiled at her friend.

"Thank you, Pam." Kay's chin wobbled but she caught herself in time before the tears began again.

Dermot opened the kitchen door and came in with a tray piled high with tea things. His face was lit with an expression of accomplishment. "I managed to find everything. And here it is, the tea. Will I pour now?" He set the tray down on the coffee table and kept up what was for him, a stream of chatter that was completely out of character, as if by doing so, he could add a sense of well-being or perhaps lessen his own feeling of guilt. He had apologized so many times to Kay that neither of them wanted to hear the same words spoken again.

"I've made a bit of toast now," he began. "It's not too burnt. Well maybe it was, but I've scraped off the burnt bits, so it doesn't look too bad. And you'll need to keep up your strength today you know, because there'll be a fair amount of people at the funeral, to say nothing of the wake now."

Kay and Pam looked from Dermot to the burnt toast offering and glanced at each other, unable to keep down a sudden rush of nervous giggles. The giggles turned into laughter which became almost hysterical. Dermot looked decidedly offended as he offered the plate of toast, each slice layered with a thick smothering of butter.

Pam took a slice and held it out to Kay between thumb and forefinger. The two women howled with laughter. Pam almost dropped the toast, but Dermot snatched it back.

"Well I don't know as it's anything to laugh about." His face was a picture of the aggrieved host. "There's nothing wrong with it." To emphasize this, he took a bite of the toast.

It was so crunchy from being overcooked that the entire slice fell apart in his fingers, leaving him with a pointy bit sticking out from the corner of his mouth. One small crumb still held between his fingers, as the rest of the slice fell to the floor.

Kay mimicked the way Dermot held his fingers and laughed until she fell back among the cushions holding onto her stomach. "Oh! Oh! Thank you, Dermot. That was so funny. Oh! I needed that."

Tears and laughter had drained all the emotion out of her. She sighed. "I think I can probably take a shower now without crying into the water." She offered a blotchy-faced smile to Pam. "Will you wait for me while I get ready?"

Pam wiped the corners of her eyes with a tissue, still chuckling to herself. "Aye. It's what we're here for. Isn't it, Dermot?" She included him in a conspiratorial wink that helped him recover from his deflation. Pam patted Dermot's hand, her approval bringing a smile from him at last.

Kay went to shower. As the bedroom door closed behind her, there was a murmured conversation. Sean came out of the bedroom, his eyes blinking owlishly in the bright sunlight.

"Sean." Dermot acknowledged the presence of the older man.

"Dermot." Sean nodded back. "I'd best be off home and see to the caves and things before the wake.

"It was good of ye to do the sitting," said Pam.

He waved her off. "Ah tis nothing. Tis only what's expected and happy I am to do it for the sake of both of them." Sean shuffled through the front door and paused to stretch himself in the warmth. "Tis a fine day for it so. And the walk up the lane will do me joints good, I'm fair cramped after it." He shuffled off towards his cottage, his step quickening as his joints loosened up.

Pam became all business. "Now! Dermot let's get organized. You clean the kitchen and maybe get the fire ready for lighting as soon as we return from the church." She stopped and looked at him inquiringly. "Would ye mind doing that now?"

"Ah sure, I don't mind at all." He grinned at her. "I'm happy to be useful." He gathered up the tea things and headed back to the kitchen.

Pam strode out of the front door. "I'm off to find the little madam and get her back here. We'll need to be ready for the wake soon, so we will."

As it happened, Aoife was just at that moment coming back into the yard. She still wore her pyjamas. She looked as though she hadn't had any attention given her for several days. Her curls were tangled and unkempt, her face smudged with dust and general lack of the application of water.

"Hello now Aoife." Pam was welcoming but brief, efficiency was her focus right then. "Where have you been?" She didn't wait for a response but took the child by the hand and ushered her through the living room and into the second bathroom.

"I don't need a bath," protested Aoife as Pam closed the door behind them.

"Ah sure you do. Don't you know ye have to look clean and presentable for the wake and the day that's in it." The sound of the shower running, muffled all further conversation.

Kay took her time getting ready, pausing often beside the open coffin which took up most of the available space in the bedroom.

Liam was laid out in the coffin, dressed in his best suit. He wore a tie that was correctly fastened which was unusual, because he could never get his tie properly knotted and preferred if he could, not to wear one at all.

The priest had wanted to wind the customary rosary beads around Liam's hands, but Kay had drawn the line there. "He was not a heathen father, but neither was he a church man. I'm doing this wake because Liam was Irish and so is Aoife and because I think he would like the send-off you know. But rosary beads would be taking it a bit far."

Kay had also vetoed the suggestion of candles at the head and foot of the coffin. "I can see the point of lighting the candles while we're in the church," she'd said. "But not here. I'd be worried about burning the place down for one thing." Nor had she allowed the covering of mirrors. Too weird she had decided. She thought it again now as she glanced in the mirror and reached for a hairbrush.

Keeping up a stream of comments to Liam, she told him mostly about how tidy the room was now that he wasn't around to mess it up. "What will I do without you, silly man?" she admonished him. "You filled my days with cleaning up after you."

Kay brushed her hair, wet from the shower. "Look," she told him, taking the wet towel from around her body. "This is what you do with the towel after a shower." She held the towel up so he could see, were he to open his eyes. "You hold it out like this." She demonstrated. "And then you drape it over the radiator like so." Kay smoothed the towel over the radiator. "Can you see how simple it is? Now why couldn't you do the same?"

She thought about this for a moment. "Did you think you were still living with your mother maybe? Is that what it is with men like you, the untidy ones? Did your mother clean up after you all your life until you left home?" She left off talking to Liam then and reflected to herself. "That must be it. I'll have a word with her when I join you both on the other side there, so I will."

She caught herself then and turned back to Liam. "Look at me using the Irish vernacular and saying, 'so I will'. Next thing I'll be saying 'to be sure, to be sure'."

She wagged an admonishing finger at him. "And I suppose you'd just make fun of me and say it was about time I realized I was in Ireland."

Kay nodded at Liam to emphasize her point and then added another thought. "And don't think I'm just going to stick around because you wanted us to come and live here. I haven't made up my mind about that yet. I know you wanted Aoife brought up in the land of her ancestors and all that, but it's up to me now boyo and I haven't decided one way or the other … Yet," she added.

As she chatted with her husband, Kay pulled open drawers and fished out underwear. Holding up a lacy black bra, she held it out for him to see.

"You always liked this one. I'll wear it for you, today shall I?' She cupped the bra around her breasts and fasted the hooks at the back. "Nice wide hooks you said. Easy to unfasten." She nodded at him as if he had demurred. "That's what you said!"

Kay straightened the bra. "Actually, I bought the bra because the hooks were easy to fasten, rather than unfasten." She looked at Liam. "Who's going to take this bra off now Liam? Who's going to swirl it around his head and throw it across the room?"

From the living room came the sound of a shovel banging around as the fireplace was cleaned out.

"No one, that's who," whispered Kay. She stood up and pulled her panties into place.

Leaning over the coffin, she placed a kiss on Liam's cold lips. "There's no one to love me Liam. No one who will love me like you did with lots of silly laughing. Who am I going to laugh with? It's just me and Aoife now."

Pam's voice could be heard in the next bedroom, her voice cajoling and persuading as she encouraged Aoife into getting dressed.

"And maybe Pam too," amended Kay. "I have a good friend there. Why should I give that up?" she asked herself.

She turned to Liam. "If I leave Ireland, I lose that you know. Do you know how hard it is to make a friendship as solid as mine and Pam's? Friendships between women are not to be sniffed at." She sniffed then as if trying it out. "So, I might stay," she told her husband. "I haven't decided yet."

*****

Kay sat quietly on the purple couch, looking down at her hands. Pam and Dermot clucked about in the background with Aoife on their heels. Listening with half an ear, she thought they sounded like a family, a mother, a father and a child.

There was a noise from the bedroom and the door opened as two men backed out carefully, holding one end of the coffin and giving quiet instructions to whoever was holding the other end.

Kay watched, hypnotized as the casket made its way through the living room and out through the front door to the waiting hearse. She sprang to her feet, reaching the coffin just as the door was closed on the back of the hearse. "Where are you taking him?" she asked redundantly. She knew where they were going. To the church. She had asked only because she needed to hear the sound of her own voice and to claim ownership of this man, her man, before he was taken away.

Pam was beside her now, a hand on her arm, a gentle voice in her ear. "It's just for a short while now Kay. We'll follow Liam down to the church."

*****

The funeral must have been an hour or so but to Kay it passed in a blur.

Aoife reached up to whisper questions in her mother's ear, but Kay didn't respond. She could hear Aoife's voice but only as it were from a great distance. She was mostly focused on Pam's calm voice on the other side of Aoife. Pam's voice was the single-most thing to help her through these last terrible days. Eventually the child turned to Pam for answers. Their two voices became a constant drone of high and low, a background to the priest who led the congregation in prayer, in standing and sitting to order.

Through all of this, Kay sat unmoving as if glued to her seat. She was only half aware of her surroundings, focused as she was on the casket at the foot of the altar.

A choir sang somewhere in the background. Kay thought it sounded beautiful. A few people walked past her with a faint aura of perfume to speak at the pulpit. She thought dimly that she should probably listen to what they had to say about Liam. But it seemed to Kay, as if a veil surrounded the space between herself and the casket, that all else existed outside of that tunnel.

It was a surprise when, at the close of the service, Kay felt an elbow beneath hers, urging her to stand. She looked up to see Pam's kind face and followed her to stand beside the coffin with Aoife.

Mourners passed slowly before her. Kay followed the gaze of the mourners as the first person looked into the casket. But she forgot to look up again and so it was, that she blinked when the casket was suddenly closed. Liam's face became lost to her for all time.

It was not the custom here in Ireland, but it was what Kay wanted. Liam was cremated. Kay wanted this because she felt strongly that his ashes should be scattered in the field behind the house. He would become a part of the good earth and of the grass and wildflowers that grew there. She and Aoife could visit him by simply stepping outside the kitchen door.

*****

By the time the mourners began to arrive from the church, the fire was lit and the cottage was bright and ready for action, if a wake could be considered as action.

The food Pam had organized at the pub arrived, along with those who had prepared the food and who now doubled as servers. They moved to and fro, keeping the table replenished with cake, fresh sandwiches and small tasty pies kept hot in the oven.

The kettle seemed to boil non-stop as more and more tea was required, mostly by the women as they sat or stood about. The room suddenly looked small as there were so many mourners crowded into it and so many cups clinking against saucers and mindless chatter about cake and sandwiches.

The men mostly stood outside in the front yard of the cottage. There were comments on their good fortune at having Pam provide the drink for the wake, her being a publican an all. Out here, away from the admonishing eyes of their women folk, bottles of beer were passed about easily. To give the mourners easy access to the alcohol, Pam had temporarily installed a small fridge outside the front door so they could help themselves.

The conversation was about Liam and how glad they were, that he had come home to Ireland and brought his child back with him to be raised in the old country, if that was the wish of his young wife there. They went on to talk of cows and sheep, about whose turf was still to be cut, about how warm the weather was lately and how it was good for footing the turf as it dried in the sun. However, it was generally agreed that it was not necessarily good for the crops which must still be grown and needed the rain.

Aoife flitted about like a butterfly from group to group, enjoying the unexpected attention. The women stroked the soft curve of her cheeks, the men ruffled her curls.

Kay stuck close to Pam or Pam stuck close to Kay. Either way, Pam kept an eye on things and gave quiet direction to her helpers about what needed doing and whose cup needed filling.

Kay responded to conversational small talk as best she could. The well-intentioned villagers had nothing but kindness in their hearts towards this young widow, come as she had lately to their community.

She could have been considered a 'blow-in' as they often referred to those not born or bred in the community. Yet, Kay held a special place in their hearts because she was not one of those who visited Ireland and left again, never to return. She had proven herself to them already because she had brought Liam back and he was one of their own.

Not only that, but she had also brought her child and that child had an Irish name and heritage. If it was up to them and their good wishes, and many of them felt it was, then the general hope was that Kay would stay and bring up her child among them.

"Will Aoife go to the village school now, will she?"

"Um." Kay hadn't decided which school Aoife might attend. She had been leaning towards the girl's school in Sligo but that was an hour's drive each way. Without Liam's support, Kay was thinking the journey might become a bit of a strain after a while. "Maybe."

Another guest chipped in "They've a strong group of teachers there so. And it'll be good for the children to have a new girl join them."

Yet another added, "It's a small school but it's a fine school."

Kay considered this as she let the conversation wash over her. A small school meant Aoife would probably make a friend or two. Certainly, it would be a help for the child, as she was never one to bother much with friends. Aoife seemed to get what she needed in the way of social interaction from her parents and from …. imaginary friends lately.

Hmm, she told herself, friends would be a good thing, especially local friends. It would help Aoife become more socialized. For that was how Kay viewed her daughter's visits to Nell's cottage, as if Aoife were creating imaginary friends because she hadn't made any of her own.

Strange she thought, as a plate of cake was passed from one guest's hand to that of another in front of her. Strange that Aoife would dream up an older imaginary friend rather than a young friend, a child.

A plate of sandwiches was held out in front of Kay, the voice belonging to the arm holding the plate floated down from somewhere above her. "Eat a bit now Kay. You need to keep your strength up so."

Kay nodded absently and took a sandwich. The plate moved on. She nibbled at the edge of the sandwich.

The noise around her seemed to rise to a crescendo and then suddenly there were no mourners.

To Kay's surprise, she could hear birds singing and Pam's voice from the kitchen calling out orders to the caterers who moved quietly about, cleaning up and putting the place to rights. Kay looked around in surprise. Where had everyone gone? Was it over so quickly? She realized she was still holding the sandwich she had nibbled. How long had she been holding it?

*****

It had been a long day and Kay was glad to be tucked up in her own bed with Pam offering her a sleeping pill and a glass of water. She took the water but refused the pill. "Aoife?" she enquired.

"Aoife's already asleep. I'll be here in the morning bright and early," promised Pam.

"Not too early," complained Kay as she fell asleep. "You're always waking me up."

"Hush now and sleep mo chara daor, my dear friend." soothed Pam.

Checking in on Aoife's room before she left, she could see the child was fast asleep and breathing steadily. Pam walked around the cottage, turning off lights, making sure the little nightlight was left on in the hallway in case Aoife woke in the night. Children often needed the comfort of a nightlight, she told herself.

Dermot was half asleep on the couch. He got up sleepily and pulled himself into wakefulness to drive Pam back to the pub. "You know ..." he began.

"Go on?" said Pam.

"I was thinking about how Liam died." Dermot shifted in the driving seat. "You know how I feel responsible."

Pam stopped him. "Don't say that. You weren't to know what would happen. Whoever that guy was, he'll likely be long gone from this place."

"I suppose so." Dermot wasn't ready to forgive his own part in the tragedy.

Pam was adamant. "He's the one to blame. And he won't show his face around here again." She placed her hand on his arm. "I don't want you to think that you're to blame Dermot. That's a crippling thing to impose on yourself. I don't want that for you. Okay?"

"Okay. I'll try," he promised.

When they climbed out of the car at the pub, Dermot took hold of Pam's arm beneath the elbow in a show of support. She looked up in surprise, then gave him a tired smile.

Dermot said, "You're a wonderful friend to Kay."

"She's like a sister to me. We hit it off the moment we met. I'm just happy I can be here for her right now." She patted his arm and they entered the pub together. Dermot nodded toward the bar and asked, "Will you have a drink Pam?"

Pam shook her head. Instead, she took him by the hand and led him upstairs.

CHAPTER 23 – THE CURSE

Kay lay on the bed for a long time, her mind playing through the events of the past week, over and over again.

She kept coming back to the fact, that this guy Mac who was involved in the accident, hadn't been seen since. She wondered again if it could possibly have been her Mac. "My Mac?" she said out loud. "My Mac would never do such a thing." That was what Pam had said. Surely Pam was right, and yet … What if it was him? What would be his purpose in doing such a thing? Revenge, because Liam had won Kay back? She shook her head. Her Mac wasn't like that. But how would she know really? It had been six years and even then, it had been a matter of weeks they had known each other.

Kay knew at an almost cellular level, that she and Mac were bound together for all time. She should be able to trust him. Yet, she mused, weren't myths filled with stories of betrayal.

A thought occurred to her. She could ask him direct, go to the hawthorn grove and call him to her. She could find out. She paused only a moment or two. She would find out!

Wearing only her robe and slippers, she ran to the kitchen door and flung it open. Not stopping to change into wellies against the possibility of mud in the field, she headed away from the cottage.

Hesitating only briefly with her hand on the gate into the meadow, she slid the bolt back with a clang, stepped through and closed the gate. Even in her haste, her tidy mind ensured that any sheep grazing there might not escape through the field, passed the cottage and into the lane.

It was a clear night. The sky was filled with stars that together with the half-moon, spread light across the meadow. She walked in ever quickening steps until she reached the great ash.

As she stepped up the slight incline, she held onto a low hanging branch. Strangely, the wind which had been gentle as she crossed the meadow, was now strong, so that her hair blew back from her face. Her robe strained against her body as if the wind had been summoned to deter her from entering.

Kay set her chin and stepped into the circle. The wind ceased immediately. She looked back with surprise that there was no evidence of the gale that had encircled her only moments before.

Unnerved but determined, she placed one foot in front of the other until she reached the center of the circle.

"Mac!" She whispered. "Are you there?"

She listened but there was no answer.

"Mac" she said a little louder. "I need to talk to you." Still nothing.

Kay closed her eyes and clenched her fists in concentration. "Mac!" She called as loud as she could. "Please come to me."

There was a rustling sound from the far end of the circle. It seemed to come from where the little stone menhir sat hidden in its bed of hawthorn.

Kay opened her eyes. A figure walked steadily towards her. She gasped. A myriad of feelings ran across her breast. Fortitude rose uppermost. Determination shone from her eyes, which narrowed at the confrontation to come.

The figure continued to move. The hawthorns seemed to crowd close, casting many shadows, yet she knew. It was Mac.

"Caer," his voice was quiet, serious. His body language, although in shadow, seemed subdued.

"Tell me." Kay stifled a sob as it rose in her throat. Her eyes filled with tears, but she shook her head angrily to force them back. "Tell me you had nothing to do with Liam's death."

There was silence between them.

"Mac?" She questioned, dreading his response.

Mac sighed from deep within his chest. "Caer," he said "I … "

Kay's eyes open wide "It was you?" A strangled sob left her throat and gushed out of her mouth. "It was you?"

"No! It was given to me, but I could not do it. Yet, I cannot deny that I was involved."

Kay pulled back her right arm and shot it with the full force of her grief up and into Mac's jaw. Mac took the blow, not moving or turning away. "Caer." Mac turned his head from side to side, as if searching for escape. There was none. His hands lifted to grasp her shoulders, but she pushed them away, screaming now.

"You knew? You knew my Liam was to be killed? Why Mac? Why didn't you stop it?"

"I did Caer. But another came in my place." He shook his head in despair. "I should have known. I should have realized they would send another."

Kay's mouth contorted. Her tears spread through the air as she sobbed. She was tortured by the very idea that this man she had loved, still loved and had lain with, knew that Liam was to be hurt and had done nothing to stop it. She pummeled his chest in agony. Sobs poured from deep within until her throat ached with the force of her sorrow. She sank exhausted to her knees, "Why?"

Struggling himself, not to break down, Mac fell on his knees with her. She looked at him, her hands held up in supplication. "How could you let it happen to me? To us? To Liam and me?"

Mac struggled for self-composure. He knew there was nothing he could say that would heal the gash in her heart nor mend the wound between them, yet he tried. “Caer, he … Liam. He threatened my people. He found a way into our world. He found it and he was going to use it and he was so close. We could not allow it to happen. I was told to come here to dissuade him. And I tried Caer, I tried. I even came to you in a dream. I confronted Liam near the grove. But he would not listen, not to you nor to me. It was as if he could not stop himself.”

Kay was deaf to his reasons. “Your stupid people were threatened by my Liam? How does that even make sense?” He was killed for this? And you knew! And by doing nothing, you killed my Liam! You!”

Kay grabbed Mac and tried to shake him, but the strength of his body was like a rock. She wanted to hurt him. She lifted her hand and smacked his face again and again. Mac didn’t move. He took the blows, know that he deserved the punishment.

Kay paused in her delirium and sank back onto her heels, her head hanging to the earth.

Knowing it was pointless but still wanting to explain, he lifted her limp body and held her to his chest as she continued to sob quietly.

“It was not my decision Caer but it fell to me to carry it out. I could not do it, but another came in my place. I was not expecting that, but I should have done. Therefore, it is my fault and the fault of no other. But I do know this, I pleaded with Liam to abandon his quest, to give it up, to return to America. But Caer he wouldn’t listen, he couldn’t listen. He was mad with the need to complete his quest …”

He broke off and bent his beautiful head, sobbing with his Caer for the loss of the man she had loved and for the loss of Caer to himself that he knew was inevitable.

They cried in each other's arms until there were no more tears to shed between them, silent in the aftermath of hopelessness. Kay could feel the beat of Mac's heart and the strength of his arms as they held her. She pulled back away from him and stood. Wiping her eyes on her sleeve and her nose too for good measure, she stepped away.

"Mac," she began.

Mac interrupted her. "Caer, I must tell you." He hesitated. "They know about Aoife, that she is one of us." Kay gasped in shock. Mac swallowed and went on. "They will come for her Caer."

Kay became very quiet. Her body began to slowly collapse again.

Mac continued. "It may not be today, or tomorrow. But they will come. You should leave here if you do not want this."

"I will not permit it," Kay whispered. "Nor will I run away." She drew her body to its full height and began in a small but steady voice. "Maccan of the Tuatha de Danaan." Her voice gained strength as she continued, "I curse you for the curse you have brought to me and my family."

Mac looked at her in amazement. Admiration and fear struggled to gain the upper hand in him.

Kay continued, "I curse you as you have cursed me. As I will desire Liam's love with no chance of holding him close for the remainder of my life, I curse you to desire my love with no possibility of attaining your desire. Not until the day you make amends for what you've done." She sobbed again but her voice remained true. "And because you can never make amends, you can never have me."

"Caer." Mac reached out his arms to her, from where he still knelt on the ground.

Kay stepped back. "Nor can you ever come near me again until that time. Never!"

She turned and ran from the grove, the apple blossom of her perfume lingering on the air behind her.

Mac stumbled to his feet and moved to follow her but was held by the very curse she laid on him. Throwing his arms up to the moon and with a great cry of pain, he bellowed “Caer! Oh! My Caer!”

CHAPTER 24 – ANOTHER GUIDE

Aoife woke to a tapping sound. She ran to the window. A daisy chain lay on the window ledge. She knew instinctively that it was from the lady. Opening the window, she retrieved the flowers. Using the mirror, she solemnly and carefully arranged the flowers on her head like a crown.

Without bothering to change from her pyjamas, Aoife padded through to the kitchen. Mommy wasn't doing anything, just staring into the coffee pot, watching it drip into the waiting jug. Aoife put her hand on Mommy's arm. "What will we do without Daddy?"

Kay opened her mouth to speak but closed it again. She was exhausted from her confrontation with Mac. It had led to a sleepless night during which she reasoned it was not likely they would come for Aoife so soon. She could not shake the apathy and grief that now threatened to overwhelm her.

Aoife watched her mother's face, wishing she'd been allowed to use the healing poultice on Daddy. As she considered this, a thought came to her mind. Perhaps things could still be fixed.

"Mommy!" she said with childish authority. "I think I know what to do." She turned and ran out the kitchen door, pausing only to pull on her wellies.

Aoife ran across the field, avoiding the potholes by jumping over them and skipping around the scratchy reeds. At the gate, she didn't bother opening it but climbed up, swung herself over and jumped down the other side.

As she skipped across the meadow, sure that she had the solution, she allowed a song to begin humming itself into life at the back of her mouth.

At the ash tree, Aoife put out a hand to grasp the knobbly tree trunk. Pulling herself up to the top of the bank, she sang the chorus of the song she'd been humming, bringing her arms above her head for the finale that she sang out to the sky.

Excited to meet the lady and present her solution, Aoife jumped down the bank and into the Faerie circle.

Skipping to the center, she climbed onto the moss-covered tree trunk. As she waited for the lady, Aoife jumped lightly from one foot to the other and began another song.

Because it was such a pretty view, Aoife faced the gap in the hawthorn that led beyond the Faerie circle towards the river. Preoccupied, she didn't hear the lady approach. It was her perfume that reached Aoife first, followed by a slight rustling of leaves as they lifted in the breeze at her passing.

Eiru looked round.

"Hello Aoife. What a beautiful song." Eiru sat on the tree stump throne.

"Hello lady," said Aoife and sat down beside her. "I've been waiting for you."

*****

Kay remembered to breathe. A long sigh escaped her as the aroma of decaf coffee reminded her to begin the day. She blinked and took hold of a cup, steadying it with one hand as she poured her decaf. Sipping, she wandered aimlessly about the cottage, pausing here and there for long moments where she didn't seem to think at all, but merely existed between one sip and the next.

*****

Eiru and Aoife ran through the grove, trailing lengths of daisy chain that fell apart as they waved them through the air like streamers above their heads. Each wore a similar crown of flowers. Aoife's heart was light. She was certain the lady could fix her Daddy.

Around and around they ran until Eiru collapsed across the great tree trunk and Aoife threw herself across her warm, perfumed body.

Heaving with exertion, they lay for a long moment in the sun, until they could once again hear the orange-chested chaffinch trill its song.

At last, Aoife slid off her soft cushion, onto the warm grass. Eiru sat up to watch her. Aoife's face was serious, her head turned to one side. Her eyes were filled with curiosity, a question clear on her face.

"Why did my Daddy have to die?"

Eiru reached out and held Aoife's smooth chin in her hands. She studied the small face for a long moment then leaned down and pressed her lips against the soft cheek. She spoke quietly, close to Aoife's ear. "Some have to leave this earth early because they are so brave and determined that the world cannot hold them."

Aoife turned her head, the young eyes looked earnestly into hers. Eiru gently wiped a tear from the child's face. "Your father was such a man. You can be proud of him for that. Are you proud of him Aoife?"

"Yes." Aoife nodded her head and gulped back her tears.

"Remember him that way Aoife."

Aoife put a hand on the lady's arm. "I am proud of my Daddy, but I don't want to remember him. I want you to fix him. I want him back."

"Oh, Aoife." The lady's quick intake of breath should have been a warning to Aoife. "I can't do that."

"Of course, you can." Aoife nodded encouragingly at Eiru. "You told me you've lived a very long time. Many, many years you said. Right?"

"Well, yes that is true. But …"

"So!" Aoife spread her hands and shrugged her shoulders. "So, you know a lot of things. You must know how to fix him."

"It is not that simple Aoife."

"It's okay if it's hard. I'll help you," she assured Eiru. "We can even try the charcoal poultice. I know how to make it. I'll show you, okay? Let's go to my house now. Come!" She pulled on Eiru's arm.

Eiru became very still. Hawthorn leaves and blades of grass alike, became still with her. Birds stopped calling to each other. All of nature seemed intent on the gathering of power that was now required by Eiru goddess of the Tuatha de Danaan.

Aoife was transfixed. She held her breath, her whole being focused on the change she could see taking place within Eiru. There was something powerful happening, something magical. She hoped it was the magic needed to bring her Daddy back.

Eiru held Aoife's eyes with her own. Into Aoife, she poured her deep understanding of nature, of the earth and the creatures that live in it, of birth and life and death, of the fullness of the earth and of how flowers, plants and all earth's creatures pass from our sight to become part of the great cycle, of the rain that pours itself upon the earth so that all is reborn to replenish the earth and of how Liam's ashes would be spread across the field in the land he so loved and would become a part of forever. Silently, Eiru gave this gift to Aoife, imbued her with the knowledge that was Eiru's right to give and Aoife's to receive.

Knowledge, understanding and acceptance flooded the child's mind. Emotions passed fluidly across her face as she experienced the pain of tragic loss, followed quickly by the certainty of promise. In that long moment, Aoife was given the rights of a light bringer, a walker between the worlds. Quite what that meant, was not made clear to Aoife in that moment, but the rights were given, and Aoife knew the power of it as it circled about her, requesting that she accept all she had been given.

"I will," said Aoife, breaking the silence within the grove.

Eiru quietly summoned the warm breeze to gently brush the sunshine against Aoife's face. Aoife became aware once more, of birds singing, leaves rustling and grass moving almost imperceptibly. It was, she thought, as if she had become part of the grove, that the grove was her and she was the grove. She stepped backward. The grove and all within it moved with her as one. Aoife gave an experimental twirl. Again, the grove moved as she did so that as she turned, she could discern no space between herself and all that was within the grove.

"And you, my sweet girl," said Eiru, "It is time you learned how fortunate you are, for you have been adopted into the tribe of our people"

"Tribe of our people," repeated Aoife slowly, looking up into the slanted blue eyes of Eiru.

"Have you not noticed how alike we are Aoife?"

"Our eyes are the same," observed the child.

"Yes. And in many other ways, we are the same."

"Will you tell me?"

"I will not only tell you Aoife, I will teach you many things, even the secrets of our people. We are Fae you and I."

Aoife's eyes widened. She whispered, "You mean the fairy folk?" At Eiru's slight nod, Aoife said "I used to think fairies were small but then I found out they're tall like me. Well, like Mommy."

Eiru laughed softly. "We are of the Tuatha de Danaan, a noble race who have lived in this land almost from the very beginning."

"Oh!" Aoife said, not fully digesting this. Even with the understanding she had just been given, still to her childish mind, one thing was more important than the other. She voiced this. "So, am I adopted to the fairy folk." She waited, head on one side, green eyes wide.

"You could say that Aoife. In fact, you have understood it well. You are and have always been adopted in the tribe of the Tuatha de Danaan."

Aoife nodded. There was a calmness to her now, a serenity that had not been there before. "And is it a secret?"

Wise in the way of secrets and how a child might burst to declare it, Eiru counseled. "Well Aoife, it is a secret but also it is not a secret. For if you declare this to friends, they might think you strange and that you think yourself above them. Can you see that?"

"Yes," agreed Aoife slowly nodding her head. I'd rather have friends than tell a secret that would make me unpopular.

"Ah! And is being popular very important to you?"

Aoife surveyed the lush green grass at her feet, studying the primroses scattered here and there in clumps of pale yellow. When she looked up, her eyes were clear, and her brow unfurrowed. "I don't care too much about being popular. But I do like having friends."

"But Aoife," Eiru laughed. "I am your friend." She took hold of the child's hands. As she made to pull Aoife into another merry dance, Eiru added "And I am your guide."

"Another guide? I have two guides?"

Eiru let go of Aoife's hands. "Another guide?" she repeated.

"Nell is my guide too. She told me that. She's my anamchara." Aoife blinked and brought her hand up to shield her eyes against the sun.

A look of displeasure passed across Eiru's face. Aoife felt the moment stretch out so that it seemed the two had become still once more, within a moment of pink-tipped eternity. Then Eiru's smile came back and the leaves on the trees began to wave again in the breeze.

A blackbird flew across the circle, just above their heads. Eiru acknowledged its message with a brief nod in its direction, for the blackbird like Eiru, held the gateway to the innerworld as well as to the otherworld.

"Well," Eiru seemed to weigh her words carefully. "You shall have all the friends you need for your journey."

"Where am I going?" asked Aoife

"Why, on this journey of your life of course." Eiru seemed to sparkle in the sunlight as she turned her blue slanted eyes down to meet those of her ward. She began to lead Aoife towards the menhir stone. Aoife's chestnut curls and Eiru's honey blonde hair lifted in a gentle breeze that warmed them as they walked.

There was a cave, set into the deep thickness of hawthorn bush beside the menhir. Aoife had not noticed it before. The darkness of the cave was lit from within and Aoife was thrilled with the very adventure of it.

"Are we going in there?"

"Yes, sweet girl. The time has come."

"Time for what?"

"For you to come with me into the place beyond."

"Will I come back here to Mommy?"

"You are to become a walker between the worlds," Eiru's response didn't quite satisfy Aoife. It was as if something niggled at the back of her mind.

Aoife looked up as a robin flew across the circle and perched in a tree. The robin made her think of Nell. She remembered Nell had said they would come for her. She wasn't sure who 'they' were, but she looked from the robin to Eiru, wondering if the lady was one of 'they' that Nell had talked about. She was not afraid, for the gift Eiru had given her had taken fear of the unknown away forever. Yet, for a moment, she wished she were older so that she could make sense of exactly what was happening. In the event, Aoife stood still, refusing to move as she considered her situation for a moment, before answering the lady.

"The robin is here. Nell said I had to be careful, so I'm not sure I should go to the other place today Lady." Aoife pointed at the robin now flying from tree to tree toward the ash at the other end of the grove. "Look. She's going to Nell."

Aoife looked back at Eiru and said matter of factly, "The robin always takes me to Nell's place. She probably has soup she wants me to drink. I don't mind because it tastes quite nice and it's got vegetables in it, so it will make me strong. Well that's what Nell says, and I think she's right because Mommy always says that too."

Eiru seemed surprised, but then began to use her voice in a sweet, persuasive lullaby way. "Let the robin go Aoife. Your place is with me."

Aoife felt entranced, relaxed and compliant. She took a step towards the menhir, then stopped and looked over her shoulder. Eiru, her golden silver gown shimmering in the sunlight, smiled her wide smile. Her honey-gold hair shone like a crown about her head.

"Well." Aoife considered a moment. "I suppose I can visit Nell later and tell her about the place beyond. She'll probably be very interested I think."

Eiru merely smiled and moved ahead of the little girl. She turned slightly and beckoned, her slanted blue eyes encouraging, bewitching.

As they drew closer to the menhir, Aoife stopped again.

"But," she says, "Will I need to tell Mommy that I'm going?"

"No," said the lady, her voice like honey. "Because you are one of us."

"Yes I am." Aoife thought it through. "Mommy will be happy when I tell her about it. She likes stories." Aoife held the Lady's hand and looked up into her face. "Mommy always tells me a story at bedtime. Maybe this time I can tell her a story instead. She'll like that."

Eiru merely smiled. Aoife looked towards the cave. "Ooo!" she said, admiring the lighting within the cave. "It looks like candle stars in a tree trunk."

Kay's voice was heard in the distance. "Aoife!" There was a pause and then "Aoife! Where are you?"

Aoife paused as Eiru continued to walk. "That's Mommy," she said unnecessarily. She looked up at Eiru, her sweet little mouth a questioning rosebud.

Kay's voice came nearer now. "I need you back here." And then closer and more urgent. "I need you back here now. Aoife!"

Aoife let go of Eiru's hand. "I have to go to Mommy." Not wanting to offend the lady she said, "Maybe I'll come with you tomorrow okay."

"But you must come with me now. It is time. You must come and take your place where you belong."

Aoife stood rooted to the spot. She looked up at Eiru with confidence. "I want to go with you. I know I will go with you someday but not today. Mommy needs me, especially now that she won't have Daddy to talk to the way she could before."

Aoife leaned up and kissed Eiru on her pale cheek. Then, like a young deer, she sprang and was gone, running across the grove. She scrambled up the bank beside the ash tree and down the other side. Across the meadow she ran until she was caught in Kay's wide-spread arms.

Together they looked back toward the circle. It was as if the hawthorn had parted briefly to allow Kay to see into the grove. Eiru could be clearly seen standing in the entrance to the portal, which was not visible to Kay moments ago. There was a dark cavern behind her with strange otherworldly lighting emanating from it.

"Mommy look." Aoife pointed.

Kay stepped slowly backward. She pulled her child close to her chest, so that Aoife naturally wrapped her legs around her mother's waist. Kay turned and ran, stumbling but not quite falling, across the meadow.

Aoife continued to speak, her voice jerky as Kay jogged up and down in her haste. "It's okay now Mommy. I know Daddy had to go because my people had to be protected. He's not really gone. He'll always be with us in the field you see. And then the lady wanted me to go with her to where my people live. And I was going to go, but then I remembered that you still need me, especially with Daddy gone to 'plenish the earth. Then the robin came. It was going back to Nell's and I remembered she said I needed to be strong and have courage. The lady said Daddy had courage too. And then you called me. I really wanted to go with the lady but it's ok, I'll go tomorrow instead."

Kay merely adjusted her hold on Aoife. She tucked the child's legs under one arm, gripping her shoulders with the other so that Aoife's face was tight against her mother's chest. Kay ran through the open gate without stopping to close or secure it.

Stumbling into the cottage, Kay wild eyed, finally stopped. She slammed the kitchen door by pushing it sharply with her backside. Her breath came in great gasps.

"Mommy you're hurting me."

"Sorry darling. I'm sorry." Kay allowed Aoife's struggling body to slide from her arms but kept a light hold on one arm as she turned the key in the kitchen door. Pulling Aoife after her, she somehow got them both to the couch and pulled Aoife down beside her.

"It's all right darling," Kay told Aoife over and over again, stroking her arms. She noticed her daughter's eyes getting bigger at her mother's alarming behavior. She calmed herself.

"Aoife, you must promise me you will never go with the lady.

"But Mommy!" said Aoife, she's really nice. She wants me to go with her to the other world. She says I'm going to be a walker between the worlds. Doesn't that sound lovely. I think I should like that very much."

Kay took a deep breath. "Now Aoife," she began. "I want you to tell me all about it. Tell me everything, right from the very beginning."

CHAPTER 25 – THE TRADE

That night, as Kay listened to Aoife's tale of how her relationship with the lady had developed, she wondered where she had gone wrong. It was true that Aoife had unusual gifts that had led Kay to give her wide parameters of freedom. Yet she was forced to question whether or not she had instilled enough of a healthy fear of stranger danger in her child.

Kay felt of sense of horror that Aoife had so glibly struck up a friendship with both the lady and her imaginary friend Nell. At the same time, she wanted her daughter to be brave and strong and to have the freedom to develop her unique powers and view of life. In this conflicted state of mind, Kay listened as her daughter expressed how both her friends had helped her understand why her Daddy had died. Kay was glad of that, but there was no way she was going to allow the Sidhe to take her child.

Kay held Aoife close, enjoying the still babyish feel of her skin and limbs. She stroked Aoife's hair and read her an extra-long bedtime story until she was certain Aoife was asleep. She needed time to think.

Kay paced up and down the corridor outside her child's room, unwilling to close the door on her daughter or to leave her.

Recalling a memory, Kay went in search of a small box she had left here at the cottage before leaving for the States six years earlier.

Rummaging about in the bottom of the wardrobe, she found what she was looking for. It was a small box of midnight blue, tightly bound with pale blue twine and fastened with a neat little bow. It was quite difficult to unfasten, so firmly she had made the knot back then.

Kay was obliged to take a pair of scissors and cut the twine. Lifting the lid of the box, she peeled back the layers of tissue to reveal an amulet of gold and silver, fastened by an antique hook onto a long silver chain. On the amulet was an intricately crafted Celtic design of two swans, their necks wound about each other.

Kay lifted the jewelry out of the box and splayed it on her open palm. The silver necklace spilled over the edges of her hand, bathed in light as it gently swung there.

The necklace had belonged to her own great grandmother who had lived in Ireland over a hundred years previously. Family lore passed from matriarch to daughter down the years told the story of an enchanted mist. This necklace was gifted by an Irishman so handsome, with his green slanted eyes and dark looks, that he was held to be mystical, like a creature of mythology. Or so the tale went.

When Kay had first heard the story, she was fascinated that her great grandmother had not stayed with this supposedly beautiful man, but actually fled from him and from Ireland, to take passage across the sea to America.

It was said within the family, that things had been complicated by the fact that her father had insisted she marry a man he had chosen for her, some farmer from a nearby village.

While Kay understood that the social mores of her great grandmother's time were restrictive where women were concerned, she could never fathom why her great grandmother had not married the man who'd given her this necklace. Judging by the quality of workmanship and the purity of the metals, it must surely have meant, the man she loved had considerable financial means.

Why, wondered Kay, had her great grandmother not disobeyed her father and stayed with the man she loved. For she must have loved him, or why would she have accepted his gift. And he must have loved her, else why give her such an expensive gift.

These had been questions she could not understand until one winter, six years ago, she had stood at the edge of the same mist and with that same man. She had known him simply as Mac.

He had seen this very piece of jewelry about her neck and had assumed, rightly, that Kay was related to its original owner, her great grandmother.

The thing that was not expected though, was this gorgeous man, as she had thought of him back then, had mistaking her for his lost love Caer. At first, she thought he had confused the name Kay with Caer. She had thought perhaps he had an accented way of pronouncing her name. And then there was the question of how old he actually was, if he had been in love with Kay's great grandmother. But then at the edge of the mist, none of these things had actually voiced themselves in Kay's mind until the moment when he had convinced her that she was the Caer he was searching for, that she was actually the reincarnation of her great grandmother.

Later, when she had reunited with Liam and returned to the States, she had thought for a while that the experience must have been a dream. Such a thing could not possibly have happened.

Kay discovered that she was pregnant and as the months went on, she had the strangest feeling that the child was not Liam's. Gradually, she began to believe that the moment of Aoife's conception was at the edge of the mist, with Mac. It was not until Aoife was a few months old and her long slanted green eyes blinked knowingly at Kay, that she was finally convinced. They were Mac's eyes and how could she deny that.

Kay sighed. And now it had come to this. She had returned to Ireland with Liam against her own better judgement and she had lost him. Was she to lose her daughter too? "Not if I can help it!" She snapped.

Throwing the necklace into the air, she caught it deftly and closed her hand around it in a fist. She had thought to wear it as a talisman for what she intended to do tomorrow night but instead, she realized she must gift it to Aoife.

Kay walked back and forth in the corridor outside Aoife's bedroom, pausing occasionally to look into the room, to reassure herself that Aoife was still there.

The silence of Kay's vigil was broken only by the noise of the fridge. It tended to hum when the motor clicked on, noticeable only at night when the cottage was quiet.

Kay's slippers made a scuffing sound on the carpeted floor as she continued to pace. At last she became aware of the clock ticking, which drew her eyes upward to the clock and beyond that, to the window. It was 3 am, still dark outside. She made her decision.

Kay tiptoed into Aoife's room and slipped the necklace over her daughter's slender neck, her fingers resting momentarily on the soft pulse. "This is yours now," she whispered.

Carefully controlling the deep sigh that wanted to free itself from deep within her soul, Kay quietly left her daughter's room and padded purposefully into the living room.

Grabbing pen and paper, Kay sat down at the dining table to write a letter. She took her time about it, making sure she had left nothing out that needed to be included. It took her many minutes as she looked over it and made alterations. She then wrote a second letter, similar to the first but addressed to her lawyer.

Kay began to fold the two letters but paused and unfolded them again. She added the date to them both. She checked the name and addressees of both letters, then re-folded the pieces of paper and thrust them into the envelope. Kay propped it on the table, against the large pasta bowl that was too big to fit into any of the kitchen cupboards, then stood back a moment to look at the envelope.

Suddenly, Kay grabbed the envelope and tucked it hurriedly behind a jug on the dresser that Liam had screwed to the wall. This was where he kept the mishmash of ornaments he had collected from various junk stores over the years.

Kay crept into Aoife's room and lay down on the carpet beside her bed. She pulled a throw rug over herself to keep warm while she waited. Her eyes began to close immediately. Kay shook her head. She could not allow herself to sleep, she told herself sternly. What if they came for Aoife and she slept through it? She would never forgive herself. She pushed herself into a sitting position and watched Aoife's Disney clock in its interminable tick-tock of time, passing so slowly that it seemed she must have aged, a year.

Dawn came slowly. Kay watched impatiently until an hour after dawn. Unable to wait any longer, she got up off the floor and walked into the kitchen.

Kay set the kettle to boil water for decaf. While she waited, she pulled up the blind on the kitchen window and looked out onto the morning.

Several sheep had trotted into the field through the open gate from the meadow. Kay hadn't realized, but she had left the gate open in her haste the previous evening.

Three lambs gathered at the trunk of an alder tree nibbling at the loose bark at its base. Two adult sheep chewed the grass at a little distance from the lambs. At the movement of the blind, they stopped and looked in her direction. They regarded her steadily for almost a minute. Eventually, as Kay did not move, the sheep returned to chewing the grass.

It would be a sunny day. There was not a cloud in the sky. Birds sang melodious and playful. Checking the front yard, Kay noticed birds still flying in and out of the feeders, despite the fact the Liam was no longer around to fill them.

It was several moments before she noticed the kettle steaming madly. It had switched itself off but not before the kitchen was moist with steam. The gray tiles were wet in the gap between the counter and the cupboards above.

Kay sat at the dining table sipping decaf and glancing at the clock often until finally the hands reached 7am. Pam's alarm was set for this time every day.

Taking out her phone she messaged Pam. "Can you take Aoife tonight?"

Several minutes passed during which Kay gazed at the screen, willing Pam to respond. Finally, the screen lit up and a text appeared.

"Good Morning to you too."

Kay thumbed another text. "Good Morning. Can you take Aoife tonight?"

"Are you all right Kay?" The question came back quickly.

"I'm fine. I just need a little time alone." Kay waited, her body hunched and stiff with barely suppressed tension.

"Sure, I'm happy to help. Wanna talk?"

"Later." Kay typed quickly, not wanting to elicit a phone conversation. "Aoife just walked in clamoring for breakfast," she lied and added a smiley emoticon to give the impression all was well.

"Drop the little Darlin' off whenever you're ready."

Kay breathed out in a long-drawn sigh of relief. Her limbs were finally freed from their self-imposed anxiety.

When Aoife, waking at last, came into the kitchen yawning and rubbing her sleepy eyes. Kay pasted a welcome smile on her face and hugged her daughter with a false attempt at bright cheerfulness. “Good Morning my sweet. What would you like for breakfast?”

“Pancakes.” Aoife said, her little mouth warm against Kay’s cheek.

She held her daughter for a long moment, drinking in the smell of her childish innocence. “Pancakes it is.” Kay let go of Aoife by degrees, her arms stroking along her shoulders and down her arms to pause momentarily at her still pudgy hands. Kay caressed her daughter to the ends of her fingers before breaking the connection. She stood then and prepared to cook the last breakfast she would ever make for her child.

“Look what I have Mommy,” Aoife pulled the necklace from inside her pyjama top. “Is it from you?”

“Ah yes.” Kay licked her lips for they were suddenly dry. “Let me tell you the story of that necklace. Kay told the tale, being sure to leave out any details which might shock the child, and careful to tell only the romantic bits. It was a once upon a time story, that left Aoife gazing down happily at the necklace as she held it in her warm hands.

Carefully avoiding the field and the meadow beyond, Kay led Aoife through a day with happy chatter, games and fun.

Together they baked chocolate chip oatmeal cookies. Aoife stood on a chair with Kay’s big apron wrapped around her as she mixed the ingredients. By the end of it, Aoife’s hair and face sported blobs of cookie mixture, as did the apron and also the floor.

While the cookies baked, Kay made a game of stacking the dishes in the dish washer and cleaning up the counters.

They enjoyed the cookies in the front garden where they sat under the alders. A picnic basket sat between them, to which Kay had added cheese and tomato sandwiches along with a flask of tea.

It was altogether a lovely day, a day to remember. Kay stretched and leaned back against the cushions which she had piled against a tree. Aoife nestled in her lap and together they watched the birds swoop down onto the feeders they had filled that morning.

Sometime in the afternoon, Kay and Aoife drove through the country lanes to Pam's place.

The pub was fairly busy. Several children sat outside, waiting for their parents who were inside the pub. The children seemed happy drinking lemonade and munching from packets of potato crisps.

After giving Pam a wet kiss on the cheek and armed now with her own can of lemonade and packet of chips, Aoife had run off outside to visit with the children there.

"Now." Pam leaned her elbows on the counter and fixed Kay with her eagle eyes. "Rough night was it?"

Kay looked at her friend with a start then realized Pam assumed she was still reeling from Liam's death. And so she was, but not in the way that Pam imagined. "Yes," she told Pam. "It was rough. I just thought, if you could take Aoife tonight …" her voice trailed off. She waited.

"Of course, I will." Pam put her hand over Kay's. "Anything you need. You know I'm here for you."

Kay sighed, her breath coming out in a whoosh. "Thanks Pam. I'm so grateful for all you've done for me, and for Aoife."

Pam shrugged her shoulders. "What are friends for!"

"Seriously Pam."

"Seriously Kay. Anyway, the little darlin's grown on me, so she has."

"She's comfortable with you."

"She certainly makes herself at home." Pam laughed. "You know what she said the other day?" Kay shook her head. "Told me I'm her second mommy and that Nell is her third mommy. Funny little thing she is."

"About that," began Kay.

"Ah! Don't even worry. Sure, she'll grow out of it in time so."

Kay hesitated. "I left an envelope for you on the dining table."

"What?" Pam was confused.

"I mean, I forgot to bring it with me. It's …. a thank you card."

Pam smiled. "No need. I love you Kay. Don't you know that? You and Aoife both."

Kay stepped forward and gave her friend a hug, squeezing her tight.

"Ah! Go on wit' you." Pam laughed. "You need to sleep. You should have taken that pill when I offered it to you the other night." Pam nodded her head, gently admonishing her friend.

Kay tried a watery smile. "I think you're right. I might take it tonight," she lied. She gave Pam's hand a quick squeeze and left the bar.

Turning at the door, she saw Pam still watching her, concern written all over her face. Kay smiled again at her friend and went outside.

Stopping at the car, she looked around. This was the place where Kay and Mac had walked away into the mist. If she had not gone toward the mist on that night, none of this would be happening. She and Liam would still be together. He would here by her side, not dead and spread all over the field behind the cottage.

And Aoife … Kay looked at Aoife sitting with the other kids, swinging her legs and chattering, her curls bouncing around her face in the sunlight.

Aoife would not have been born as this Aoife but as some other version of herself. She would have been Liam's child and not Mac's. "Aoife but not Aoife," mused Kay out loud.

Kay's heart was full as she looked at her child. Aoife belonged here, in the land of her father's. Kay believed this and would fight to ensure that it came about the way Kay planned for it to be.

Kay snapped back to the present. She couldn't allow herself to stop and think. Her path was decided. She opened the door and slid behind the wheel. Putting the car into gear, she drove out of the carpark into the brilliant green of an Irish afternoon.

Once at the cottage, Pam ran about doing chores. It was partly to pass the time until the night should come and partly as if everything must be in perfect order, which she felt it must.

Laundry was done, dishes put away, floor swept, furniture polished, beds made, and windows cleaned. She even watered the hanging baskets, for they didn't always get sufficient water from the rain, protected as they were by the eves of the cottage roof.

At last, everything was ready. Kay showered and changed into jeans and sweatshirt. It could be cold at night and the midges were often still active well after dusk.

Kay made up her face. She even smoothed out her silky blonde hair with heated straighteners. She did all this to give herself confidence.

Lastly, she took the envelope down from the shelf and placed it in a prominent position on the dining table.

As dusk lengthened into night, Kay slipped out through the kitchen door, closing it one last time before heading across the field.

She was careful to shut the gate that led into the meadow and to slide the bolt home in a final act of closing the door on her life.

Licking her lips to give herself courage, she turned towards the shadow that was the grove of hawthorn. The moon was rising, it was a clear night again. She could see her way across the meadow quite easily.

The grass felt sweet and succulent as it brushed against her ankles. The sheep that could often be found here during the day, did a good job of keeping the meadow trimmed. Right now, she couldn't see the buttercups and daisies that were strewn through the grass. Yet, it was somehow comforting to know the wildflowers were there, unseen and yet still beautiful.

As she reached the edge of the great shadow of the ash, Kay stretched out her hand, feeling for the trunk of the ancient tree. Finding comfort in the rough bark beneath her hand, Kay walked up the rise that heralded the entry to the circle.

Stopping just on the downside of the bank, she was in the thickest part of the grove. Kay listened for a long moment but there was nothing but empty air. The darkness of the grove held a forbidding stillness.

Hesitant but determined not to come off as weak, Kay walked carefully but with purpose through the dark grove to the tree stump. Hauling herself up, Kay stood straight and peered into the darkness. The tress seemed to close in on her in a way that sunlight would banish instantly.

Rousing herself, she called "I want to talk to you. Eiru! Lady! Whatever your name is." Kay's voice died into the silence. There was no response but the sighing of a gentle breeze.

She repeated herself. "I want to talk to you. Now!"

A breeze flickered lightly through the hawthorn trees, playing with the shadows as the moon lengthened its path within the circle.

Kay waited for what seemed a very long time until at last, the emotional roller coast of the past week seemed to crash down on her.

She stumbled down from the tree stump and sat down on it. She put her head in her hands and wept.

Gradually, she became aware that she was not alone. A gentle rustling through the grass behind her caused her to pause in her tears, face still in her hands.

Was that a perfume she could detect? It smelled of turf set fresh into drying stocks, of the heather that covered the peat bog, of new mown grass on a summer's day and of woman at her most fertile.

The hair stood up at the back of Kay's neck, extending along her arms. The nerves on her back tingled. She slowly sat up, shaking with fright as the presence and the perfume enveloped her.

The rustling sound continued to approach from behind her and then stopped. It was so close that Kay felt she could reach out and touch whatever might be there. Her skin crawled. She berated herself for being cowardly and sat up ramrod straight.

Unable to bear the anticipation any longer, she turned.

A shimmering form stood in the moonlight. Not so close that she could touch it, yet not so far that she could not reach out if she would dare.

It was enough that the figure did not move, nor did it speak. For a long moment, Kay merely looked. Her eyes felt round as saucers.

It was the one Aoife called Eiru, the lady. It was the woman that Kay had seen yesterday. Only now in the moonlight, the hair and garments of the woman had a silvery glow that seemed to flicker as the breeze cast shadows from the trees across her face and form. "What is this?" asked Eiru.

Kay swallowed hard. She dragged up her courage from deep down. It balled up with the terror in her chest and produced the righteous anger of a mother, threatened with the loss of her child. "I demand that you leave my daughter alone."

The figure before her said nothing, merely waited, almost mocking in its silence.

Kay spoke on while she still had the anger within her. "I want Aoife to have a normal life. She needs the grounding as a normal human being before she discovers who she is. I need her to have that." There was no response. "Please!" added Kay.

Eiru finally spoke. "We cannot leave Aoife here for you to stamp her indelibly with a loathing for her people. Aoife is Aos Sidhe of the Tuatha de Danaan. She must take her place among us."

"It's too soon for Aoife." Kay repeated her demand. "Take me. Take me instead of Aoife,"

Eiru again said nothing.

"I know you mean to take her. I am offering myself instead." Kay's fury began to dissipate in the face of an immovable calm emanating from Eiru.

Kay began to stammer. "If-if you don't take me in her place and agree to my terms, I will take Aoife far from here tomorrow and I will ensure she never sets foot in Ireland again."

The air around Eiru rippled. Kay could not see the woman's face in the darkness but then she turned her head to look down at Kay. At this movement, the moon cast its light across the planes of her face, so that Kay could see the eyes glint. A deep fear balled itself inside her belly.

Eiru stared at Kay for a long moment. "If you thought you could do that, why did you not leave today?"

Kay's words came in a rush with her breath and voice all raggedy. "Believe me, I-I thought of that. But I want Aoife to grow up here, where her father is."

Kay's voice faltered as the moonlight glinted across Eiru's face. Kay saw one eyebrow lift sardonically. They both knew the true identity of Aoife's father.

Kay could not allow herself to be intimidated. She pulled herself together. "Liam was her Daddy. The only father Aoife has ever known. It would be good for Aoife to grow up here. I want that for her but only if you agree to my terms." Her voice faded. How could she have thought she could make a deal with this woman, with these people.

"Why should you trust that I will keep my part of the bargain?" asked Eiru.

When Eiru spoke the words of negotiation, Kay knew such a deal was possible. She swallowed her fear and spoke up. "Because I know the Tuatha de Danaan are a people of high moral character." Kay's mind brought the quick thought that the high morals of the Tuatha de Danaan hadn't stopped them executing Liam. She pushed this thought away. What was done was done. It was up to Kay to save her child now. She went on, "I believe the Sidhe hold to a principle that binds you as a people to your word."

The shimmering form was silent, seeming to consider Kay's words.

"T-take me in her place."

Eiru laughed mockingly. "And who will raise the child in your absence?"

"I have a close friend. She lives in the village and will never leave here. I've written that she must take Aoife and bring her up knowing the mythology and history of her ancestors. This friend will do that because that is the way she was brought up herself, to believe in and respect the Tuatha de Danaan. She knows all the history and, and everything," Kay ended, sounding lame even to herself.

Eiru spoke again. "If I do this, make this exchange, you realize you cannot enter in your present form and expect to return into this time?"

"Will there be an opportunity for me to return here?" asked Kay. It was not an option she had been aware of.

"It may be required of you," was all the information Eiru seemed inclined to provide.

Kay bowed her head in the moonlight, mulling over this new information. So, I can return here, she thought, but I have to change my form.

A memory suddenly struck her. "Well then, if I can't go in my present form, consider this. Am I not a shape shifter? Am I not the Caer, that Mac," Kay almost choked as she spoke his name, "Am I not the Caer that Maccan searched for through all Ireland?"

"Caer Ibormeith." Eiru pronounced the name of The Maccan's lover in full. She appeared to consider Kay's offer and then dipped her head in apparent acquiescence.

Turning away then, Eiru began to return the way she had come. After she had gone a little way, she looked back at Kay. "Come!"

Eiru walked on and Kay followed toward the mouth of what looked like a cave. It was as Aoife had pointed out just a few nights earlier, all lit up like candle stars in a tree trunk.

Even as she followed Eiru, thoughts continued to whirl in Kay's mind as she thought of Aoife. How would her daughter feel in the morning when she realized Kay had gone? Would Pam be able to cope with the task of being a mother? Was she doing the right thing? How would she know it had all worked out? A cold hand gripped Kay's heart yet, she trusted Pam with her whole heart.

As she entered the passageway behind Eiru, Kay noticed that her own body had begun to shimmer just as Eiru's had in the circle only minutes before. It was as if the air moved with them, iridescent as a dream, that appeared to dance from and around them in soft gentle waves.

Kay tried to still her pounding heart. There was a ruffling sound, as of wings unfolding. She looked down at her body. "Wait! Are those feathers?"

EPILOGUE

Pam heard the sound of a motorcycle turning into the carpark. “Is that Dermot back again?” she muttered, looking at the clock. “He’s only been gone 10 minutes. That man can be so forgetful.” Pam smiled, pleased with herself, for Dermot often returned soon after leaving for work, just to give her a kiss and then head out again.

The door of the pub swung open. Heavy footsteps sounded on the floorboards.

Pam quickly stuffed Aoife’s school gym clothes into the washing machine and shut the door. She’d need those tomorrow. Aoife had been with her and Dermot for six months now. Pam loved her new role as a mother. The three of them had become a close family unit.

Adding a capful of laundry liquid, Pam turned the dial and pressed the on switch. “I’m coming Dermot,” she yelled and quickly checked her face in the hall mirror. “You’ll do,” she told her reflection.

“What is it this time?” said Pam as she ran lightly down the stairs, ready for his kiss.

She almost fell off the bottom step. A tall man, with broad shoulders and darkly attractive looks waited for her there.

“Hello Pam,” said Mac. “I’ve come for my daughter.”

You just finished:

The Secret of Clonacool

Carole Mondragon

What Happens Next …

Look for Book Three in the Tuatha de Danaan series

The Key to Clonacool, *coming in the fall of 2020*

Printed in Great Britain
by Amazon